The Survivor of Babi Yar

The Survivor of Babi Yar

by Othniel J. Seiden

1980

Typesetting by Enkidu Press, Boulder, Colorado
Printed in the United States of America

Library of Congress Card Number 80-51028
ISBN 937050-02-4

To Sue, Greg, Eric, Kurt
for your faith, I dedicate this book with love

Prologue

The place, Babi Yar, is real. The atrocities herein described were real. They took place, not only at Babi Yar, but throughout Europe and Western Russia, wherever the paths of Jews and Nazis crossed. The people about whom this book is written are, or were, real, but their characters in the story are composites, for there were millions of them, and each had a story that deserves telling. The atrocities that occurred to those people happened over and over and over, again and again and again . . . fourteen million times . . .

And out of the holocaust emerged two categories of Jews: those few who survived and the millions who perished. And regardless of which group any specific Jew fell into, that Jew at some point was left with a perplexing question, "Why me?" It was surely the question that flashed across the minds of those who suffered and died; more often than not, it was also the question for those who survived. They could not help wondering why they were saved, when so many others— women, children, the elderly—were murdered.

"Why me?" It is a question that demands answering. I think that I have found my answer through this book. It is simplistic, perhaps too simplistic, but it answers the question for me— possibly because I need desperately to have it answered. For only if I find an answer can I continue to believe that God is benevolent, merciful and just.

The Author
1979, Denver, Colorado

PART I
CRIME OF COMMISSION

1

Solomon awoke in a small enclosure—the space under a stairway—dimly lit by a lantern. He felt weak. Any movement was painful.

Where am I? How did I get here?

He was lying on a cot, naked to the waist, under a clean sheet. He felt under the sheet and found the undershorts, not his own, unfamiliar. Above, what appeared to be the underside of a landing, the stairs angling down to his feet; at his head, a high wall about a meter from the end of the cot; to the right, the cot stood against another of the walls, an outside wall of cold stone, like a foundation. The undersides of the stairs were wooden, the wall at his head and the one to his left, an arm's length from his cot, stucco or plaster. The floor was dirt.

Am I a prisoner?

He looked around for an exit. He was able to make out a small door at the base of the tall wall beyond the head of his cot, not more than a meter high and no wider than a man's shoulders. It was not made to enter or exit conveniently.

He remembered a massive crowd of people. Fleeting, confusing . . . he was terrified.

"What is this place?" The words barely escaped his throat. His mind was a blank.

From somewhere beyond the walls, he heard the sound of a door opening. Then footsteps on the landing and stairs above him—heavy, bold steps. The lantern swung. Eerie shadows moved on the walls.

They're coming for me.

Again, that image of crowds. Fierce pain tore through his whole body as he tried to move toward the foot of his cot. He didn't have the strength to move to the end of the chamber away from the door. He felt resigned. His eyes followed the invisible footsteps from the bottom of the stairs to where the closed door stood, half hidden in shadow. He heard something being dragged along the floor, but he didn't hear the door swing open. Quietly, a figure maneuvered, with some difficulty, through the low entrance. Its features remained obscured. Solomon lay frozen as the figure waited in darkness.

He's not in uniform, Solomon thought with relief. He has no weapon.

The figure turned toward him. "It's about time. You've been sleeping like the dead since I found you."

What does he mean? Where am I? Why can't I remember?

"Don't be afraid. My name is Ivan. Ivan Igonovich. Do you feel anything?"

Solomon shook his head feebly.

"I found you two days ago, in a ditch along the road. I've never seen such a mess. Mud, blood, filth caked all over you." The figure was animated now, gesturing with his arms and massive hands as much as the small chamber would allow. "I thought you were dead. But, when I jogged you, you mumbled. Then you fainted again. You've been mostly unconscious ever since."

Solomon managed, "I don't understand. Where am I?" Some of Solomon's fear melted. The lantern light in the small room was too weak for Solomon to make out Ivan's features clearly, but the deep voice was gentle. Though the man looked powerful enough to crush him with one hug, Solomon's terror faded to a nagging anxiety.

"You are safe," the stranger reassured him. "We have you hidden. We've gotten some broth into you, but you've been delirious. Do you remember anything at all?"

Solomon tried. He couldn't seem to focus.

"You spoke of a pit of death. German gunners. Piles of death. What does it all mean?"

Solomon nearly cried out, "The Germans were shooting us. All of us. Shooting us in the ravine."

"What is your name?" Ivan asked. "What do they call you?"

"Solomon Shalensky. I am called Sol by my friends—if any of my friends are still alive."

"How old are you, Solomon?" Ivan asked, calmly.

"Eighteen. Eighteen on September the third."

"Tell me more. Where did all this take place? You spoke of a ravine."

"At Babi Yar, near Kiev. The Germans killed all of us in the ravine."

Ivan stared in astonishment. "What do you mean they killed *all* of you? And how did you get here? Kiev is over ten kilometers to the south."

"I don't know how I got here. I must have crawled. . . . I think I crawled at night." Solomon's voice dropped and his speech slowed. His mouth became dry and his heart started to pound. "They thought I was dead. I was buried. They killed us all."

"Who?"

"All of us. All the Jews."

"A pogrom?"

"No. They just took us to the ravine and shot us down with machine guns."

"Were you and your friends . . . a resistance group?" Ivan's voice was suspicious.

"No. They took all of us from Kiev and shot us in the ravine. All of the Jews from Kiev. They shot us."

Ivan shook his head. "You must be mistaken. There are thousands of Jews in Kiev!"

"All of us," Solomon repeated. "Thirty thousand in two days. I was among the last. I was buried with the rest."

Ivan stared a long time. "You're tired." He gestured toward the cot. "Rest, Solomon. You're safe here. I'll come back later with more broth, and we'll talk."

Ivan left Solomon alone under the stairs.

2

Solomon tried to put things in order. Where must I start? Suddenly he was crying. Mama, Papa, my sister and brothers— they must all be dead. And Grandpa. All dead. His tears came in a torrent now. He cried until it hurt. "Oh, God," he whimpered. "Why me?"

His face was still damp when Ivan returned an hour later with some broth. There was black bread, too. Broth and bread. Solomon was amazed that he was hungry.

3

Ivan watched Solomon eat. His eyes gazed at the boy's face. Could it be true what he has told me? What part is exaggeration? He was a mess when I found him. He's truly been through something horrible.

"How is it that you've hidden me in your home?" Solomon asked. "It's not usual for a Russian or a Ukrainian to hide a Jew."

Ivan felt a moment of hostility. "Not all of us are like that!" Then he realized that Solomon had reason to be curious. "When I was younger, I saw the aftermath of a pogrom. I saw the organized slaughter of Jews in their village. Sixty-three Jews were killed in their shtetl one Easter. I don't know how many were maimed and injured. Their homes were burned and their shops looted. The so-called Christians claimed it was vengeance for the Crucifixion." Ivan's gaze fell to the floor as a frown of disgust wrinkled his forehead. His eyes closed.

"Since that day I have never placed foot inside a church. Once I worked for a Jew, too. I was treated fairly and decently. But I had no idea you were Jewish when I found you. I thought perhaps . . ."

"What?" said Solomon.

"I thought you were a resistance fighter. I had no idea that the Jews were special enemies of the Germans. But, if I had known, it would not have made any difference."

7

"How is it that you have a secret place like this in your home?"

"It was the home of the Jew I worked for—a Zionist. He built this secret room to hide his family, should a pogrom have come this way. He was always afraid of a pogrom. He had survived one as a child and had never gotten over it. Several years ago, he decided to leave Russia for Palestine. One night, he and his family stole out of Russia. They took only what they could carry. He left me all of this for my loyalty during the years I worked for him." Ivan looked about the little chamber. "It will probably get some more use now."

After a short silence, Solomon asked, "How will I ever be able to repay you?"

"Never mind that. Tell me, do you remember any more now than you did before?"

"A little has come back to me." A distant frown crossed Ivan's face. "It is all so unreal, like a horrible dream."

Ivan waited for Solomon to continue.

"It all seems so impossible. We actually thought we were being liberated by the Germans. We thought that the cultured Europeans were going to liberate us from the tyranny of the Ukrainians and Russians. No more pogroms, no more poverty, no more anti-Semitism, that is what we thought. We welcomed the Germans. I don't understand how it happened."

4

Over the next twenty-four hours, life and strength returned to Solomon's body. He still slept most of the day and night. But when he slept it was only for an hour or two. In his waking moments, he remembered.

Ivan looked in on Solomon frequently. Each time he brought more food and broth. "You must have fluids," he said. "You body's as thirsty as a sun-dried fish. Eat the broth. Solid food is not so important. And use lots of salt."

As time passed, Solomon noticed that Ivan was adding more solids to the broth—potatoes, carrots, cabbage—and always there was the bread. Fresh-baked, warm, reminiscent of that his mother baked. And, except for the few times Ivan came in wearing his nightshirt (the only way Solomon knew night had come), the two talked. During the nighttime visits, Ivan only placed the food next to the bed and briefly asked whether Solomon needed anything else. Once he added some fuel to the little lantern that continually lighted the small, secret room. He also checked the chamber pot by the bed, but Solomon had been too dehydrated and starved to produce much waste. In three days, he'd emptied out only a little urine.

On the morning of the fourth day, Ivan brought Solomon a hard-boiled egg, some salt, milk, meat and bread. Solomon ate heartily. Ivan couldn't have realized that this was far better than Solomon was used to eating. Solomon came from the poor part of Kiev, where life was hand-to-mouth, and on some days the hand never reached the mouth. Bread and potato soup were often all his family had to eat for days on end. Eggs were a luxury, milk a delight saved for the young. Tea was always available, and meat was on the table perhaps once a week, in very good times. Various vegetables were to be found steaming on the table when they were in season and so plentiful that their price was forced down, or if they had grown in the little garden his mother labored over. But often, even the vegetables from the garden could not be eaten by his family. If they would bring a good price at market, like the eggs their few chickens laid, they would have to be sold, and cheaper foods would be purchased for the family with the money they brought.

"You look much better today," Ivan said. "Today I think you should get up and venture out a little."

"Is it safe for me to go out? I do not want to jeopardize the safety of your family." Then he added, "Though I've heard no one else around here."

"I have only my wife here now. My children have grown and have moved out on their own. This small farm could not support their families, too. I have three grandchildren, also," Ivan said with pride obvious in his massive grin. He had strong white teeth, none missing, a rarity among the people of the Ukraine. His round face seemed to glow with his pride, eyes sparkling. "You have heard no one else because you are not directly in or under the house. This room is in a storage cellar. As for my wife, she helped me get you down here, but you were delirious. We cleaned you up." He laughed softly. "It was almost too great a job for the both of us. But she was a nurse before she settled on this farm with me, so it's she who is mostly responsible for your recovery. You will meet her soon."

Again, Solomon said, "I don't know how to thank you both."

"Eat now, thank later. I'll bring you some clothes that my wife packed away from our sons when they were younger. There was no hope of getting the blood and filth out of your clothes. They were not fit for rags. All we could do was burn them.

Ivan left the room. Solomon ate. Ivan returned in a little

while with some clothes. Solomon put them on. They fit loosely, but Solomon had never before had clothes that fine. He had always had hand-me-downs or used clothes that his parents had bought in the marketplace. These clothes were hardly worn and didn't have a patched place on them. Solomon could not remember ever having clothes that weren't patched or mended. "This is too good of you," he remarked. "Surely you have something less fine. I feel it is too much to give me such fine clothes."

"So for what would we save them? They fit no one in the family, and it will be fifteen years before my grandchildren will grow into them. I can think of no one who needs them more than you right now."

Solomon graciously accepted. As he dressed, he looked at each garment, and felt the fabric with his fingers—softer than any he had ever worn before. Then, realizing Ivan was impatient to get outside, he dressed quickly.

"Now, let's get out of this little place. You've been cooped up here long enough. You will come back in here to sleep, or if the Germans come calling, but the rest of the time you will be outside or in the house. You should be safe enough, now that you can move about on your own."

Solomon followed Ivan through the small opening in the wall into a fruit cellar full of vegetables, fruits and sacks of grains. Ivan pushed a box in front of the small opening. It was impossible to see or even guess that there was a room behind the wall supporting the stairs out of the cellar.

They climbed the steps and came out into the light. Solomon was temporarily blinded. The last light Solomon could remember was the day he and his family were taken to Babi Yar.

"See?" Ivan said. "You should be safe here, for the time being."

Solomon looked about. The storage cellar had been dug after the house was built. Its entrance was about ten feet from the house, so that in bad weather they didn't have far to go to get their supplies. It was located at the rear of the house, so that if trouble came from the road, about 200 meters distant, the family could enter the cellar without being seen; the house was between the cellar entrance and the road. Solomon could see that the cellar was built, not for storage, but to hide people.

The house was small. It was built of native stone and wood. It wasn't a large farm, but, according to Ivan, it was bigger than most in the area. Ivan was obviously a man of means. He had two cows, several pigs, chickens and geese. Solomon could not be sure how much land Ivan had, but much of it had been tilled. Most of the crops had been harvested. The area was surrounded on three sides by a forest and on the fourth by a dirt road.

"I have never seen such a big place. It is really all yours?"

"All that has been cleared. It represents years of hard work. We are proud of it, Sosha and I."

They entered the house.

"It is good to see you again," Ivan's wife, Sosha, said after they had been formally introduced. "I have not seen you since we cleaned you up. I hope your strength is returning."

"Yes, I feel much better. There is no way I can ever thank you sufficiently."

Sosha was an attractive woman. Her blonde hair, high-lighted by the whiteness creeping into it, was pulled straight back and rolled into a bun. She had a round, full face and skin reddened from hours of work out doors. Her skin would have been as brown as Ivan's, had her complexion not been fair. Instead of tanning, her skin had a blush to it. Perhaps an inch taller than Solomon, she had a typically big-boned Slavic build. Though her hands were rough, her warm smile made her almost girlish.

Solomon had just recently finished the food Ivan brought to him, but Sosha ladled out two bowls of potato soup from a pot that constantly simmered on the wood stove and placed them on a large rough wooden table for Solomon and her husband. The three sat down. She took a glass of tea for herself.

Sosha realized that she'd never seen Solomon in full daylight. His hair was light brown. When Ivan had carried him home that first day, he took him directly to the cellar, where the dim light made his hair look nearly black. I must have washed it a half-dozen times to get the filth and blood out, she thought. Now she could see the uneven patches where she'd had to cut out some of the tangles.

"I'll trim your hair later this afternoon if you like," she said to Solomon. "Ivan is due for a trim, too. I can do you both today while it is still warm outside."

"Thank you, but that's not necessary," Solomon answered, apparently surprised by her proposal.

"Nonsense. I enjoy cutting hair."

I'll have to fatten him up a bit, she thought, though he's huskier than he appears in those baggy clothes. He must have been a handsome fellow. How penetrating his brown eyes are. Thoughtful. Even now they sparkle. We'll get the stubble off of him, too—it makes him look so gaunt. He certainly doesn't have Slavic features. His ancestors must have migrated from the south, perhaps Italy, Spain or Greece, someplace Mediterranean.

"Tell us," Sosha said, "What do you recall now?"

Glancing at Ivan, Solomon said, "Much has come back since you first asked me. The more I remember, the more horrible it becomes. I find myself wondering if it really happened. But it must have happened. I could not dream such horrors."

Solomon paused for a moment, apparently trying to organize his thoughts.

5

"The shelling was almost constant in our part of Kiev, as it was all over the city and the surrounding villages. We lived with it day and night," Solomon began. "The earth shook. Many families dug trenches in their yards and moved into them. The city officials even recommended it. We stayed in our home. My father insisted that God would see to our safety if He meant for us to survive."

"We could hear the explosions from here," Sosha interjected. "But it never came here."

Solomon hesitated. A tear formed in his eye. He cleared his throat.

"For several days, we began to see an increasing number of Russian troops running from the front. They would occasionally stop and beg for civilian clothes. Anyway, out of the growing retreat came rumors that in a matter of days the war would end for us and the front pass us by. The Communists and their officials left the city along with the retreating soldiers. Most of us that remained, I think, felt that living under German occupation would be better than life under the Bolsheviks. We certainly preferred it to the constant bombings! We were—if not openly, at least secretly—looking forward to occupation. Not that we weren't afraid, but only afraid as one is when he awaits a new experience which he knows nothing about. Afraid like children on their first day at school.

"On September 19th, everything suddenly stopped. The silence was frightening, almost painful. For the first time, I realized how relentless the explosions had been. For a long time we sat, paralyzed by the silence. Was it just a lull? Would it start again? Were the Bolsheviks gone forever? Were the Germans here? Perhaps the Russians would counterattack (we doubted that, but no one knew).

"Then we heard—first one, then another voice, and another: 'The Germans are here! Bolshevik rule is over! Come out everyone! The war is over! The Germans are here!' We could hear people running outside. Some were cheering as the Germans entered. Once outside, my family and I could hear the noise of trucks, and we ran toward it. The crowds grew as we approached. It was breathtaking. We looked up and down the main road through Kiev. As far as we could see in both directions, trucks loaded with soldiers. None marching nor walking. There were artillery pieces in tow and occasional motorcycles with side cars. And, every so often, a polished, open-roofed car with officers went by. How different from the Russians who'd retreated through Kiev over the previous days! This was an army. They didn't even look like they had been in battle.

"As more and more of our citizens came to watch, the procession took on the mood of a parade. The soldiers waved and smiled, at first at the girls and children. The children cheered and the girls laughed, blushing, and then waved back. Soon, everyone was cheering, calling out words of welcome."

Sosha asked Solomon whether he wanted a glass of tea. He nodded and went on.

"It took a long time for all of the trucks to pass by. Then there followed enormous supply wagons pulled by the largest draft horses I'd ever seen. The wagons were loaded with food and ammunition. Looking up, I realized that this was the first time in what seemed like ages that no German planes were dropping bombs, no shells falling out of the sky! It seemed a glorious day. My father kept saying it was the beginning of a new life.

"Everyone was curious, the Germans included. I'd never in

my life seen so many cameras! The Germans took pictures of everything; the trucks, the people, our bomb-damaged streets where houses and buildings still burned and smoldered. They took pictures of each other." Solomon paused, shaking his head.

"It was fascinating. The feeling was of wonder and freedom! On Kirillovskaya Avenue, a number of buildings had Soviet flags waving in front of them, and as the crowds moved past they pulled the flags down and trampled them into the ground. Some flags were burned and their burning cheered. Had the Russians counterattacked to retake the city, I think we Jews would have fought the hardest against them.

"As the day passed, there was more and more activity. The Germans were busy establishing quarters. They were all over the city. Many went about fully armed, seeking out foolish partisans who stayed behind. They had help from the citizens pointing out Communists and partisans. Many who weren't partisans were picked up simply because they'd been pointed out. It was a bad time to have enemies. I don't know where they took those people. They were just rounded up and taken away. Maybe they also went to the ravine."

Sosha placed the tea in front of Solomon and another glass before Ivan.

"As the fervor of the crowds grew, they became a mob. I think it started with the pulling down of the Soviet flags, most of which were on stores and buildings owned by party members. After all, who else but the Bolsheviks could own a business? Soon the mob started breaking windows and looting. Then, quite suddenly, it didn't matter who owned the property. There were goods of all kinds to be had for nothing—for the taking—by people who were used to having nothing. In minutes, stores and businesses were stripped of goods, fixtures, equipment—everything. People fought over things they couldn't even use. It was insane. The Germans watched and laughed, and if there was something they wanted, they took it from the looters."

Solomon sipped some tea. His story poured out.

"Not everyone who was in the city stayed when the Germans

came. Over the next few days, a good number of people left with what they could carry, most in the middle of the night. Their property was quickly claimed by those who remained. Of course, the better homes and buildings were taken over by the Germans, whether the owners abandoned them or not. If the Germans wanted a headquarters, they requisitioned it, meaning they kicked the owners out. The same happened with livestock and food. Cows, pigs, grain, chickens, ducks, geese . . . anything the Germans wanted, they took. Sometimes, if the owner argued, the Germans would give him a slip of paper telling what was taken, telling him to take the paper to the commander for payment. That usually satisfied the owners, until they found out the receipts were worthless. Of course, by that time their property was long gone, or in a German stomach. No one was terribly shocked by this treatment. It was not really any worse or different from the treatment we'd received from the Bolsheviks for years.

"September 19th came and went. Most of us went to bed that night happier, full of hope. Before that, I think only party members might have known the feeling. How soundly you can sleep when you go to bed with hope!"

How sensitive he is, Sosha thought. "Where were you educated? You express yourself so well."

"Yes, you speak as if you went to a fine private school," Ivan added.

"Very private," Solomon replied. "Since the government never saw it necessary to provide an education for the poor Jews of Podol, we had our own school—as it has been for centuries, either by tradition or necessity—taught by our own scholars. And my grandfather was a learned man. Many hours he spent with me, nights, weekends, reading, tutoring . . ." Solomon returned to his story.

"When we got up on September 20th, the German flag was everywhere. It too was red; only the swastika replaced the hammer and sickle. September 20th was a day of settling in— the Germans into Kiev, and us into our new situation. That night, we again went to bed hopeful.

"I think it was the next day that we saw the first of the notices posted. All property that had been looted had to be returned to the Germans. All surplus foods had to be turned over to them. All radios, weapons, military equipment and supplies had to be given up as well. The disturbing part of the notice stated that failure to carry out the instructions was punishable by death. 'Anyone not carrying out this order will be shot,' it said.''

Sosha placed bread and cheese on the table. "Wouldn't you like to rest for awhile?" she asked.

"No. I want to go on."

"What happened on the afternoon of the 24th?" Ivan asked. "Late that afternoon we heard some tremendous explosions from the direction of Kiev, and that night the sky was aglow. We thought for sure the Russians were counterattacking. It was as if the war had started again."

"Let me think . . . the 24th. Yes, it was the 24th that Kreshchatik Street was blown up."

Solomon took a bite of bread, then a larger one of cheese.

"The Germans had taken over the fine buildings on Kreshchatik, in the area of Proreznaya Street. They had taken over the Continental Hotel, the Doctor's Club, and the party offices deserted by the Bolsheviks. The Bolsheviks must have anticipated the Germans' grand taste—or their greed. Kreschatik Street was the finest area in the city, ideal for the needs of the occupation.

"Anyway, as soon as the Germans were settled in, the partisans blew them up. On the 24th, around four o'clock in the afternoon, there was a series of explosions at measured intervals."

"That's right, that's what we heard!" Ivan interrupted. "It was in the late afternoon, and we heard explosion after explosion."

"You heard them blow up the Kreshchatik!" Solomon nodded vigorously. "The explosions continued through the entire night and all of the next day. In fact, they didn't stop until the 28th of September. It looked as if all of Kiev would burn to the ground."

"It is still burning," Sosha said.

"Still burning?" Solomon asked, surprised.

"Yes," Ivan answered. "At night the sky is red over Kiev from the flames."

Solomon looked at Ivan with disbelief. "But that is more than a week of burning!"

"Yes, and from the glow it puts off into the night sky, I think it will burn at least another week. They must not be fighting it. Just letting it burn itself out. Probably too dangerous to fight the flames, or maybe nothing left worth the risk of saving."

Sosha studied Solomon. He seems about average height. He's slim, but strong, I think; athletic looking, maybe he played soccer in happier days. I'll put a few kilograms back on him and he'll be as good as new. Even now he moves with grace and conviction . . . not in the least clumsy, but he still shows some weakness. The telling of his story must be difficult for him. How horrible. . . . He does have a handsome and sensitive face. He's pale now, but I can see that his complexion is normally dark. Goes with his brown eyes and light brown hair. Those eyes . . . they want to say so much. In spite of the poverty of which he speaks, he's been well educated. People of the book . . . probably learned a lot from his parents at home. Yes, he looks of Mediterranean extraction, but not so much Jewish . . . Maybe among Jews he would look Jewish, but he could be a Greek Orthodox as well. He has a square chin and jaw and high cheek bones. A thin face, long, may not fill out even after I fatten him out again. He stands straight. Full of pride.

Ivan and Solomon were still talking about the fire that would indeed continue in Kiev for two more weeks when Sosha interrupted. "Are you sure you wouldn't like to rest a while?"

"No, I feel quite strong. It is good to just be out of that little room," Solomon said.

6

"It was on September 28th that the most terrifying notice was posted. The Germans placed it all over Kiev. Its message spread like the plague. Those who didn't see it themselves soon heard about it."

"What did it say?" Ivan prompted.

"As I recall, it said, 'All *Yids* living in or about the city of Kiev, or in its vicinity, are to report no later than eight o'clock on the morning of Monday, September 29th, 1941, at the intersections of Melinkovsky and Dokturov. You are to have with you all documents, money, valuables. Bring warm clothing, changes of underwear. Any Yid not following this demand, or who is discovered elsewhere, will be shot. Any civilian entering dwellings evacuated by Yids or looting their property will be shot.'

"The appointed location, the corner of Melinkovsky and Dokturov Streets, was near the cemeteries. The old Jewish cemetery was also in the area. Actually, the Germans had misspelled the names of both streets—they were supposed to be Melnikov and Deztyarev—but the message got across. The next morning, the intersection was a mass of humanity. Most people arrived very early. If they were to be deported, better to get there early and get a good seat on the train. Most expected that they would go by train, for the location was also near the freight yards, which would make loading easier.

"Some of us were very upset, assuming we were being

deported because of the explosions of the Kreshchatik. Everyone knew that the partisans and the N.K.V.D. had planted those explosives in the basements of the buildings before the Germans arrived. Now the Jews were being blamed. To be deported for acts perpetrated by the Bolsheviks! But there was no arguing with the Germans.

"There was much speculation among us. The message had said to bring warm clothes. Did that mean a cold climate? It dispelled the hope of some that we'd be sent to Palestine, which most considered wishful thinking, at best. How long would the train ride be? It did say to bring a change of underclothes. Why not more belongings? Well, obviously they couldn't expect to take all the belongings of tens of thousands of Jews. First they would move out the people, later their possessions. Besides, what did the Jews have worth taking? Most were poor as mice; in fact, mice lived better. The Germans were allowing us to take what money and valuables we could carry. And it put many Jewish minds at ease that the Germans were not allowing homes to be looted. Of course, there were always the pessimists, who assumed the Germans were planning to loot the homes themselves."

They finished eating. Sosha suggested they continue their talk outside. "You need to get some sun and fresh air, Solomon. Let's go outdoors."

Solomon shielded his eyes from the bright sun. He sat down on the back stoop, tea glass in hand. Ivan sat on a bench next to it. Sosha followed with a tray of cheese, bread and the *chinik* and set it on a stump. She sat down on the bench next to Ivan.

Solomon went on with his story.

"We lived in the *Podol*. It was quite early, still dark out when the noise of the first Jews to leave their homes awakened us. They upset my mother; she was afraid all the seats would be taken, that our family might be separated. People who came late could not hope to be seated together, she told us. She rushed us along, my brothers and sister, my father and grandfather and myself." Suddenly, Solomon broke down sobbing.

Sosha tried to comfort him. "Why don't you rest a while? You needn't go into any more."

"No, I want to go on. I have to tell it all. You must know what these Germans are really like." He gulped down more of his tea, and when his glass was empty Ivan picked up the *chinik* and poured the glass full again. Solomon continued. "As you know, the *Podol* is the poorest part of Kiev. Each of us carried a bundle we'd made up the night before. There was nothing of any value left, not that we were taking anything other than sentimental treasures. We certainly had no savings or jewels. All that we earned went to feeding our large family. We wore most of our clothing. Our furniture the Germans or looters could have, if they wanted it. Our home, I realized as we left it, had been only what our family made of it. I mean, without us, it was a terrible run-down shack. We all felt that if we could stay together, we could make as fine a home anywhere they sent us." He paused. "Except for me, they are all together now." There was a silence as Solomon sobbed again for a few moments. Sosha, too, was silently crying. "I am sorry," he said to her, "but I feel compelled to go on."

Ivan put his arm around Sosha. His left hand, in a gesture disguised to look like a scratching, wiped away moisture beneath his left eye.

"The streets were terribly crowded. Everyone headed toward the designated intersection, slowly, because of the congestion. Not all were Jews. Many were just curious citizens; others were neighbors and friends helping us carry our belongings. Some had their things piled high on wagons that jammed up the narrow streets even more. There was no hope of reaching the corner by eight o'clock. Our only concern was to stay together. We selected points along the route where we'd wait for anyone who accidently got lost.

"From the *Podol*, we had to cross the Dnieper. It was half past eight before we arrived. After crossing the river, the crowd became even more impossible. There were often such bottlenecks that we couldn't move at all. Frequently we would just sit down on our bundles, waiting for the crowd to move on, at times for thirty minutes or more. Others sat down, too. Many out of frustration, ate food they had packed for their trip.

"The torment of deportation was deepened and made more terrifying by the acts of some of the citizens who came to see us off. What Jew has not been stung by the barbs of anti-Semitism? But that day. That day the bigots had no inhibitions. They spat on us from balconies. I saw one woman empty her chamber pot upon the procession. Insults, laughter . . . rotten vegetables, stones and bottles . . . all plunged into the stream of Jews. Now and then someone would dash into the crowd, grab an elderly or weak Jew's bundle of possessions, and run off with it. At first other Jews would try to stop them, but the Germans stationed along the way soon brought them to a halt! The pursuers were struck down with gun butts.

"It was late in the afternoon before we got to the appointed spot. A barrier had been placed across Melnikov Street, and a number of Ukrainians stood about to see that all traffic passed the barrier in only one direction. They didn't seem to care who went beyond the barrier, but they checked everyone who tried to come back. To come back, papers had to be in order. You had to have proof that you were not Jewish. All the Jews had their papers as instructed by the German proclamation, but many of the other Kievites did not carry theirs. Some went through the barrier to help their Jewish neighbors carry belongings, or simply to stay near friends until they were safely on the train. Those who later couldn't prove they were not Jewish were detained. Non-Jewish men, of course, could show they were uncircumcised and passed through. Women had a more difficult problem.

Sosha was blushing. Solomon said, "I'm sorry. I shouldn't have been so blunt. . . ."

"Don't be silly, Solomon. You forget, I've raised three boys, and Ivan is no saint. Tell your story however you must."

"I guess there is no delicate way to tell it." He paused.

"Dusk came and we were stopped at the barrier. 'That is all for today,' a German shouted. 'The rest of you will be put on tomorrow's trains.' The streets were cordoned off and we spent the night there on the roads—thousands of us—guarded by hundreds of Germans and Ukrainians with dogs and machine guns.

"The night was cold and sleep was impossible. All night long, dogs attacked those who tried to escape. Shots rang out. There was no way out . . . no way to resist.

"At dawn, the procession started again. We passed by the old Jewish cemetery. Many of us wanted a last look at the graves of loved ones, but a German soldier blocked the gate which was closed off with barbed wire. So, as we passed the long brick wall of the cemetery, many stopped and prayed. Most of the elderly knew they would never return to Kiev. 'Who will visit the graves? Who will care for them?' my grandfather moaned. 'We cannot even say goodbye. My children, promise me you'll return and visit the graves. Tell my dear Sara that I wanted to say goodbye. Tell her they would not let us.' He cried as I had never seen him cry before. Even when his Sara, my grandmother, died, I did not see him cry as he did that day. He leaned against the brick wall and started to pray.

" 'Move on, you old Yid!' a German shouted. Then he gave my grandfather a push and knocked him down.

" 'You German bastard!' my oldest brother shouted, lunging between the soldier and my grandfather. 'Keep your filthy hands off him. I'll teach . . .' He was felled by a blow from a club-wielding Ukrainian. The German and the Ukrainian laughed. 'That'll teach you Jews a little respect,' the German said, walking off.

"My mother and father jumped to his side. We all thought he was dead. He lay there, the back of his head bleeding. My grandfather stood up, too stunned to know what had happened. The rest of us had to struggle to contain one of my brothers from also going after the German.

"Finally, my brother moaned and moved his head. 'He is alive!' my mother exclaimed. 'Oh, thank God, he is alive!' She took a handkerchief and pressed it over his wound. He hadn't fully come back to his senses when another German came along and herded us on. My brothers and I had to half carry him along, at first. Then, enough strength for walking came back, though we had to guide him. He was dizzy and sick to his stomach.

In the excitement, my sister had her bundle snatched. We

looked about and caught sight of a Ukrainian woman running toward the barricade. There was no hope of getting to her through the crowd, but when she reached the entrance, she was asked to produce her papers. She had none with her. Carrying the stolen bundle, she was even more suspect. She apparently couldn't convince the Ukrainian guard that she wasn't a Jew who'd thrown her papers away in hopes of getting out. A German officer was called over, but he didn't believe her either. Finally, she was dragged back into the crowd, swearing and shouting until one guard slapped her hard across the mouth. They finally released her about twenty meters ahead of us. There was still no chance to retrieve the bundle, but we tried to keep an eye on the bitch, hoping we'd be able to get it back on the train.

"The crowd was moving faster now. There was less noise and talking. There were more Germans standing about, aiming us in one direction. We assumed we were nearing the train. We wanted very much to get on board. Then perhaps we could rest. Mother could attend to my brother's injury. We could eat a little of the food we had been saving. Though hungry and exhausted, we'd remained together!

"But now that there was less noise, we could hear gunfire in the distance—machine gunfire. There was no continuous firing interspersed with explosions as in battle. It was intermittent, at almost regular intervals. There were perhaps twenty or thiry seconds of shooting, followed by thirty to forty seconds of silence, then another thirty seconds of firing. As we moved, the gunfire grew louder and we all became nervous. 'It's just maneuvers,' the Germans told us. 'We are having troop maneuvers further up in the ravine. You need not be concerned about it. It is only a training exercise.' And we believed them. What else could it be?

"After we'd gone—I don't know how far—the crowd started to slow down, and then we stopped. We stood for a few seconds, then moved a few steps again, then stopped, and then moved forward. This went on for some time. 'They're taking us a train-car load at a time,' someone said. It made sense. The rails were just ahead. We still could not see the train, but neither could we see the front of the crowd. We continued to move and stop, move and stop.

"Finally, we came to a place where the number of Germans nearly tripled. There was a slight bend we couldn't see around, where we'd apparently have to go. We moved again, and this time the Germans stopped us, letting the group ahead of us disappear around the bend. The Germans and many Ukrainians passed among us, taking our coats, jackets, sweaters—all of our warm overgarments. They also took our bundles. Some tried at first to resist but were beaten until they relented. After the first few beatings, we realized it was stupid to resist. There was little in our bundles to fight for, anyway. 'You will get your things back when you reach your destination,' we were told. We knew how unlikely it was that they'd ever match the bundles with the proper owners, but we had no choice. They told us to move on. It was chilly now. The long, late afternoon shadows fell over us. A brisk breeze had begun, bringing with it the measured, intermittent gunfire: the sound was louder now."

7

Solomon's voice lowered. He was silent. He put his head in his hand, closing his eyes. A very low moan came from his throat. He shook with sobs. Then he cried openly. Sosha came to his side and put her arms around him, pulling his head to her chest. "Please, Solomon, rest now. Don't try to go on."

Solomon couldn't stop crying. For a long time, Sosha sat with him. At last she released her embrace, and he wiped his wet face on the sleeves of his shirt.

"Please, Solomon, don't try to go on," she repeated.

"I must," Solomon flatly insisted. "I must tell it all, now." He took a long drink fron a fresh glass of tea Ivan handed him, wiped his eyes once again and cleared his throat.

"As we rounded the bend, we saw that there were even more Germans. Ukrainians, also. Just ahead of us the corridor formed by the soldiers—perhaps two meters wide, through which we'd have to pass—suddenly narrowed. There was no way out. About every ten meters were Germans with short-leashed dogs. The rest of the soldiers, German and Ukrainian alike, held clubs or whips. There was no way out!

"Once in the corridor, we were made to run. Women, children, the old. Made to run. Whips lashed the air and struck us. The clubs crashed down. Many fell, each one tripping and toppling others. The dogs were set on to those who went down. Many couldn't get up and the dogs ripped them open. There was blood everywhere.

"We ran as hard as we could. Some were trampled to death, I think—small children, the old . . . the weak. Some parents carried their children through. A few tried to turn back when they realized what was happening. By the time we were a few meters down the corridor, most of us were dazed.

"I don't know how long that corridor was, but at the far end, we stumbled into a large clearing. Stunned beyond pain—and worse, beyond any chance for resistance—we stood in that clearing bewildered, bleeding, uncomprehending—like cattle. 'Take off all your clothes! Off. Everything off!' Again the command came: 'Take off all your clothes! Off. Everything off!' Not one of us moved until the soldiers started to rip clothing off; then it started to sink in. 'Everything off. Your shoes, your stockings, your filthy underclothes. Take off everything, you filthy Jews!'

"We began to take off our rags. We dropped our things where we stood. In a few moments we were all naked. Children sobbed. Women wept. We all looked at the ground, not wanting to see each other. I didn't want to see my mother and sister. I remember a small child crying near me; I picked her up. She pointed toward her father. I took her to him and he held her close. We bled and shivered and stood helplessly while the Germans and Ukrainians laughed and amused themselves.

"When everyone was naked and the Germans had passed among us to make sure we didn't have any rings or jewels, they herded us together. 'Now move, fast. Go through that opening!' Ahead of us were two high mounds of earth, and there was an opening between them. To get through, we had to go single file.

"If I live to be a hundred, I will never forget what we saw when we passed through that opening."

Solomon stared vacantly. Sosha wondered whether he remembered they were there with him. Then he began to speak almost without emotion, as if the voice were not even his.

"We entered a ravine. It looked to have been a sand quarry in Babi Yar. To the left was a very narrow ledge which ran along a sandstone cliff. To the right was a flat plateau, and on it— aimed at us across the ravine, were a number of machine guns.

They weren't deporting us. They were killing us!

"They marched us out. Someone up front who refused to go farther was immediately shot with a pistol and pushed into the ravine. My eyes followed him down: it was the first moment I realized the ravine was full of bodies. Hundreds of bodies!

"My eyes came back to the path. It was covered with blood, very slick. We walked along that path in the blood of our people.

"Then we stopped. A machine gun started to fire. It moved toward me from the front of the line and I saw people tumbling into the pit like dominoes, one after the other. I suddenly thought of my family and called out, 'Mama, Papa! Where are
. . .

"I slipped and fell. I struck my head and slid into the ravine.

"The next thing I remember, it was dark—very dark. The machine guns were silent. Now I heard another sound. Shoveling, men talking, dirt falling. Then something fell on my back. It was cool and moist. A second, a third time I was struck. A fourth time I was struck, this time on my half exposed face. I was just about to scream out when I heard a moan and then a pistol shot. The moaning stopped. I bit my tongue. The next shovels of dirt fell past me. More was pitched into the ravine, but it didn't hit me. It was dark and late; the diggers were tired, so they were just covering us lightly. I lay still. Close by, there was a moaning; one light passed over me, then another; then a shot rang out. The moan stopped. The lights moved on with the shovelers. Several more shots rang out to finish off someone who'd moved or moaned. I lay very still. The ravine continued to move under me as the bodies settled. Soon, the stench of blood, urine and excrement, sweat and vomit reached my nostrils. I gave thanks to God, for my life, while below me and all around me my people were dying."

8

Ivan and Sosha sat stunned. Solomon took a long drink of tea. His gaze fell toward the ground.

Ivan finally said, "God was with you, Solomon. God was with you that day."

They were words that could only have been spoken in retrospect. Surely, few there at Babi Yar that day could have thought God was with them. More likely their thoughts cried out, God, why? Why have You turned against us? Why do You let them kill the women and children, the elderly? Why do You have them kill us? And me . . . why me? And then Solomon thought, Yes, God, You were with me that day, but were You also with the others? What of the tens of thousands of others? Why only with me?

"You must rest now," Sosha said. "I insist. I'll not listen to another word until you've rested."

"Yes, now I do feel tired. I think I will rest."

"Lie down over there in that hay. The sun will be warm and good for you," Ivan suggested.

"Thank you, I think I will." Solomon was asleep in a minute.

9

Sosha carried in the tray of leftovers, and Ivan followed her with the *chinik* and glasses. "I think I'll hitch up the wagon and drive toward town," he said.

"Today?"

"Now."

"Why?"

"Close to Kiev I might be able to find something out. We must know more about these Germans. I still don't understand how all this could have happened. I have to ask some questions."

"Ivan, be careful. If you reveal that we are sheltering Solomon. . . ."

"Don't worry, Sosha, I'm not a fool. I think I'll go talk with Retski. He lives near Kiev, and he is always arguing politics. If anyone knows what's going on, he'll know."

Ivan was gone for almost four hours. When he returned, Sosha woke Solomon and put supper on the table. Ivan related what he had learned that afternoon.

"Retski confirms that people are being massacred every day at the ravine. He says it still goes on from dawn to dusk. He says it has not stopped since the 29th of last month. But what I couldn't believe is that he is in sympathy with the shootings. 'Good riddance with the Bolshevik's and the Jews,' he kept saying."

"Are his sympathies with the Germans?" Sosha asked.

"You know Retski. His sympathies are with no one. He calls them fascist pigs, whatever fascists are. He is against all political groups."

"How does he explain what has happened?" Sosha asked.

"Retski had, as usual, a long explanation, but it is probably mostly true."

"Do you think he had any idea that we are hiding anyone here?"

"Believe me, Sosha, when I tell you I was very careful, especially after I learned of his feelings about the ravine."

"Go on with what he told you," Solomon prompted.

"Well, according to Retski, the stage for the Babi Yar massacre was set long before the Germans came here. According to him, it had its beginnings when Hitler and Stalin made a secret pact in 1939."

"And how does Retski know about secret pacts?"

"If it has to do with politics, Retski finds out. And you know that in these matters he's usually right. Anyway, he said it was a situation of one tyrant dealing with another tyrant, and, as usual, their subjects would pay the price.

"Hitler and Stalin had agreed that if Russia did not interfere with the Nazi invasion of Poland, they would divide the country up between them after the German victory. Stalin would get territory, but, more importantly, he felt he was buying security on his Western border. Some bargain! The only problem, Hitler is even less honorable than Stalin. His forces invaded Western Russia on that entire front.

"We Russians knew only what the government wanted us to know of the Germans. Stalin did not allow the Soviet Press to reveal much about Hitler's activities in Europe. The little that did get into our papers was praise of the 'secret ally.' I try to tell this as much in Retski's words as I can recall.

"The average Russian, who is just educated enough to know there is a Europe outside of the Soviet Union, realized that Europe was the pinnacle of civilization. Compared with the terrible poverty the Russians experienced, the worst ghetto in Europe seemed glorious. Under the Czars, the Soviet citizens lived in constant fear, hunger and suffering. With the revolution brought about by the Bolsheviks all this worsened, so that they lived with their starvation, in terror and utter hopelessness.

"Now the German war machine is turned against the Soviet Union. The poor Soviet peasants, villagers and citizens dread the war, but they don't so much dread the Germans. The shellings, bombings and gunfire terrify them, but the advancing German army does not. As the retreating Russian troops clog the roads, most of us Soviets feel relief. As the army retreats deeper into Mother Russia, the Communist leaders and party members vanish with them. To the civilian and non-party Soviets, the Germans appear as liberators. Jew and Gentile alike think of the Germans as here to replace the barbarian Bolsheviks. The Germans that built great museums, universities and industries, that fostered great poets, artists, writers, musicians, scientists, physicians and philosophers are here to transform our slums.

"When the well-equipped, well-dressed, efficiently organized German army enters an area just vacated by a limping, tattered Russian army, it only reinforces the general feeling of liberation. The people line the streets to watch and welcome the Nazis. The occupations means an end to the shooting, shelling and bombing. The end of a short war—and of Communist oppression and poverty.

"To the unwary Jews . . . they think it might bring an end to anti-Semitism and pogroms. After all, they only knew of prewar Germany, where the Jews had found relative success, freedom and assimilation into German society.

"So in the first few days of occupation the Germans were enthusiastically welcomed. This is the way it was in Kiev on September 19, when the German troops paraded into our capital city of the Ukraine."

They finished supper, and as Sosha brought a fresh *chinik* to the table, Ivan asked Solomon, "Do you feel up to finishing your story?"

"Yes, I'd like to get the rest told, if you are ready for it. There isn't much to tell."

Sosha sat down and poured tea.

"I think I told you that we were being buried. Anyone who moved or made a sound was shot. I lay still for a long time, afraid to move, hardly to breathe. I was only under about three or four inches of dirt and sand. My face was mostly uncovered. I was naked and cold. I listened. Silence. It was time to escape.

"I raised myself up. The dirt must have been keeping me warm. The cold bit into me. My eyes could not adjust to the dark. If there was a moon, its light was not falling on the ravine—an advantage if there was a guard about. I groped my way over the piled-up bodies. The thin layer of dirt could not disguise the carnage. My hands touched now a thigh, now a face, now a riddled chest . . . all chilled and sticky with blood. I was afraid I might vomit and some soldier might hear. But my stomach was empty. I crawled.

"Then I came up against one of the sandstone walls, which one I couldn't tell. I stood up. I felt for the top but couldn't reach it. Then, I tried to walk across the bodies, using the wall to balance and guide me. At every stop I reached up for a handhold. Loose dirt kept giving way underfoot. My toes pressed down on the soft bodies. Soon the cold, disorientation and despair all gripped me. I could find no way out!

"Then I had an idea. I bent down and reached into the earth and grabbed a body. Limp and heavy, there was no lifting it. I got down on my knees and dragged it onto the body beside it. For the moment I was thankful for the blackness of the night. I felt, grabbed, and dragged another body upon the first. Then another. Another. Another. It took a long time. Finally, I climbed on top of the pile and with all my strength pulled out of that ravine.

"I stood on the narrow rim off which we had been shot. The blood on the path had dried and was no longer slippery. I remembered the dropoff was to my right when we were marched in. Now it was at my left. Then I began to crawl slowly, stopping often to listen. At last I reached the large dirt mounds that formed the narrow entrance to the pit. Again I listened. Silence.

"I escaped into the field where they'd made us undress. I could see better, but that brought with it the fear of being seen.

I stayed in the shadows and looked around. There was no sign of life. Then I saw what I hoped was a pile of clothing. The Germans and Ukrainians had looted the confiscated clothing, then placed them in piles—to be picked up later, I suppose. I rummaged through a pile near me and took whatever fit and put it on. In a pile of hundreds, I found two shoes—not a pair, as you know—that fit well enough. I felt warmer.

"I crossed the field toward where I remembered the woods being. Passing under the branches, I could feel the terrain steepen. I didn't dare stop climbing. Fatigue pulled at me and the climb was slow. Many times I tripped, fell, ran into trees or brush, but I kept climbing.

"At last I was out. A clearing let me look back. From where I stood, I could see across the ravine. On the other side, the entire sky was lit by the fires that still raged in the Kreshchatik. Babi Yar was just a deep black hole. There were a few fires below where German or Ukrainian soldiers were encamped, or maybe where other Jews waited for tomorrow's 'deportation.' My fatigue caught up with me. I found some underbrush, crawled beneath it, and fell into a deep sleep."

Sosha interrupted, "Are you sure you want to continue?"

"Perhaps a little more tea. . . ."

Ivan picked up the *chinik* and felt it. "This has cooled off. There is more hot tea in the samivar."

Sosha took the pot to refill it. She returned and refilled Solomon's glass. He sipped and went on to tell how he awoke with a start in the morning. It was the sound of machine gun fire that brought him back from sleep. He could not see the pit, but he knew what was happening. Twenty or more seconds of firing, a brief silence, then firing again. How many would die today? He peered out of the bushes. No one was in sight. He crept out and stood up. Looking across the ravine toward Kiev, he could see people sitting on the other side, looking down into Babi Yar. Some of them had picnic baskets and blankets; many had their families with them. They were having a wonderful time watching the slaughter of Jews.

Solomon ran across the small clearing at the top of the ravine and into the woods. He ran until he was exhausted, tripping over stones and stumbling through the underbrush. Finally, he fell headlong into the wild growth. He lay there breathing deeply for a long time while his senses returned. This would not do. He had to move with caution. What if he ran into Germans? He would be right back at Babi Yar. Maybe they would shoot him on the spot. He decided that if he were captured he would try to escape and force them to shoot.

Getting up, he leaned against a tree. From the sun and the shadows and the distant sound of the shooting, he determined the direction in which he wanted to go. Babi Yar was surrounded by Kiev and its suburbs. The least habitation lay to the west. He put the sun at his back and started to move with caution, staying in wooded areas as long as they lasted. In a short time, he came to a sparsely-populated area. He avoided roads, cutting across fields and gardens. Soon he had passed through the only populated part of his escape route.

Now he had large, uninhabited areas to cross. He took to the woods, to ditches. When there were fields, he selected unharvested ones so the crops could offer him protection. Where there were only harvested fields, he went out of his way not to cross them. He followed hedge rows and windbreaks. Occasionally, he would glean a potato or an onion or beets from the edge of a field.

Thus he traveled into the night until he tripped—exhausted, thirsty and in shock—into a deep ditch. He was unconscious before he hit the bottom and there he lay, half dead, until Ivan found him at dawn the next day.

Now Ivan would talk.

PART II
SIN OF OMISSION

10

The Roman Catholic Church came to Russia by way of Poland. Its greatest influence was, therefore, in Western Russia. Though not a large population, most of the Roman Catholics in the Soviet Union now fell under German occupation.

Father Peter Rochovit had his parish in the countryside surrounding Kiev. It was a poor parish, his congregants mostly peasants. Not only was the economy hard on them, as it was on everyone in the Soviet Union who was not a Bolshevik, but in the Ukraine the Roman Catholic church was a minority church. The Bolsheviks discouraged religion, and the Vatican considered communism its most dangerous enemy.

Father Peter was the second of six sons born to a peasant who came to the Ukraine in 1897; he was born in 1910 in the parish he now served.

The Roman Catholic church was central to Peter's family's existence. Peter had been attracted to the church at an early age. He found in it an escape from the harsh life in the Ukraine. He became a favorite of the elderly priest of the parish, who encouraged Peter to pursue a life of service to God.

Because the parish was poor, the church school provided only a basic education. It was adequate for most, since most peasants considered formal education a luxury. If a child learned to read, it was a great accomplishment, although literacy did little to help provide for a family. If one member of a family could read, then that family was no longer illiterate, and it did not seem important for more than one member to learn the skill. In the Rochovit family, Peter had the greatest aptitude, so he'd been chosen to get the education.

After Peter finished his schooling at the church school, the old priest arranged for him a scholarship to divinity school in Poland, with the understanding that he'd return to his district and follow in the footsteps of his mentor. Peter went to Poland at the age of seventeen. At the age of twenty-two, in 1932, he returned as a priest to his parish. When the old priest died in 1935, Peter took over the parish and served the people he'd known and loved since childhood.

Father Peter believed in what he preached and lived by his teachings. In spite of his youth, he had good judgment and considerable wisdom. He was an avid historian and an insatiable reader. His knowledge of other religions was vast. His interest in political philosophies was also deep, and he was concerned with the dangerous policies of Bolshevism. He felt, as did the Vatican, that communism was the greatest threat to the Roman Catholic Church and to other religions.

Even though Peter kept up an active correspondence with several priests in Poland with whom he'd gone to school, he had no idea what German occupation would mean to the people of the Ukraine. His colleagues in Poland did not write to him of political matters. He was a victim of the same news censorship that kept all Soviets uninformed. When the Germans came to occupy Kiev, which included his parish, he too saw them as liberators, believing they would lift the yoke of religious persecution off of all the faithful, but especially from the Roman Catholics, since Hitler and many of his top officials were Roman Catholic.

He also believed that the industrious and cosmopolitan Germans would bring his people new opportunities to throw off the heavy burdens of poverty and ignorance. But after the Germans entered his parish on September 19, 1941, he and his parishioners heard only the distant sound of machine gun fire, carried on the wind from Babi Yar.

11

"What are your plans now?" Ivan asked Solomon on Tuesday morning, October the 7th.

"I don't know."

"You are welcome to stay with us until you decide," Sosha told him.

"Thank you. I appreciate all you've done, but I'm endangering you by staying here. If the Germans found me here, they'd shoot us all. I can't put you to such a risk."

"We have not even seen a German, yet. I don't know that they will come this far from the city," Ivan said.

"Oh, they will get here. As soon as they have the city secured, they will come."

"Well, we'll see," Ivan said. "Anyway, until you decide what your next move will be, you'll stay with us. We'll all be safe enough for the time being. You can sleep under the steps. During the days you can help me with the chores. We'll keep our ears open and an eye toward the road."

Ivan was right; another week passed and still the Germans did not come to the farm. Because they were fighting the Russians on an enormous front, the German army could not stretch its ranks enough to put soldiers into the rural areas. They concentrated their forces in cities and strategic villages.

During the third week Solomon decided he would join the resistance and do what he could to avenge, in some small way, those who died at Babi Yar.

12

Not until October did Father Peter find out what all the gunfire was about. He couldn't believe it; the Germans were, after all, a cultured people. Even the Bolsheviks would not have dreamed of killing thirty-four thousand Jews! Of course, pogroms had killed a hundred thousand or more over the past few centuries, but that was not the same as shooting thirty-thousand men, women and children and heaping their bodies in a mass grave. On the other hand, he thought, it wasn't that different at all.

Father Peter was troubled. How could he confront the atrocities? By Saturday, October 4th, he had not yet found the answer. What stand would he take at mass tomorrow?

On Sunday, Father Peter gave a scathing sermon condemning the German atrocities at Babi Yar. His parishioners were shocked. Some had an attitude of "good riddance to the Yids." Others were disturbed by the actions of the Germans, but they were not ready to stand up for Jews. No one stayed after church to talk with Father Peter about his sermon, as was usual on Sunday mornings.

On Monday morning, a German staff car pulled up in front of the church. The officer got out and entered the church. It was empty. He went out and walked around to the back. There he found Father Peter pumping a bucketful of water.

"Good morning. You are Father Peter Rochovit, I must assume."

"Yes, I am. Can I help you?"

"I am Major Hans Oberman. May we talk?"

"Of course. Please." Father Peter pointed to a bench and the two sat down. He wondered which of his parishioners had reported his sermon.

"Several of your parishioners have remarked to us about your sermon yesterday. I must say that we are surprised and disturbed by what we have heard."

"Surprised? Disturbed? I do not understand why this should surprise you!"

"Your remarks went against official church policy."

"I do not believe so."

"Please," said Oberman. "The official Catholic policy is well known. It was set out clearly in 1933 by the Vatican, in an agreement with our Fuhrer. It is only because of that agreement that you have not been arrested." The German paused.

"Please go on. I am not aware of this agreement and would like you to give me the details." Father Peter knew the German could offer no details because the agreement story was a lie.

"You priests amaze me!" the German said arrogantly. "Here we are doing efficiently what the Roman Catholic Church has been doing piecemeal for centuries, and you all seem so astonished."

Father Peter was speechless.

"Why do I shock you? After all, the Catholic Church was trying to rid the world of Jews long before there was a Germany. The Crusades were blessed by the Pope; anti-Semitic policy was built into the Christian doctrine by Paul, the founder of your faith. You know as well as I do that the ghetto was not an invention of the Germans. We have just improved on the concept."

"Surely you can't compare . . ." Father Peter began.

"If you will just recall," Oberman interrupted, "the first ghettos appeared in Venice, toward the end of the fifteenth century. After that, the Roman Catholic Church established ghettos for the Jews everywhere that it had sufficient influence over local governments. And it was the Roman Catholic

Church that passed ordinances that Catholics could not work with Jews or deal with them, driving them out of many professions and occupations. The Roman Catholic Church has reminded the world for centuries that Jews are nothing but tyrants and congenital enemies of Church and State. Understand, Father, I have no argument with those facts. What I find disgusting and hypocritical is that you speak out against your own policies, when someone else carries them out for you!"

Father Peter was stunned. He was well versed in history and knew he could not argue these facts with the German. These were facts not openly discussed by churchmen . . . delicate matters, best left undiscussed. Well then, thought Father Peter, what of this agreement? "Tell me of the agreement you mentioned."

"The fact of record is that on July 20th of the year 1933, your Pope, Pius XI, signed a concordate between our Fuhrer and your Vatican. The Roman Catholic Church agreed to keep its priests and the influence of the Church out of politics. Your sermon yesterday certainly did not uphold your Church's side of that agreement. I think you will admit that it is your obligation to support the policies of the Vatican. Am I wrong?"

"No, you are right. I must uphold the policies of His Holiness. I do, however, question your interpretation of this agreement—*if* it exists."

"Oh, I assure you, it exists. Without question it exists. I would suggest that you contact your superiors and make yourself familiar with your obligations in these matters. The Vatican knows that what Hitler and the Reich do is for the best. You should have faith in the wisdom of the Church. When the Vatican agreed to keep out of our politics, our Fuhrer granted complete freedom to the educational and religious policies of the Church. We have certainly lived up to our end of the bargain. We are a very understanding people, however, and we realize that your comments were probably provoked by a lack of insight. We felt that this dialogue would help you to understand the situation better and remedy the problem. I am sure that after you have had a chance to consider all that I have said, you will find it in your heart to give your parishioners a better sermon next Sunday. I am sure that they would be only too interested in the real facts of the matter. Admit that you spoke hastily! They will have nothing but the deepest respect for you then. We are, after all, doing what is best for you and the rest of the world. The Vatican understands that; surely you cannot doubt that wisdom."

Father Peter was silent. The German appeared satisfied.

"It has been a pleasure to meet you, Father. I am sure you see the validity of my statements. Remember, we are in this struggle together—the Reich and the Church—to rid the world of the Bolsheviks and the Jews. Both are a threat to civilization. Both are a threat to the Church."

Oberman got up and continued with small talk as they walked to the front of the church where the staff car awaited. Father Peter didn't hear a word. Major Oberman thanked Father Peter for his audience and departed. On the wind, the sound of gunfire from Babi Yar continued.

13

Solomon's decision to join the resistance was the easy part. How was he to contact the resistance? Resistance organizations did not make their whereabouts generally known. There was no way to know who their contacts were, no way that Solomon could make his intentions known. He asked Ivan whether he had any idea of how to contact a resistance group. Ivan could think of none.

After a few days, Ivan decided to go to Kiev. On the way he would stop off with some neighbors and talk to them. He would discuss the occupation and get some feeling of their sentiments. Perhaps he could get a lead or an idea of how to make contact with the resistance. He would have to be very careful not to arouse suspicion. While in Kiev, he would take some produce to market. The marketplace was a trove of gossip. He had yet to meet his first German soldier. This trip would afford him his chance. And he could also find out more about the events of Babi Yar. Solomon, too, was interested in what more had happened there since his escape. Sosha in the last minute decided to go with her husband. She could be another source for information. Gossip was far more prevalent among the women.

It was agreed that while the Igonovichs were at Kiev, Solomon would stay out of sight. He decided that he would hide himself in the woods behind the farm during the day. If they were still gone after dark, then he might go into his small hidden room. He departed for the woods and Ivan and Sosha left for Kiev.

Solomon had wanted to explore these woods for some time. Early in his stay, he'd thought it would be wise for him to know his way around the area. He might be able to find not only an escape route but an alternate hiding place; he might even build one. It was just a matter of time before he would be discovered if he stayed at the farm.

The day was warm for autumn. This was the first time since his recovery that Solomon had ventured away from the immediate surroundings of his hideaway. It was like a holiday. It had always relieved the drudgeries of the *Podol* when he had a chance to go out into the woods; it was much the same now. The few birds not yet migrating chirped and were answered by the chatter of squirrels. Sunlight trickled through the trees, making bright patches on the forest floor. The dry, fallen leaves rustled underfoot, releasing a strong scent of fall.

He had walked about a quarter of a mile when he came across an old trail. In days past, trails led from village to village, but when the villages were deserted, victims of urbanization, trails fell into disuse.

The layer of leaves on this trail was thick and undisturbed. The path was obviously seldom used. Solomon would follow it as far as he could. He decided to follow it to his left first. He reckoned the direction to be north. The morning sun was to his right and a little to his back. It threw a long shadow of himself toward his left and slightly in front of him. It amused him to have such good company.

When he had walked about a kilometer, he came upon a small stream. The ancient footbridge was in disrepair, the left-hand railing gone and three-quarters of the planks of its floor were missing, or broken through. Solomon balanced his way across on the mostly-exposed log that was the left support of the narrow bridge. On the far side of the stream the trail took a sharp right and followed the river. Solomon missed his shadow, which was now behind him. Every once in a while he would turn to see whether it were still following him. At one point, he caught himself talking to it. "We must stay together, you and I. You are my only remaining *mishpocheh.*

Solomon followed the trail along the stream until it ended at a small ravine. He could see where a bridge had once been, but it had long since collapsed. Its remnants were lying below. The ravine was perhaps fifteen meters deep, its sides steep, but not too steep to negotiate. It was perhaps thirty meters across, and Solomon could see where the trail continued on the other side. It occured to him that this would be an ideal area to explore for a refuge. It was obvious that no one ever used this path anymore. Certainly the Germans would have no idea of its existence.

He climbed down into the steep walls, and at the bottom he looked back up. It didn't look as deep from there. Instead of climbing back out the other side, he decided to explore the ravine. As he looked around, he realized he'd left his shadow on the top, for the sides kept out of the sun. "I will pick you up later. Wait for me up there in the warm sun!" he called out. As a child, he'd had a little stuffed bear, and he remembered talking the same way to it. When he had his bear, he always had a friend. Now, aside from Ivan and Sosha, he was totally alone. As far as the world was concerned, he was dead.

If the trail on which he had just come ran east, then this ravine must run north and south. Since he had been traveling north before the trail turned, he decided to explore the ravine to the right first. This would take him south. "Let's see. I'll be doubling back, keeping me closer to the farm than if I went farther north. Better I should know the terrain around the farm well rather than to spread out too far." He estimated that he had traveled one or two kilometers north and about two kilometers east of the farm. If he now turned south, he would be staying within a two-to-three-kilometer radius. "If I could find a good hideaway in that range, it would be perfect." He'd be near someone he trusted—near a place where he could get provisions—yet far enough away to hide without jeopardizing his friends.

The dry creek bed he was walking in was probably one that flowed only with the winter run off, or when occasional heavy rains caused it to flood for a few turbulent hours. As he made his way north in the ravine, he wondered where the stream that the trail had been following went. It made a turn south a few hundred meters back, where he and the trail crossed it by some stones that had been placed there. It now occurred to him that the stream and this ravine must both empty into the same body of water. . . . "Perhaps the Dneiper River. It would be behind me, to the south. How far? It would be good to know. Someday that might be an escape route."

He traveled an estimated kilometer and came to a small cave. It was at a curve in the ravine, along the outside wall of the turn. Its entrance was under a shelf cut by centuries of rushing water. It was a hole about one meter high, five or six meters wide. It would give excellent protection, except from floods. Then it could be a death trap. Stooping down, Solomon went under the sandstone shelf to the low entrance. Crouching even lower, he crept inside. Once inside he could stand up. It was a rather large chamber—a geological bubble, hollowed out by wind or water. When his eyes became used to the dim light streaming through the entrance, he noticed something else. At one end of the cavern—a rise. The floor at that spot was about a meter and a half above that of the rest of the chamber. Perhaps it would be safe there even during high water. The thought excited Solomon. He went back toward the entrance where the light was better. He looked carefully at the walls there. His excitement increased. The water line appeared to be no higher than a meter. It did not go more than a few centimeters above the top of the cave entrance.

"It's like submerging an inverted glass into a bucket of water. As long as the glass remains inverted and air can't escape, the water stays out."

Solomon emerged from the cave with a wide grin on his face. The sun was higher in the sky now, and it could reach the bottom of the ravine. Solomon was happy to see his shadow had rejoined him. He went about a hundred meters back down the ravine. He noted a spot where it would be easy to climb back out of the little gorge. In a short time he was back on top, at the edge of the forest. He sat down by a tree and took two turnips from his pocket. "Lunch time," he told his shadow. As he sat eating, his mind raced. He would come back here with provisions and store them in the cave. Also, he wanted to find or make a more direct route to this place. He calculated he had traveled about five or six kilometers to get here.

"If I could go directly through the woods, it might not be more than one or two kilometers. The farm must be almost due west."

He got up and started through the woods. His shadow, shortened by the noon sun, walked abreast of him to his right. It dodged in and out, disappearing and reappearing in the shadows of the trees. But as the sun moved into the west, his shadow started to fall behind him. "Too bad you can't keep up," Solomon laughed over his shoulder, "but I'm in a hurry, and I can't slow down for you now. You'll have to do the best you can."

14

Solomon came across the path after only about a half an hour. He turned left on it.

He had gone about half a kilometer when he saw something he didn't recognize—a large boulder in the middle of the trail which he had to veer around. "I've come too far!" He backtracked for about a hundred meters then decided to turn into the woods again. "The farm can't be too far. If I don't run into it, I'll at least come to the road that runs in front of it." He marked the trail at this point and turned left into the forest. Moments later, he found himself at the edge of the woods, behind the farm, almost exactly where he had left the property that morning.

He was just about to start across the field when he heard someone shouting in German. He dived back into the woods. Crawling behind a tree, he held his breath and listened. Again he heard German. He didn't understand the words, but he knew there were at least three persons. His heart pounded fiercely. What could he do?

"Compose yourself. Relax. You're safe here in the woods. They have no reason to suspect you're here."

Slowly, he turned onto his stomach and crawled to a small clump of brush at the edge of the woods. Hidden there, he made a surveilance of the farm. No one, but the voices continued— three, then a fourth voice, then a fifth—all from in front of the house. One by one, five soldiers came around from the other

51

side of the house. They were looking into windows, annoyed to find no one there. At the back of the house, they saw the cellar's entrance. One man opened the door, pointed his gun down the stairwell, and called into the empty storage room. He listened, then slowly started down, pulling a flashlight from his belt, while one of the other Germans stayed at the door with his gun ready. After a minute, the first emerged again. They all went on, leaving the door open.

Now a few more soldiers appeared—ten altogether. One was obviously an officer. He barked commands left and right, and the others made themselves busy. They searched the house with the same caution as they'd used in searching the cellar. Then the officer pointed out the few animals that were grazing, pecking and wallowing about the farm. As he did, an aide at his side made notes on a clipboard. Probably send a truck out to get them, Solomon thought. They all went back around to the front of the house, and in a few minutes, he heard motors start, vehicles driving off.

Solomon remained where he lay for the rest of the afternoon. Not until Ivan and Sosha returned after dark and he saw the lights go on in the house did he come out of the woods. Even then, he advanced toward the house with care. He looked into the windows before he knocked and entered.

He told them first about the search of the premises. Then he told of his explorations. He warned that the Germans would probably be back soon to confiscate the livestock. He insisted that it was time he move to his new home in the ravine. Ivan agreed that they should put some provisions in the cave, but he was not so sure that Solomon would have to move there permanently—at least not yet.

The day had been exhausting for everyone, and they decided to retire. They would talk further tomorrow.

15

Father Peter could not get the German's visit off his mind. Over the next few days, he'd become more and more disturbed. Each day he could hear the intermittent gunfire from Babi Yar. The only respite was when the wind occasionally blew towards Babi Yar; then the sound was carried away. But Father Peter knew they were still busy with their loathsome work.

"Dear God," he would murmur, "how long can they keep that up? How many people are they killing? They killed all of the Jews of Kiev in the first few days. Who are they killing now?"

These questions haunted him. He could not reverse his stand in his next sermon. The German's words bothered him day and night. Father Peter knew that the historic facts about the Church were true. Anti-Semitism was a product of early Christianity, and it had been kept alive by the Church ever since. It was a fact that the Church had to accept but preferred to sweep under the rug. As a historian, he could not deny the truth, but he did not like having these facts pointed out to him by Major Oberman. In spite of all this, he could not believe his superiors expected him to sit silently while Jews or any others were being slaughtered like so much livestock. He would write to his bishop for advice.

He lay awake two nights composing the letter he would write. Over and over he wrote it in his mind. But before he had a chance to put his thoughts down on paper, he received a letter from the bishop. Word of the sermon had gotten to the superior churchman. The letter did not contain the history lesson the German presented, but it did express an unquestionable reprimand for the stand that Father Peter had taken in his last sermon: "It is not our place to mingle in politics. Our place is to teach the word of our Lord, Jesus Christ. Political matters are to be left to those who govern, and now, that is the occupation forces of the German Reich. They are our allies in the Church's struggle against Bolshevik oppression."

He crumpled the letter and threw it to the floor.

He knew he could not bring himself to reverse the stand in his sermon. He struggled with his conscience. Finally, he decided that his next sermon would be on a subject completely divorced from the problem. The subject selected was a simple commentary on a Bible reading, in no way connected to the events of the time. Since his bishop had left no doubt about the position he was taking, Father Peter decided to take unprecedented action. He would write directly to the Vatican for guidance. He would not say more on the subject until he heard from the Holy See or his representative. That was as far as he could make his own conscience bend. He put down on paper the thoughts he intended to write to his bishop. But this letter was going to His Holiness, Pius XI. Father Peter wrote and rewrote that letter, perhaps twenty times, until he thought it was just right. In it he explained in great detail his controversial sermon and his defense of it. He also discussed in great detail his encounter with the German officer. Then he asked for enlightenment on all agreements and policies of the Vatican and the Roman Catholic Church in regard to the activities of the German Reich. He closed his letter asking for specific guidance: How should he advise his parishioners to live under the occupation? How should he behave toward the occupation? And what about the activities at Babi Yar?

His answer would be long in coming.

16

After breakfast the next morning, Solomon and Ivan went to the cave. They followed the landmarks Solomon had set. They had no difficulty finding it, and the jaunt took them only about half an hour. They estimated that, if pressed, it could be done in fifteen to twenty minutes. Between them they decided which provisions should be taken to the cave. Then Solomon suggested they make a small enclosure in the woods to keep some of the livestock hidden. The Germans would surely be back to confiscate the animals.

"Why let those bastards find all of them? After all, Ivan, you could say you had sold some of the animals."

They agreed, and on the way back they selected a spot. It was by the stream that the trail followed, so that the animals could have water. In the afternoon they returned to that spot with tools, cleared an area and built a makeshift fence. This done, they herded a few of the animals from the farm to the corral. They hurried, knowing the Germans might be back anytime . . . certainly in a few days.

The next day they made several trips to the cave, each time carrying supplies until they had enough provisions to sustain a person for weeks without need to leave the cave. All the time they were working, Solomon wondered whether he would be the only one who might have to use the cave as a refuge.

Ivan and Sosha told Solomon all about their trip to Kiev. They had no leads on how to contact a resistance group. The people in Kiev were all extremely cautious, afraid to talk openly of their feelings. No one trusted anyone else. The city was completely without Jews now. All had been killed at Babi Yar in the first few days of the slaughter. The few who were not murdered had escaped the city or were in hiding. The killing at Babi Yar continued. The sick, the insane, the lame, captured communists and soldiers—anyone not following the German edicts to the letter was being taken to the ravine. They were also bringing people to Babi Yar by train for extermination. There was a curfew in Kiev now, and anyone on the streets after the appointed time was shot on sight. Each morning, women, children, men were found where they'd fallen, killed only because they were on the street after dark.

The people who in the beginning greeted the Germans as liberators now feared them . . . hated them.

"How foolish the Germans were to make potential allies into staunch enemies," Sosha said.

"No one speaks of resistance," Ivan said. "If such a move is already under way, no one admits being part to it. Too many are willing to sell information to the Germans."

"I know the feeling," Solomon said.

"Sosha did hear one bit of gossip that might be a lead. In the marketplace, she heard some women talking about a sermon that had been given by a Roman Catholic priest, Father Peter. It seemed he had condemned the Germans. The gossipers said he was sure to end up at the ravine for his comments, but so far the Germans had only reprimanded him. Perhaps he's changed his view to save himself. "Anyway," Ivan continued, "it would be dangerous to see the priest at this time. He might be under surveillance. A visit could endanger him, as well as the visitors. If we can't find another way to contact the resistance, and if the priest is not in custody—and does not change his sentiments—perhaps he might be a lead in the future. We'll have to wait."

Two days went by. Ivan and Solomon were moving some stones from a corner of the field near the woods at the back of the property. Ivan suddenly stood up straight. "Listen!"

"What is it?"

"Listen! I hear a truck."

Solomon heard it now. It was very near.

"Quick, run into the woods," Ivan whispered. "There isn't time to get to the cellar."

Solomon turned and ran the few meters to the trees. He dived to the ground and found himself near the same brush from which he had watched the Germans the other day.

"Stay hidden," he heard Ivan say. "I'm sure it is the Germans. I'll see what they want. Probably they are coming back to get the animals."

Ivan started walking toward the house. There was the squeal of worn brakes. A door opened and slammed shut; German and Ukrainian voices sounded. The motor idled. Now Ivan could see the truck on the road in front of the house. Solomon could not see it, but all the sounds reached him.

Two Germans got out of the cab, and three Ukrainians jumped out of the open back of the truck. They had been riding there with several animals apparently picked up at other farms. Ivan met Sosha as she came out of the house, and they walked together toward the approaching men.

The Germans spoke neither Russian nor Ukrainian. The German who was not the driver—a corporal—spoke to one of the Ukrainians, who acted as an interpreter. He, in turn, spoke to Ivan in Russian.

"We are here as representatives of the German occupation forces. We have come to collect your livestock, as decreed by the commanding officer of the occupation forces of the Kiev area."

"I do not understand," Ivan replied. "You just want to *take* my animals?"

"It is everyone's duty," the Ukrainian replied. "If you do not cooperate, it will be hard for you."

"But animals are my living! What are we to do if you take our livelihood?"

"You will survive. We must all make sacrifices. There can be no exceptions. Now, enough talk! Let us do our work. This list states that you have five pigs, three cows, a horse, and several chickens, as well as geese. Where are they?"

"You are mistaken, sir. As you can see, we do have chickens and geese. Out there is the horse, but we only have one pig, and no cows."

"This list states you have five pigs and three cows."

"But we are poor! Such livestock would make us wealthy. Where did you get such a list? Surely there is some mistake."

Sosha was terrified. What if they didn't believe Ivan? What if these were the same Germans that searched the farm? They would know. Ivan was taking a terrible chance but it was too late now. And what if they saw the cow dung in the field? The Ukrainian spoke in German. They looked at the list together. They looked at Ivan. They talked again, then the German spoke curtly and turned for the truck. The German driver followed him, leaving the three Ukrainians to round up the animals. Sosha was visibly relieved. Ivan said he would help; he wanted them out of there as quickly as possible. The horse and pig were no problem, but the chickens and especially the geese were another story. The men gave up after catching only half of them. Satisfied, they drove off to the next farm.

Ivan turned to Sosha as the truck dwindled into the distance. They smiled.

17

The church was full on Sunday. Father Peter didn't know quite how to interpret it. Were they there because they were in sympathy with him? More than likely they were there out of curiosity. Would he speak out against the Germans? He wondered who in the gathering had reported to the Germans last week. His eyes fell upon one stanger in the crowd, too well-dressed to be Ukrainian. They were not going to depend on his congregants. Germans. Well, if they wanted fresh material for charges and arrest, they would all be disappointed.

The sermon was no more inflammatory than the mass itself. As the worshippers departed the church, the traditional line of parishioners formed to compliment the priest on his service. The well-dressed man was in the line. He spoke Russian but with a German accent. "A fine service, Father. I especially enjoyed your sermon. I want to continue attending your services while I am stationed here. It will be wonderful to hear such a sermon each week!" He tipped his hat and departed without waiting for an answer.

Father Peter was relieved. He had feared that the Germans would demand a public retraction of his stand, and he could not do that. He hoped the German's superiors would be satisfied. But all this was only a stall. Sooner or later the matter would arise again. The Germans were not going to change. Every day the winds carried the sounds of gunfire. He could not continue to ignore that sound. He would eventually be forced to restate his feelings. he would have to do that much, regardless of Church policy.

Days passed. No reply came to his letter. The gunfire continued. He could not escape it. From dawn to dusk, Father Peter heard each report as life snuffed out. How many shots could be fired in a single day? Thank God the days were getting shorter. If each day was even a few minutes shorter, how many lives would that save? How many times could a machine gun fire in two minutes? Ten . . . twenty . . . fifty? That was significant. If ten, twenty, or fifty lives could be spared because it grew dark a few minutes earlier, then how many would die each day in the twelve hours that the guns were active? He began to feel responsible for the deaths of all the people who died on each day of his silence. Silence condoned the crime. But what would his speaking out do? Nothing but add him to the thousands in the pit.

Still there was no reply. How much longer could he continue to wait. If he didn't get answers soon, the pressure of his conscience would force him to act. If the Church did not show him the way, perhaps God would.

18

Three days later, God replied.

A man appeared at Father Peter's door. Father Peter was so eager for a sign—some approval to act—something that could free him from his guilt. He was sure that this was divine guidance. But he had to be careful. It could be a trap. How could he be sure the Germans were not setting him up? He knew the consequences of trusting the wrong man. Arrest would come immediately. This would be one way for the Germans to discover his true sympathies. But Father Peter was at the limit of his endurance. Here was a chance to act. If it were a trap, then let it spring. He welcomed the man in.

Gregor Kirtzof was the name of the man who appeared at the church that day.

"Good morning, Gregor. How pleasant to see you. It is...."

"Father, I will come directly to the point. I heard your sermon two Sundays ago. We all know your sentiments. I want to tell you there are a number of us who feel as you do. We realize that you are in danger from the Nazis if you speak out again. We know that you can say no more than you have. In fact, we implore you not to speak out again. There is a small but growing group of us who intend to act against the Germans. If there is any way in which we could serve your cause—so that you are not endangered further—I will be happy to serve as your contact."

Father Peter invited the young man into his personal chambers.

Gregor Kirtzof lived in Kiev proper. He was the eldest son of a blacksmith and apprenticed to his father. The family business made a meager living, but by Soviet standards they lived well. The family was large; Gregor had four brothers and two sisters. So the forge had nine to feed. The Kirtzoffs were a religious family. The few Sundays they didn't show up, the church seemed a little emptier, especially when the hymns were sung. Father Peter had known the family since he was a child.

Father Peter closed the door to his humble apartment, which was attached to the back of the church. He poured two glasses of tea and they sat down at a small table.

"Tell me, Gregor, what is it like in the city?"

"Terrible! Worse than under the Bolsheviks. The Germans may not threaten the Church as much as Bolsheviks did, but they are not what we believed them to be. How can a cultured people be so uncivilized? They have no regard for human life."

"I have heard shooting every day. Can they really be killing so many?"

"Yes. In the first two days, the Germans slaughtered over thirty thousand Jews. Since then, all of the rest. There were one hundred thousand, Father Peter! Ten percent of all Kiev!"

"But surely some have escaped."

"A few may be hidden, but they would be very few. Any Kievites discovered hiding Jews are also killed. Their bodies are stuffed into Babi Yar at the ravine, but most of them are publicly shot in the city along with the Jews they were hiding. It sets an example. Always after a public execution a number of Jews turn up, deserted by their benefactors."

"So it is true, then. I cannot believe it," Father Peter said.

"It is not only Jews they are killing. They shoot prisoners of war, captured partisans, communists they discover, ex-officials of the previous government who did not escape the city, and, worst of all, people they round up at random."

"You mean to tell me they just pick up people?"

"Reprisals for breaking their rules!"

"No questions? No trials?"

Gregor laughed. "Trials? The nearest thing that they have to a trial is torture and interrogation. That is reserved mostly for partisans who might have information the Nazis could use."

Father Peter sat stunned. He had known it was a terrible situation, but, like many, he had hoped that much of what he had heard was rumor.

"Once they swooped down on the Kreshchetik," Gregor continued, "and arrested the first hundred men they found on the street. They took them off to Babi Yar and shot them to pay us back for a German soldier who was found dead one morning. They might drive into an area at night arrest all of the people in a house or apartment building. The sound of motors or brakes terrifies our people."

"Terrible," Father Peter murmured.

"It is not just the fear," Gregor went on. "What little food there is is rationed. For a few ounces of flour or stale bread, we have to stand in line a full day. All food stores and livestock, if we had any, were confiscated during the first days of the occupation. And food is not all they have taken. Radios, weapons, tools, good clothing, blankets—all have been confiscated." There was a short silence. "And there is the curfew. We must be indoors between six p.m. and five in the morning. They might drive into an area at night and arrest all of the people in a house or apartment building. The sound of Bang! They're shot. I think the Germans consider it sport, like hunting squirrel or rabbit."

"It is truly a wonder that I was not arrested for my sermon," Father Peter said. "It is surprising the Germans had such patience with me."

"That is why you must not say anymore. You cannot know whom to trust. A great many people would sell information to the Germans for an extra ration of bread. Besides, there are more important things to do."

On this point, Father Peter could not contain himself. "Who spoke to the Germans about my sermon?"

"I don't know. But you were the talk of Kiev that day. The Germans may have heard of it from a second or third party."

"I see."

"The Germans will watch you closely, but I don't think they will move against you if you keep your course! It is said they try not to interfere with the Catholic Church. Apparently Hitler made a pact with the Vatican. He is Roman Catholic, you know."

The priest was shocked to find the Nazi-Vatican agreement was such common knowledge. If it was so well known, why had his superiors not replied?

19

His Holiness, Pius XII, was born in 1876, as Eugenio Maria Giuseppe Giovanni Pacelli. After his education, he entered the Secretariat of State in Rome in 1901. He was appointed professor of ecclesiastical diplomacy at the Pontifical Ecclesiastical Academy in 1909. He held that post until 1914. During that time, in 1911, he was also made undersecretary of state in Rome. In 1917, he was appointed Archbishop of Sardes and apostolic *nuncio* to the Bavarian court at Munich. In 1920, he became *nuncio* to Germany and in 1925 he moved to Berlin. He became Cardinal Pacelli in 1929 and Secretary of State in 1930. It was in that capacity that he negotiated a concordat between the Holy See and the Third Reich.

That agreement was signed by him and Hitler's Vice-Chancellor von Papen on June 20, 1933. In that concordat, the then Pope Pius XI agreed to keep the Church and its priests out of Hitler's politics. In return, Hitler would not interfere with the policies of the Vatican and the Roman Catholic Church. Though Franz von Papen signed the concordat with Cardinal Pacelli, he was cordially welcomed by His Holiness, Pius XI, who then took the opportunity to express how pleased he was that Hitler and the German government were so uncompromisingly opposed to communism. The Vatican considered itself a full partner in Hitler's battle against communism and thus blessed the Third Reich. The Vatican's prayers went out to give the Third Reich Godspeed in attaining its goals. The

Vatican ordered its Bishops to support and swear their allegiance to the Reich. "In performing my spiritual duties, I will endeavor to avoid all acts which might be detrimental or dangerous to the Third Reich," were the concluding words of the churchmen's oath.

In 1939, Cardinal Pacelli became His Holiness, Pius XII; he supported the agreement that he had negotiated and signed for the Vatican six years earlier. The great majority of bishops and priests supported the agreement. There would be no public condemnation of the acts of the Nazis from the Roman Catholic Church.

When Father Peter Rochovit finally received his letter, it came from a secretary of the Vatican. It was impersonal and gave him no specific guidance for his situation. There was enclosed a copy of the July 20, 1933, concordat. A brief cover letter declared that the enclosure would explain the position of the Church. It emphasized that the Third Reich was doing what was best and necessary in the common struggle against communism. Father Peter was reminded that his duties were to be concerned with spiritual and not political matters of his parish.

Father Peter Rochovit decided he would not be able to support the dictates and position of the Church.

20

Four days had passed since the Germans confiscated Ivan's animals. No more Germans had been seen in the area since. It was nearing dusk, and Solomon was entering the woods behind the farm. He was headed for the corral to prepare the hidden livestock for the night. He had just gotten to the trail when a sound stopped him in his tracks. It sounded like a mumble, but it had a strangely familiar ring to it. Again, he dived into some underbrush. He listened. The sound continued. It came from deeper in the forest, between the trail and the cave. Cautiously, he started toward the sound.

Creeping perhaps fifty meters, he found himself at the edge of a small clearing. What he saw was too unlikely. I must be dreaming, he thought. In the clearing were three men dressed as peasants. Ukrainians. Two silently rested against trees, while the third man produced the sound that had brought Solomon there. It was not quite dusk, but the forest held out the fading light, and it was properly dark for the evening prayer—the evening *Amidah, Maariv,* chanted daily by all Orthodox Jews.

Here in the forest, Solomon had found another Jew! Probably three Jews, at least one of whom was orthodox in his observance, saying the three *Amidahs* each day . . . *Sheehrit* in the morning, *Mincha* in the afternoon, and *Maariv* at evening time. Solomon kept himself from running into the clearing; he didn't want them to flee before he could identify himself. More importantly, if they were armed and on the run, they might shoot before asking questions. At that moment he thought of the safest way to make his presence known. Softly, Solomon started chanting the *Maariv* as he had done daily with his father, brothers and grandfather.

The two men sitting came to their feet. Suddenly to hear evening prayers coming from the trees! The *davening* Jew almost choked on his words. They all stood dumbfounded as Solomon walked, chanting, into the clearing. Without stopping his prayers, he walked to the side of the *davening* Jew and continued his chant to its completion. The other Jew joined him as soon as he had composed himself.

After they finished the prayer, Solomon introduced himself. They told each other of their recent plights.

The three men were Ukrainian Jews who had been conscripted into the Soviet Army. They had come from various units captured by the Germans. Upon seizure, the first thing the Germans did was separate the Jews from the rest of the war prisoners. They were loaded on trucks, under guard, to be taken to an execution point. All three men had been on the last truck of the convoy, along with about fifty other Jewish prisoners. Realizing they were to be executed, they decided unanimously to try to escape if the opportunity presented.

There was only a motorcycle with a sidecar and a machine gunner following the end of the convoy. Each truck carried four Germans: two in the cab, a driver and an armed guard, and foolishly, two, both armed, in the back with the prisoners. The captives were told that anyone talking would be shot, but there were too many in the truck for two soldiers to watch. In very discreet whispers, they made and passed their plans. Approaching the Kiev vicinity, they passed through a series of forests, where the roads twisted and curved quite severely. It was the best chance they would get. At a predetermined signal, they made their move.

Their actions were lightning swift. They hit the two guards who had been lulled into carelessness by the long, boring ride. They stripped their weapons from them in seconds and threw the limp bodies off the back of the vehicle into the path of the motorcycle, which had been following too closely. In the reflex swerving and braking of the motorcycle to avoid the bodies, its riders were distracted enough to let the prisoners get off the first burst of gunfire . . . killing the cyclists instantly.

At that moment, the other prisoners jumped over the sides of the truck, which had slowed its speed on the curve and was hidden from view of the rest of the convoy. Most of the men were off and to the woods before the two Germans in the cab of the truck knew what happened. As the last of the men went over the side, one of the prisoners with a guard's weapon fired into the cab. Then he jumped clear and also headed for the woods. The first fugitive off the truck ran to the dead cyclists and confiscated their weapons and ammunition. In all, the whole escape took less than thirty seconds, and the last truck of the convoy was not missed until the rest reached a straight stretch of road a minute and a half later. The getaway could not have gone smoother.

Not all of the escapees stayed together, but about fourteen did. Most of the weapons and munitions were in their possession: three machine guns, two pistols and a small supply of bullets. With that they decided to carry the war to their enemy, the Nazis.

For the next three days, they moved continuously through the forest. In running from the German search party, they came across a band of Ukrainian partisans. Their paths crossed purely by accident, and the Jewish group considered it extremely good fortune. The partisans numbered in the thirties, and the Jewish escapees wanted to join forces with them.

The Jews were still in their Soviet Army uniforms, and the partisans knew these men were probably well trained, and, from their appearance, battle-seasoned men. Many questions were asked of the Jews . . . over and over, about their escape, and all that had gone on before and after. They were finally satisfied that the fugitives were what they claimed: escaped prisoners of war, Jews who wanted to join up with a partisan group to fight the Nazis. The Jews understood and respected the precautions being taken.

Not until they had convinced the Jews that they believed their story did the partisans ask them to turn over their weapons. Overjoyed that they had been "accepted" into the organization, the Jews did not hesitate to relinquish their arms.

"Now," the leader of the partisans began, "we must get you out of those uniforms, or what's left of them. Follow this man to our supply cache. He will get you other clothes and show you where to bury your uniforms."

They were led off into the woods.

Moshe Pinsker, the orthodox one, felt uneasy. The further they walked from the encampment, the stronger his uneasiness grew. He was relieved that he had not surrendered the pistol he carried under his shirt. It had a full clip of bullets in it, but he had no other ammunition.

Moshe had been near the front of the group when they started into the woods, but as his feelings intensified, he began to fall back, whispering his fears to others as they passed him. Most paid him no mind. By the time they had covered a third of a kilometer, he and two others had lagged to the end of the group. The three turned off the indistinct path. They followed the sounds of the others, but at a distance of twenty meters to the side and rear.

Moshe whispered to his companions, "I tell you, there is something terribly wrong here. I would think that the trail to their supplies would be frequently traveled. That path shows no signs of heavy traffic. I can believe that they would hide their supplies away from the main camp, but not so far away. I don't trust them and I don't know how to convince the others."

"I think you are overly suspicious, Moshe," one of the other men said. "I think we should catch up with the others."

It was at that moment that the three heard voices coming through the woods. The larger group had come to a clearing and there found three more partisans awaiting them with automatic weapons. "All right, you Jews. Get your asses over there. Men, make it fast. We have their weapons. There is no reason to burden ourselves with these Yids any longer." If there was anymore said, it was drowned out by the noise of guns. When the guns stopped, all that could be heard was the laughter and joking of the Ukrainian partisans.

The three surviving Jews ran.

Two days later, their paths crossed that of Solomon.

21

The three men were half starved. Solomon decided that the livestock would have to survive the night on their own. He took the men to his cave and told them to stay there until he returned, and he offered them all the supplies they needed. Solomon returned to the farm. That evening, Ivan and Solomon went to the cave together after checking on the animals.

The three had eaten their fill and were asleep when Solomon and Ivan got there. No glow was visible outside of the entrance, even though the cave was dimly lit by two candles. When they awoke, Moshe introduced his companions to Ivan. He seemed to be their spokesman and leader.

"Mr. Igonovich, I am Moshe Pinsker. These men are Uri Bolnik and Boris Spovinski," he said, pointing out his two friends.

"You needn't be so formal. I'm known to my friends as Ivan."

"Then please know us as Uri, Boris and Moshe."

Formalities done, the five of them got down to business.

"I suppose Sol has told you of our situation. We had hoped to join a partisan group to fight the Nazis, but it is obvious now that we will have to do that on our own. The anti-Semetic Ukrainians are as big a threat to us as the Germans. We will have to form our own Jewish resistance."

"Then I will be your first volunteer," Solomon said.

"Good!" Boris exclaimed. "What a success. We have increased our ranks by twenty-five percent!"

In that moment, Solomon felt for the first time since Babi Yar that he belonged somewhere. It didn't matter that his future was no more sure nor secure than a minute earlier. He was no longer alone. Kind as Ivan and Sosha had been to him, it was not the same. Now he was among his own people again. He was *mishpocheh*—family . . . the tribe.

"How do you plan to recruit?" Ivan asked.

"I don't know," Moshe replied. "But, if need be, we will be a four-man army."

It was decided that for the time being the cave would be their headquarters. Solomon spent the night with his new fellow partisans. He would be the go-between from the farm to the cave. It would not be wise to have too many strangers moving visibly around the area. Ivan volunteered to be the eyes and ears for the group.

"Good," Moshe said. "Better that we have gentile eyes and ears in the gentile world."

Ivan did not take offense but suddenly became aware of what they were up against. It was not just the Nazis they had to fear. They had to be wary of the entire Christian world. Many non-Jews who hated the Germans would gladly turn over a Jew to them, or simply kill them as the Ukrainian partisans had. Anti-Semitism was not a German invention; it was an invention of the Christians. In this part of the world, Jew baiting and Jew killing were not such crimes.

Sol continued to work about the farm for Ivan and Sosha. In time, the neighbors who occasionally passed would think him a hired hand and not out of place. That way he could move freely about the area. When Ivan and Sosha went into Kiev, however, he could not go with them as hired hands sometimes did; it would be too risky. Dressed in peasant clothes, he could easily pass as a Ukrainian non-Jew, but he had no papers, and too many Kievites knew him.

The four Jews did most of their partisan work at night; only Sol worked during the day, when he made his appearance at the farm. During the first few days they used morning and evening twilight to become familiar with the area.

They explored the ravine that the cave was in. Solomon and Uri explored up from the cave, while Boris and Moshe explored down. They went far beyond the point where Solomon had entered the ravine. They followed the stream bed to its eastern end, where it opened to the Dneiper River. At that point they were about twelve kilometers north of Kiev. The ravine there widened and became heavily wooded.

The ravine turned at the cave, and Solomon and Uri explored to the south. The ravine deepened as they went. At the end of about three kilometers, however, the sides of the ravine lowered again and widened until the two found themselves on some rolling, hilly pastures. Cautiously they pushed on until they worked their way to the top of one of the higher hills and one of the few that offered some trees for cover. From there they saw a broad highway leading to a sizable town perhaps a kilometer away. Then the two returned to the cave, taking about forty-five minutes at a fast walk.

Solomon reported their findings to Ivan later in the day.

"That town would be Irpen," Ivan told him. "It is not too important, except that it is on the road as you saw, which is a major route across the Ukraine. It leads to Kiev if you follow it east. It is bound to become a main supply route for the Germans."

"How far would you guess Irpen is from Kiev?" Solomon asked.

"Ten or twelve kilometers, I'd say."

That evening, all four of the partisans and Ivan followed the ravine to the south. After dark, they descended to the road and to the outskirts of the town. There was little activity there, but plenty of Germans. The Germans appeared to be using this town as a storage depot. Numerous trucks were parked there, and a number of storage buildings had been set up. There seemed to be only enough troops to guard the equipment.

"These must be supplies to be used in Kiev," Uri suggested. "They probably store them here because it is easier to protect them from theft and sabotage."

That sounds reasonable," Moshe agreed. "What do you

think they store here?"

"That will be our first project," Ivan said. "Now let's get out of here and make some plans."

They turned to the ravine and started back toward the cave. They were only about a kilometer into the ravine when they heard voices. Each man froze. The voices came again. Moshe touched his right index finger to his mouth. Then he pointed toward the top of the ravine to the left. The walls here were steep and high. Moshe signaled the men to follow. He headed on down the ravine toward the cave. After little more than half of a kilometer, he stopped.

"I think it is safe to speak now, but quietly," he said. "As we came up along here earlier, I saw a trail that seemed to lead to the top of these walls."

"That's right," Uri interrupted. "I noticed it this morning. It can't be too far. Maybe a hundred meters north of that rock outcropping we just passed." He pointed to the landmark about thirty meters behind them.

"Good," Moshe replied. "Uri, you come with me. We will try to double back on top of the cliff. The rest of you go back to the cave and wait. We should return within the hour. If we don't, do not come after us. It would be pointless for all of us to be wiped out in one operation."

An hour passed, and an hour and a half. Ivan had gone back to the farm. He did not like leaving Sosha alone. People were becoming desperate for food, clothing, or anything that could be sold or traded. More and more reports were circulating about robberies throughout the area. People who lived outside of the cities were easy prey to desperate drifters.

Finally, after two hours, Moshe and Uri returned to the cave. With them were two Jewish families along with seven unrelated Jews. Theirs had been the voices on the cliff. They had been living in the woods for several days and nights, coming from the northwest of the country. Their intention had been to escape the occupation ahead of the German advance. The families had slowed their progress and soon found themselves passed by the German front. They had then to restrict their movements to nighttime and through the woods. It was very difficult. By the time they reached this area, they realized that to reach unoccupied territory was almost hopeless. The refugees were having a meeting to decide what to do when Moshe and Uri came upon them. The two partisans had only to listen for a short while to become convinced that they were Jews. It took a little more to convince the larger group that the two partisans were Jewish. Not until Moshe *davened* for them did they believe.

Recruitment was easy after that. The partisan band now numbered twenty. Twenty-one if Ivan were included, and if Ivan were to be included, then Sosha also could be counted, making twenty-two. The two families number four and five.

The partisan group was now made up of Moshe, Solomon, Ivan, Sosha, Uri, Boris, four men between the ages of nineteen and twenty-nine among the unrelated Jews and five women in that same group between the ages of seventeen and twenty-five. The two families contained three children between the ages of three and six. Their fathers were twenty-three and twenty-seven, and their mothers were twenty-four and twenty-five. There were no elderly or sick among them yet, but one of the first things the group decided was that no Jews would be turned away from the group. The partisans would commit themselves to saving Jews as well as to destroying Nazis.

Their windfall was not without its problems. It was time to reorganize to accommodate the number now in the group. The cave was too small to house the partisans now. It could be used for storage, but a new encampment would have to be found. Also, they would have to carry out a raid immediately for supplies and food. Irpen was the logical target.

For the present, Moshe was appointed leader. He picked his next in command from those he knew best: Solomon, Uri, Boris, and one of the new partisans . . . the one who seemed to be a spokesman for them. Dovka was one of the five women among the unrelated Jews. At twenty-two she had earned a law degree. Her father had been a judge—unusual for a Ukrainian Jew in those years. Her family was one of the first to be wiped out by the Nazis. She had not been home at the time of the roundup, but her father, mother, and younger brothers and sisters were hanged in the public square as reprisals for an act of resistance. Dovka saw the terrible execution from a window overlooking the square.

Rachel was another of the unrelated women. At nineteen, she was next to the youngest of the girls. She, too, had lost all of her family. Shy and sensitive, she had developed a close attachment to Dovka, finding security in Dovka's strength.

The group had the manpower to carry out a raid against the supply depot at Irpen, but their entire armament was the gun with its six bullets which Moshe had not yielded to the Ukrainian partisans and an old rifle of Ivan's with a few rounds of ammunition. Among the new arrivals were only three knives, and these were kitchen utensils.

Moshe called the group together. He sent out several men to find a site for their new camp. He asked Ivan to go into Irpen to reconnoiter and report back. Ivan took Sosha with him. They were the only ones who had identity papers, which made them the intelligence arm of the partisan band. Then Moshe met with his command personnel to get organized. They met until mid-afternoon. By that time, Ivan and Sosha returned and told them the layout in Irpen. The men also had located what they considered to be an almost ideal site for the new camp. They would all go to look, but not until they planned their raid on Irpen. That took precedence over all, for until the raid was carried out they had no source for supplies.

The Germans were storing supplies in trucks themselves. This reduced the handling of materials and conserved storage space. As they talked, a problem presented itself. From the information that Ivan and Sosha brought back, they decided the most likely plan was simply to sneak into the town, get into the trucks, and drive out with them. The storage depots were used mainly for heavy ammunition and weapons. Ivan had counted only eight men stationed at the truck parking area. How many there would be at night was mere speculation. There was no fence around the trucks. The problem was that few of the Jews knew how to drive. Moshe, Boris and Uri had learned to drive in the army. Dovka knew how to drive, much to everyone's surprise, but she had never driven a truck. They'd tell her what she'd have to do. The only other driver was one of the family men, the older of the two. Not only could he drive, but he had been a mechanic, and he told the others how to start a vehicle without its keys. At best they could steal only five trucks, and it was doubtful that they would know what their contents were before the job was done. It would be a risky mission.

Ten partisans would enter Irpen. The other five would take care of the guards, help to hotwire the trucks, and, if they succeeded in getting away with a truck, try to learn a little about driving by watching their companions. The remainder of the band would wait at an appointed place to unload. They would then have to carry the supplies back to the cave. The empty trucks would be abandoned far away to mislead the Germans, and the drivers would have to walk back. Their companions would stay with the others to help carry. Moshe, Uri and Boris gave the others who were to go into the town a quick course on how to kill the guards silently.

At about one hour after darkness, ten partisans left for Irpen.

It took them about two hours to get to the parking area. They were amazed to find only six Germans guarding the trucks. Uri decided to make his way around the entire area to be sure that there were no more guards in the vicinity. He was back to the others in less than five minutes. While they were waiting, the others started to hotwire five of the trucks. That done, they turned to the unpleasant detail they had planned to take care of first. Moshe appointed one German to each of four groups of two partisans. He and Boris would take care of the remaining two guards, one each. Each team crept off into the darkness. They had learned their lessons well. Only one of the Germans had a chance to cry out, and fortunately he was the last to die. No one heard his brief yell except for the other partisans, who had already dispatched their victims in silence. So far the mission was going perfectly . . . too perfectly, perhaps. They dashed to the trucks, all of which started. They pulled out on the road without headlights and proceeded to their rendezvous.

"Beginner's luck," Moshe confided to his partner. There was no traffic on the road. No one followed them. The raid had not yet been discovered. Six Germans lay dead, stripped of their weapons and ammunition. A few minutes later they were at the rendezvous with the rest of their comrades. Quickly they emptied each truck. When they got to the last truck, the one Dovka had driven, they came across their first bit of bad luck. In retrospect, it was humorous, but Dovka had risked her life to take a truck loaded with condoms.

From the time they had stolen the trucks until they were emptied had taken only twenty-five minutes. The raid had gone so well, in fact, that Uri suggested they go back and steal five more.

"You are crazy," Moshe said.

"Sure it's crazy," Uri agreed. "But what better chance do we have than right now? After tonight their security will be ten times heavier. If we go back cautiously we can get five more trucks if these have not been missed."

"Let's take a chance on it," Boris agreed.

"It is crazy," Dovka confessed, "but I think it might work. If we drive back to about a half kilometer from the town and leave the trucks there on the road, we could go on foot and watch for any activity at the truck parking. If they have detected anything, we should know it before we expose ourselves."

Moshe considered for a few moments and then said, "All right. But only the five drivers go in. I'll not risk ten lives for this insanity. Maybe God has given us this night. Let's make the most of it."

Twenty minutes later they were back with five more trucks, and fifteen minutes after that the trucks stood empty behind the first five on the road into Irpen.

Dovka said, "I only regret having to take back all those condoms. If we could only have destroyed them, maybe the whole German army would get syphilis!"

22

The partisans carried supplies all night long. They couldn't begin to get everything back to the cave, but what they had to leave they were able to hide and bring in over the next few nights. They worked until an hour after sunrise, and they were about ready to drop from exhaustion. Moshe ordered them to rest a few hours.

While the others slept, Moshe, Uri, Dovka and Solomon started to take an inventory. They had gotten from the guards six automatic rifles with twenty rounds of ammunition for each. They had taken one pistol with three clips of bullets. They had also recovered five knives and six bayonets. But when they started to go through the other supplies they realized the full measure of their success.

Moshe made up an inventory list in the order the items were found:

> Blankets, wool #260
> Canned field rations #50 cases of 48 tins each
> Dynamite #50 boxes of 60 sticks each
> Lentils #50 bags—50 lbs. each
> 5,000 bullets (wrong caliber)
> 48 oil lamps (no oil)
> Medical supplies #8 cases, assorted
> Pencils #1 box of 1,000
> Typing paper #10 cases
> Shovels #1 case, short handle, 24

Emery boards #1,000
Soap #5 cases 48 bars each
Handkerchiefs #6 cases 250 each case
Dinner Bells #1 case of 60
Table salt #10 bags 50 lbs. each
Light bulbs #10 cases 48 bulbs each
Coats, winter #70
Flour #6 bags 50 lbs. each
Coffee beans #4 bags 50 lbs. each
Soup ladles #80
Shoe polish, brown #4 cases 60 tins each case
Mouse traps #3 cases, 100 per case

Moshe was disappointed that there were no weapons. There were also no blasting caps nor fuses for the dynamite, but he thanked God that they'd lost no lives in the mission.

The children had been asleep in the cave while the adults were on the mission. They awoke to find the grownups in exhausted slumber. Rachel had chosen the entrance to the cave to lie down. She was awakened by the children when they awoke. To keep them from waking the others, she decided to take them for a walk in the woods before breakfast. Quietly they slipped away down the ravine until they found a place where they could get up its side easily. Once on top, they walked into the woods. She pointed out the different trees that she could identify. They had gone only a little way when they came across thousands of chestnuts lying all over the ground. They had happened into a grove. Rachel told the oldest child to run back to the cave and bring some empty boxes.

An hour later, the triumphant children and Rachel returned to the cave with two boxes filled to the brim with chestnuts. All day long the children went back to the grove, with first one and then another adult, until by mid afternoon they had brought the thousands of nuts from the forest floor to the cave. The children would be no burden to the partisans.

23

As head of the intelligence arm of the small partisan group, Ivan started to look for sources of information. He decided to talk to "the priest" who had spoken out against the Germans. There had been no more inflammatory remarks since the first, but Father Peter Rochovit was still one of the biggest topics among the gossips of Kiev. Ivan thought something might be gained by opening a dialogue with him.

During the last week of October 1941, almost four weeks after the slaughter started at Babi Yar, Ivan made his trip to the church. There had been no let up in the gunfire from the ravine. Ivan had put off this inevitable visit because of his concern that the priest might be under surveillance. Also, many of the Jewish partisans had indicated that they did not trust any gentile. "Isn't it possible that the priest might have made that first sermon just to attract partisans and Jews for the Germans?" some of them asked. It was not a majority opinion, but it had to be considered. There was much discussion.

Ivan finally decided on his own to visit the priest. He was not concerned that he would reveal too much to Father Peter. His concern was that if he was arrested because of the meeting, the Germans might extract information from him by torture.

Early on the last Friday in October Ivan made his way to Father Peter's church. He had left his home before sunrise to get to the church by eight. He did not go directly to the church but walked past it on the road for about half a kilometer. The church was surrounded by fields. The priest's garden was in the back. To one side was a cemetery, and in front a dirt road. At about a half kilometer he turned around and scanned the entire area. There was no sign of surveillance. He walked back directly to the church, found the door to the sanctuary open, and went in. He sat down on a bench and wondered what he should do next.

Father Peter had watched Ivan walk past the church. He had watched him walk up the road and return. He'd seen Ivan turn into the churchyard and heard him enter the sanctuary. Now he sat by the window of his quarters and wondered what he would do next. There was no alternative. He would have to go and see what this stranger wanted. It certainly was not the first time a stranger had entered his church. But this one disturbed the priest. He would have to be cautious. He got up and entered the sanctuary.

"Good morning. You are a stranger here. I do not recall seeing you before, but please feel welcome. I am Father Peter Rochovit."

"I know, thank you. I am Ivan Igonovich. It is true, I am a stranger to your parish and church, but I do not live far from here. I have a farm eight kilometers north."

"You must have started out very early. Can I offer you some tea?"

"Yes, thank you."

"Let us go to my chambers and you can tell me, Mr. Igonovich, what important matter brings you here so early in the morning."

Ivan was obviously uneasy. But his uneasiness made Father Peter more comfortable. Perhaps it was because insecurity did not fit the German personality, nor that of most collaborators. But he was not reassured enough to let down his guard. When Ivan couldn't find words right away, the priest continued, "Are you a Catholic, Mr. Igonovitch?"

"Please call me Ivan. No, Father, I practice no religion."

"Well, then, you are not here for confession. Tell me, are you a Communist? Are you seeking sanctuary?" The questions were out before the priest realized it, and now he was sorry he had asked them.

Ivan was surprised at the bluntness. "I am not a Bolshevik, and I am not seeking sanctuary. But I understand that if I were, I would do well to come here. To be frank, Father, I understand you heart is in the right place."

Father Peter was very uneasy. He had put himself in a vulnerable position. "I refer to sanctuary of the soul," he said. "I . . . I . . .." he tried to find words. "I do not mean to get involved politically."

"Father," Ivan said. "I am going to gamble my life on a hunch I have heard the truth about you; then I am going to leave. You will either turn me in to the Nazis, which I doubt, or you might completely ignore what I tell you, which I also doubt. I think you will find some way to act that will help my friends and me fight the oppressors."

Father Peter was aghast at the sudden candor. He tried to hide his shock.

"Father, I suspect that since your impassioned sermon of several weeks ago, certain people have or will in the future seek you out. There are certain of those people that I am interested in."

"I don't understand," the priest said in all sincerity. "What certain people?"

"The Jews!"

The priest had expected almost anything but that reply. Why did this man want the Jews? Was he indeed a collaborator? Could it be he was asking him to turn the Jews over to the Nazis?

"The Jews? Why do you want just the Jews? How do you expect me to get you Jews?"

"Because the Jews have a very special problem. They cannot trust non-Jewish partisans." Ivan related the experience of Moshe and the Ukrainians. "They feel—and they are right, I'm afraid—that everyone is their enemy. that is why I think Jews might contact you. They have nowhere else to turn. You cannot direct them to non-Jewish partisans. It would be too risky. They might end up dead after being stripped of all they own. With us, they will at least have a chance."

Father Peter did not commit himself.

Ivan did not ask for commitment. He suddenly rose and started for the door. "Father, I have placed my life in your hands. Please consider carefully what I have said." As he was leaving, he told the priest how to find him at his farm. "I hope you will contact me and not the Germans. Thank you for your time."

It took several days for Father Peter to absorb all that Ivan had said. He went over and over the events of the morning trying to find a flaw, some clue that would tell him whether Ivan's message was truth or treachery. He weighed all the possibilities. If Ivan were a collaborator, even inactivity could be interpreted as treason by the Germans. The Germans would expect him to report the meeting immediately; to ignore it would be shirking his duty to the occupation. Well, if that were their game, then it was done with. There was no way that he could turn Ivan over to the Nazis. On the other hand, maybe they were really trying to use him to capture Jews. How could he be sure? He could talk to Gregor Kirtzof about it, but what if his partisans would also kill the Jews for their possessions? He didn't think it possible. But the constant sound of machine gun fire from Babi Yar . . . that, too, he hadn't thought possible.

24

The second week in November about an hour before sunrise a knock on the door woke Ivan and Sosha. They both sat up quickly. Sosha immediately throught something was wrong at the encampment, that the knock was a partisan's. Ivan thought first of Father Peter: Could he have sent the Germans?

There was no chance for escape. Ivan got up and went to the door and opened it. A tall, thin man in clothes too light for the cold fall night stood framed in the doorway.

"You are Mr. Igonovich? Mr. Ivan Igonovich?"

"Yes. And who are you? What do you want?"

"I am a Jew. I am a Jew sent by the priest, Peter Rochovit."

Ivan stepped part way out of the doorway and looked about. There was no one else there. "Quick, step in." He closed the door behind him.

"You say Father Peter sent you? How did he happen to send you to me?"

"He said you would know about it. He told me you would know what to do."

"You say you are a Jew. How do I know you are a Jew?"

"To the Germans I can't prove I'm not a Jew, and to you I have to prove that I am. How do I prove I'm a Jew?"

"I don't know. Say something Jewish."

The stranger looked at Ivan as if he were mad but went ahead and said a few words of Hebrew and then a few words of Yiddish. "There, does that mean anything to you?"

"No. It sounds Jewish, but I can't know for sure. I must know for sure."

Sosha was watching from the darkness of the other room.

"Wait here while I get dressed." Ivan went into the darkened room and returned a few moments later. "Follow me." Ivan wanted to get the man out of the house. He would think about his next step as they walked. He felt better when they got away from the farm. If this were a trap, getting away from the house now would not alter anything; nonetheless, he felt better about it.

"Is anyone else with you?"

"No. I am alone."

They went down toward the road and walked along it for about a kilometer. Ivan kept looking about to see whether they were being followed. He saw no one. Finally they came to a sharp turn in the road, and as they turned the corner, Ivan and his companion ran abruptly into the woods. They were about five meters into the forest when Ivan stopped. They waited for several minutes to see whether anyone came around the turn following them. When no one came, Ivan started walking again. The sun was beginning to light their way dimly through the woods. Ivan turned, and doubled back and made circles, retraced their tracks and thoroughly confused his companion. The whole time, he looked and listened for followers. None appeared.

After almost an hour in the woods, he started toward the new encampment. It took almost another hour to get there. When they arrived, Moshe and the others took only a few minutes to satisfy themselves that the newcomer was indeed a Jew, a *landsman*, a member of the tribe.

"Did Father Peter tell you that you might be walking into a trap?" Ivan asked.

"Yes. He told me you had contacted him but that he couldn't be sure it was not a trap to uncover his activities or capture Jews in hiding. I knew full well the chance I was taking. If I found Jews, I was to return to him and inform him that you were what you said you were. If I do not return, they will assume that I met with the Nazis."

"They? Why do you say 'they?' "

"The priest and the other Jews."

"There are more Jews?" Moshe asked.

"Yes, seventeen of us. We have gathered over the weeks in the woods. We did not know where to turn for help. One of our group had heard about the priest's sentiments, and we thought perhaps he could help us. That is how I have come here. If you will have us, I will report back to the priest and get the rest of my group."

The partisan band now numbered thirty-nine. It was time for another mission.

PART III
OCCUPATION
1942–1943

25

By mid-January of 1942, the partisan band contained more than a hundred Jews. Between November and mid-January, the encampment was moved three times. Each time, a large number of newcomers joined the movement. It was a precaution Moshe thought would reduce the chances of discovery or betrayal. He also decided the camp would have to be moved each time a partisan disappeared, to assure that the Nazis couldn't torture the camp's location out of their captives.

As the group became larger, moving became more difficult. But Solomon came up with an idea that would allow maximum security without constant disruption of the community life.

There should be three camps. The first camp a very mobile one where supplies can be gathered for and from missions, he explained to Moshe. They would not use it more than forty-eight hours at a time. New members could be brought in through it, and there be observed before being told about other camps. If there were a betrayal, or if someone followed newcomers, only a few partisans lives would be jeopardized. If the Germans followed a mission back to the first camp, the same would hold true; after a mission, no one would go back to camp two for at least twenty-four hours.

Camp two would be a temporary facility housing mission-eligible partisans and newcomers from camp one. The new partisans would remain at camp two until their loyalties proved unquestionable. It would look like the partisan's main encampment, and the knowledge of camp three would be kept from newcomers until they're deemed safe to go there. The second camp would be moved only in cases of capture or security leaks. Unless a major mission were anticipated, camp two would never at one time house more than a fourth of the partisan band. This would reduce the chances of a crippling raid.

The third encampment would be deep in the forest, almost a wilderness area, a day's travel from the nearest road or village. It would be the bands' permanent home until the occupation was over. All routes to this camp would be posted with lookouts. A warning system would give at least three hours to prepare for defense or evacuation. All children, elderly, and non-combatants would live in camp three. New partisans wouldn't be brought to camp three until their loyalty had been proven. When partisans were scheduled to go on a mission, they would have to leave camp three at least twelve hours in advance to get to camp two or one. Camp three would be far too remote to be the staging area for any mission.

Everyone agreed to try Solomon's idea.

For most of the Jews, camp three was the first place they had ever been free of the constant abuses of the Christian world.

Shelters at both the first and second camps were makeshift and temporary, usually leanto-type structures made of tree limbs. Sometimes trenches were dug and lived in. Any natural shelter, such as a cave, was utilized. Once in a while, they used deserted farm buildings.

The main camp was another matter. Everything had some signs of permanency. Houses had been built among the trees to give protection from the weather and the observation of men in overflying aircraft. Built simply, the houses were not unlike those used by Ukrainian peasants for centuries. The average building was about five meters by three meters and as much under the ground as above. It could be put up in a day or two by several men. First, a hole was dug about four feet deep by the dimensions of the building to be constructed. When evacuated, the hole looked like that dug for the foundation of a house, but no foundation was constructed. Instead, logs were placed on the ground at the edge of the excavation, laid upon each other to a height of about one meter, making the structure look like a short log cabin. Then a thatched roof was added. The earth which had been excavated was piled outside the logs. When completed, the houses looked like low mounds of dirt with thatch in the middle. There was a vent for smoke from a fireplace at one end of the room. Inside, it was dark. The distance from the dirt floor to the roof was about two meters, with the roof having just enough slope to carry off rain water or melting snow. The primitive structures gave excellent protection from the cold winter winds and weather. In the hot summer months, if the Jews were still there, the huts would be cool. There was such a home for each family. The unmarried men and women lived dormitory style, a house for each eight men and women. There was also a house that served as a headquarters building and one designated to be a synagogue and school. Supplies for the camp were kept in three other buildings, and there was a common kitchen, though it was used mainly by the single partisans. The families often preferred to cook for themselves. There was also a hospital building—as yet seldom used, fortunately.

A short time after the three-camp system was established, Solomon started to keep a diary. Events demanded documentation. Certainly the Germans would not keep honest chronicles of their atrocities. If there were no survivors, how would the world ever know what went on? It was a common fear among the Jews that the world would never learn the truth about their extermination. Many besides Solomon started diaries, hoping they would be found later.

The new life in the forests, the daily chore of survival, the inhumanity of the situation all produced changes in the partisans. The times made changes in Solomon, too. He now wore a beard. The warm sparkle in his eyes didn't disappear, but he developed a bitterness not uncommon to the partisans who had lost so much. Solomon's humor often turned sarcastic. It was never directed at individuals, but at the world outside the encampments. The hard work of survival made his body strong and sinuous. In the few months that ended 1941 and began 1942, he matured remarkably. People respected his opinions in spite of his youth, but then most guerrilla activity was carried out by the young. And in those first few months of forming the Jewish community in the forest, Rachel became an increasingly important part of Solomon's life.

26

Now that there was a mutual trust between Father Peter and Ivan, the priest started to send him many escaping Jews. It was a dangerous situation for the priest, but one he could do nothing about. When refugees came to him, he took every precaution, but he could never be really sure that he wasn't being entrapped. Fortunately, the Germans had so many other problems that they watched only one facet of the priest's life—his sermons. Each Sunday, the same German came to the worship service, sat attentively through the sermon, and then reported back to his superiors that the priest was being cooperative with the occupation. The reports temporarily satisfied the Nazis. Father Peter and the partisans had no way of knowing that the Germans did not consider the Churchman a threat except through his words. To them, every shadow hid an enemy observer.

Security and suspicion were problems shared by all resistance groups. But there was one matter that was unique to the partisan Jews: the policy of accepting all Jews into the community. There were no exceptions because of age, sex, health, or disabilities and handicaps. Other groups could select just those who were capable of fighting, but the Jews could not refuse refuge to any Jew; to do so would be a death sentence. Outside the partisan camp was enemy territory, inhabited by Nazis and anti-Semitic Ukrainians.

This policy actually became an asset rather than a liability to the Jewish partisans. Others had a single object in their activities: the disruption and destruction of the German war machine. The Jews had not only that goal but the goal of survival—both for the individual Jew and for Judaism at large. This difference reflected the difference between the Nazi treatment of their enemies: Gentiles were executed because of political philosophy or military actions, but Jews were executed because they were Jews. Hitler had singled out only one other group for the final solution—the Gypsies.

The policy of accepting all Jews kept the Jewish partisans human. The permanent family camp with its children, old people, and families was a cross section of society. It constantly reminded the fighters of what they were fighting for, providing a civilized place to go after they'd finished their missions. And for the refugees it was a blessing. When they finally reached the family camp, they were taken into the community and made to contribute in some way. This let them feel their lives were necessary.

Early in the formation of the family camp, a group of Jews came to the band. They had started out in Poland ten months earlier. At that time, they had numbered twenty-nine. Their original destination was Palestine. They were a Zionist youth group, and they had intended to walk to Palestine, as many Jews had done before them. For ten months, they had been eluding the Germans, being forced farther and farther south and east, until they were found by the partisans. Twenty of their number had perished.

These young Zionists intended to form a kibbutz when they finally reached the Promised Land and had trained for years in pioneering techniques. Their training was invaluable in the establishment of the family group. It would be even more valuable in the spring, when their agricultural skills would help the partisans grow their own food. Now in the winter they were already planning their crops.

At about the same time that the nine Zionists arrived there came to the family camp three Jews from Kiev. These three were very orthodox, a grandfather, nearly ninety, his son who was well past sixty, and his grandson who was over forty. They had escaped the city before the Babi Yar roundup and had miraculously survived living in the woods and with peasants; finally, Father Peter had directed them to Ivan. When they first arrived, no one realized of what extreme importance these three elderly orthodox Jews would turn out to be. Though he hadn't known them in Kiev, it was Solomon who discovered their great talent: printing.

These men represented three generations of printers and had run a family-owned printing shop in Kiev. When the Germans occupied the city, the shop was immediately confiscated—the written word being one of the greatest threats to any occupation force.

The old man had been retired and spent his time at his first love—reading. He retained much of his old skill, however. His son was a master printer, capable of the finest reproduction work anywhere. But the greatest talent had surfaced in the grandson. He was not only a master printer but a master engraver. Solomon's first question was, "Can you reproduce official papers, papers like passes, identity cards, documents, and letters?"

The youngest of the three, the grandson, answered with a chuckle that was almost arrogant: "It would be simple if we had the equipment and the proper paper; but we are here, and *it* is there."

"Are you certain that you have everything in your shop that you would need?" Solomon asked eagerly.

This time the father answered. "Our shop was one of the finest in Kiev. It was set up most efficiently. The Germans would be fools not to use it. If I'm right, there will be plenty of official paper, ink, and engravings of official letterheads and seals."

A mission was immediately planned.

The next day Ivan and Sosha went into Kiev, to the address of the printing shop. The Germans were running it. It was not a big plant. Ivan guessed that one truckload could move out everything in the building. Ivan and Sosha reported their findings back to the planning committee, and the mission was put into operation.

Unlike most of the partisan groups in the forests, this Jewish group carried out missions through the winter months—a dangerous business because tracks were easy to follow in the snow-covered meadows. Most partisans chose the best defense—to wait out the winter in hiding.

But Solomon's three-camp system allowed this group to function year round, though the partisans would have to wait for a fresh snowfall in order to move from camp to camp without leaving tracks. But it still was so efficient a system that the partisans now averaged as many as three or four missions a week.

Stage one of the latest mission was to obtain a German truck. Four partisans simply waited along the road to Irpen and selected the first solitary truck to come along that fit their needs; the Germans did not send many trucks out without convoy, but there were always a few. With this truck, the partisans got a bonus of three rifles, several rounds of ammunition, three uniforms from the occupants, two grenades, and a truckload of barbed wire. They had no immediate use for the barbed wire, but it was stored away. Everything was kept, no matter how unlikely; improvisation was the key to the partisans' survival.

As soon as the truck was obtained, four partisans initiated stage two by dressing in German uniforms from the growing captured military wardrobe. One was an officer's, the others enlisted men's. Four more dressed as Ukrainian workers—collaborators. Within an hour after the truck was stolen, the masqueraders drove it to Kiev. They entered the city at dusk. With all the *chutzpa* they could muster, they drove the main street across half the city, turned and rumbled three blocks up the proper side street, then steered into an alley behind the shop.

Hans Geller, the partisan dressed as the officer, spoke perfect German. Before escaping the advancing Nazi front, Hans lived in Berlin where he'd been a chemistry teacher. Now, Hans hopped down from a truck behind a Ukrainian print shop full of Nazis. He strode to the alley door and gave it three authoritative knocks. When it opened to reveal a German corporal, Hans mustered all the arrogance he could.

"I am Major Strauss. We have been informed that this print shop is a target for a partisan raid tonight. Quickly, we must move out everything and set a trap for the swines!" As he spoke, he motioned his crew to start moving things out, and they did. There were only three Germans in the shop at the time; fortunately, none was an officer. Overwhelmed by the invasion, they started to help moving equipment. Outside, the last man to enter the shop cut the telephone wires. The officer played his role well and did not do any work. He just kept yelling orders to keep the real Germans rattled. With ten men working, they had almost everything on the truck in ten minutes . . . everything but the presses. There were two of them—one larger and a second smaller, hand-operated proof press. In another five minutes the small proof press was on the truck.

As quickly as they had entered the building the partisans left, but not before they dealt with the three real Germans. Hans, who'd lived all his life in peace, and two other partisans, who'd also never expected lives of violence, skillfully cut the soldiers' throats. The Germans had no weapons, but the partisans took their identification papers and uniforms, leaving the three bodies clad in underwear.

Bolstered by the success of their raid, they drove back out of the city with twice the chutzpa with which they had entered. Only for a moment did Hans dwell on the thought that he had to take a life to make his mission a success.

Seven days passed before the printing press and equipment reached the family camp. Thus, the three "men of letterts," as Solomon called them in his diary, busied themselves. They had all the tools they needed, and the paper stock from the print shop proved to be official German paper. It took them one day to set up, and on the second day they were busy forging identity papers and all the documents necessary to allow the partisans more freedom and safety in their movements about the occupied country.

27

"I think I love her!" Solomon had written early on in his diary. He meant Rachel. Now, in February of 1942, he no longer had any doubts.

Rachel had a very simple beauty. She was fair and blue-eyed with long, straw-colored hair. Her tall, slim body made her look more frail than she really was. She seemed at first a shy and dependent person, but was, in fact, quite self-reliant. Though not a leader of people like Dovka, Rachel was one that leaders could rely on.

When the partisans first found her group in the woods and brought them back to the cave, she was attracted to Solomon, and he recognized it. He encouraged her, but thought of the relationship as one of protector and friend.

As time went on, though, he found she was giving at least as much as he was. Stable and attractive, Rachel proved easy for Solomon to talk with. Like many survivors of atrocities such as Babi Yar, Solomon had denied himself the necessary grieving. Rachel recognized his tenseness and undercurrent of depression and forced him to talk of his past, his loss, his guilt, his hate. Her own past was no less tragic than Solomon's, of course; no Jew at that time, in those places, had any special claim on tragedy.

Rachel was from Minsk. She was the only child of a third-generation rabbi in that city. Her mother had died in 1939 of cancer, and though orthodox tradition encouraged a widower to seek a new wife after a reasonable period of mourning, her father had not been able even to consider it. Rachel ran his household and filled in the duties of *rebbitsin* for the congregation whenever she could. When war broke out between Russia and Germany in June of 1941, Minsk had a Jewish population of about 90,000—about one-third of the city's population. On June 28, 1941, just three days after Rachel's nineteenth birthday and the announcement of her engagement to a young local merchant, Grigory Rakitch, the Germans occupied Minsk.

Shortly after the German occupation, the city's commandant ordered all males between the ages of 15 and 45 to report and register. Both Rachel's father and Grigory were included in that group. Since evasion was punishable by death, an estimated forty thousand men reported. The mass of humanity was marched to a field at Drozdy just outside the city. There the forty thousand men were divided into three groups: Soviet military men caught up in the occupation, Jews, and non-Jewish civilians. For five days they were kept in that field for processing, during which time Rachel had no news of her men. On the fifth day, all of the non-Jewish civilians who could prove they were neither military personnel nor Communist party members were allowed to return to their homes.

After the release of the non-Jews, the Germans commanded all of the Jewish lawyers, dentists, physicians, educators, rabbis and professional men to make themselves known. Several thousand men qualified, among them Rachel's father. From that group only the physicians were taken aside, and the rest were marched to a nearby forest where they were machine-gunned into a mass grave. The remaining Jews were crammed into Minsk prison. It took several days before news could be smuggled out to Rachel and the other Jewish women as to the fate of their loved ones. Rachel set aside her own grief while comforting many of the hysterical women in her father's congregation.

Not until August 20th did the Germans release the imprisoned Jews. Thousands had already died. Upon his release, Rachel's fiance, Grigory Rakitch, went to her and demanded that she prepare to leave the city with him. Earlier that day the city commandant had issued an order establishing the Minsk Ghetto, declaring that all Jews had to be in a confined area. Rachel and Grigory fled the city that night and became forest people—a new, growing society of Jews.

They traveled through the forests by night, heading south in hopes of finding some partisans. After five nights of travel, they crossed the border into the Ukraine. Though still behind German lines, they were getting closer to the front. But the front was now moving to the south and east faster than they were. Two day's travel into the Ukraine they finally came across a partisan band. Rachel had related the story to her new forest family.

"We were in the forest, lost, exhausted. I was falling asleep when Grigory shook me awake. He hushed me before I could speak. 'Someone is coming,' he whispered to me. I could hear footsteps through the dry brush on the forest floor. Grigory motioned to me to follow him into some low weeds. There was no trail. If they were Germans, our only hope was to be under cover. It sounded like a whole army approaching us. No effort was made to quiet their steps. We were sure they were the Nazis. When we could make out occasional talk between the men, it turned out to be Ukrainian. But we maintained our silence. They passed us by, and after a short time Grigory motioned me to get up and follow him again. We headed in the direction they had gone and were led by their sound. 'I want to be sure they are not Ukrainian collaborators before we make ourselves known,' Grigory said in hushed voice.

"At almost the same instant we were grabbed from the rear. Arms about our throats. Knives pressed into our ribs. 'Resist and you are dead!' I could feel the sharp point cutting through my clothing and biting into the outer layer of my skin. The arm choked off my air until I thought I had taken my last breath. Not until strong hands secured both my arms did the choking grasp free my throat. Fresh air rushed in. My heart beat like a kettle drum, but I remember thinking, Thank God it hasn't stopped. Apparently Grigory and I had been following between the main body of men and the rear guard.

" 'Search them!' one of the guards shouted.

" 'We are friendly!' Grigory cried.

" 'Shut up! We decide who's friendly. Search them!'

"I was too terrified to speak. The thought struck me that we had indeed run into Ukrainian collaborators. There were now seven of them, two more having come out of the woods when they heard the commotion the first five had made. Two held me, two held Grigory. One stood perhaps two meters in front of me, leveling a rifle at my head; another pointed his weapon at Grigory.

"The latter was the one who shouted commands at the other men. He told them to search us. One walked to Grigory and looked directly into his eyes. 'Don't stuggle. It will go easier for both of us.' His hands slid over Grigory's entire body, seeking the bulge of a hidden weapon. 'He has nothing,' the man finally announced.

" 'Look for identity papers,' the leader replied, and the man pushed his hands into each of Grigory's pockets. They were empty. Then he opened Grigory's shirt and felt around inside. He loosened Grigory's belt and opened his trousers to make sure papers were not hidden there.

" 'This one is a Jew!' In his search, the man had seen Grigory was circumcised. His tone was terrifying—anti-Semitic. 'But there are no papers.'

" 'Search the woman!' I heard. All eyes except Grigory's turned to me. His head hung tearfully toward the ground. He felt my anguish and was defeated by the knowledge of our helplessness.

"As the searcher approached me, he looked directly into my eyes as he had into Grigory's, but a sickening smirk twisted on his face. Fear rushed through my body ahead of his hands as they slipped over my clothing, slowing at my breasts, then going on down . . .

"I thought I might faint and then I heard him say, 'She has no weapon.' A reprieve!

" 'Look for papers!' The reprieve was short-lived. I felt my blouse opened up. I heard snickers. His foul breath penetrated my nostrils and a wave of nausea ran through my stomach as he stepped closer to reach around inside my clothing. His rough hands felt inside my tattered brassiere. I broke into tears, and I heard Grigory whimpering.

" 'No! Please no!' I screamed, as his hand probed inside my other undergarments. 'No! We are not your enemy! I have nothing for you . . .'

" 'Enough!' the commander said. 'Bring the man to me.' His word seemed heaven sent.

"He had been asking questions of Grigory for some moments before I could pull myself together to take notice of what he was asking. 'Are you alone? Are there more of you in these woods?' Grigory answered all of the questions, trying to convince them that we were who we claimed. 'You say you want to join us to fight the Nazis. I've never known a Jew to fight. Besides, our mission is to kill Nazis, not save Jews.' Then a shot rang out.

"I screamed, 'Grigory!' I saw him slumped to the ground . . ."

Rachel began weeping only now. Solomon tried to comfort her, but Dovka interrupted him. "Let her tell it. It is the first time she has been able to speak of the horror. Let her get it out or it will destroy her."

Solomon could hardly stand the torture Rachel was reliving, but from his own experience he knew that Dovka was right; these horrors had to be purged.

It was a while before Rachel could go on.

"After the echo of the shot died out I heard *him* tell his men: 'Use her as you like.' I heard my clothing rip and I felt the hot, smelly breath of the first man as he grabbed me." She paused, but now there were no tears. "I guess God was merciful, for I remember nothing else until you—you, Dovka," she said looking up at her friend, "until you and your band found me that night."

28

Major Hans Oberman sat in his Kiev office, upset because his superiors had warned him to curb the growing guerrilla activity in the area. At first there were only isolated incidents: the enormous explosions and fire in the Kreshchetik, a few minor thefts and killings, and the incident of Father Peter's sermon which he'd put an end to himself. These were discouraged by severe penalties to the perpetrators—death to them and their families.

But then the organized activities began. There was the raid on the supply depot at Irpen which cost six German lives and nine truckloads of goods, because of which Major Oberman had rounded up six hundred Kievites and had them shot. One hundred civilians, he made it known, would die every time a German soldier died. Surely that would deter the partisan activities, he'd thought. He was wrong. After that sabotage, raids, killings, and disruption of troop and supply movements started to occur regularly. Heavy reprisals didn't seem to disturb these partisans. Surely they were the Bolsheviks.

Now his superiors were putting the whole problem in Major Hans Oberman's lap. "Reprisals are not enough, Major," Oberman's Colonel had explicitly pointed out. "I suggest that in addition to your reprisals, you start measures to capture these scoundrels. The only way to stop these partisans is to exterminate them. They are just like rats, Gypsies and Jews. But Jews and Gypsies are easy to catch; rats are more difficult.

You might even have to get out of your office or your mistress's bed to capture them," he added sarcastically. "I suggest you make it your first order of business. Do you understand me, Major?"

"Yes sir."

"Good. You are dismissed."

This was not the way Major Oberman was used to being talked to. He was deeply humiliated. He knew the Colonel was passing on to him what he, himself, had gotten from his superiors. It had probably been passed down the entire chain of command, but it ended with Oberman, and failure to do the job would be borne by him alone. Yes, Major Hans Oberman was very upset as he sat in his office, mulling over his problem. Ordering five or six hundred people to their deaths was easy; he could do that with a signature. It could be done before breakfast. Just a simple command before leaving for lunch and a few hundred Ukrainians would pay for the crimes of a handful of partisans. Why didn't those inhuman bastards learn that their deeds were costing their countrymen's lives? Didn't these partisans value the lives of their own people? Now he would have to be inconvenienced. It would be so much easier to raise the reprisal ratio to two hundred to one, but the Colonel would not hear of it. "Capture those scoundrels," he had commanded.

Oberman decided he would have to set a trap for these partisans. Once they were out of the way, he could return to the simpler task of executing civilians.

Oberman had come from an old, aristocratic German family. He had been to the finest schools, wanted for nothing. No deep interests had led him into any profession, but he'd always hunted new pleasures, and because of that, he'd developed a broad and perverse body of knowledge. His delightful conversation made him wonderful company.

All this, in addition to his totally amoral nature, had made Hans Oberman an ideal candidate for promotion within the SS.

29

Three hundred Kievites had just been rounded up and executed in reprisal for the three Germans that were found in a gutted print shop the night before. As word of the reprisals spread, rumors popped up about the troop-transport train due to pass through Kiev in about two weeks. Fifty new pilots would pass through the city on their way to the airfields near the Russian front to replace veterans being relieved to go on furlough. These men, a special squadron, had entered flight school on a day when Herman Goering was making a formal inspection and in his honor had been named the "Goering Squadron." They had gotten much publicity, and Goering now took a special interest in them. After spending one night in Kiev, the replacements would change trains, and to pay Goering homage, preparations were made to satisfy his favorites' every pleasure as long as they were in the city. But the exact date and time of the train was to be kept secret for security purposes.

Ivan was in Kiev the day the rumor was being passed from one person to another; the next day the family camp held a conference. Ivan had gotten the news back to the partisans.

Moshe began. "Ivan has gotten word to us that a train is to come through Kiev with a special squadron of pilots, headed to the Russian front. They are known as the Goering Squadron. If we could sabotage that squadron, wouldn't that be a fitting present for that egomaniac Goering?"

"So what is to stop us?" Boris asked.

"Blowing up the train will be no problem," Solomon replied. "We are very proficient at that. The problem will be to get the date, route and time."

"That's right," Moshe agreed. "Without that information our talents are worthless. So I have a plan. I will appoint two teams. Those of you who can move about in Kiev with relative safety I am sending to gather information. Solomon, you cannot go into the city for fear you'll be recognized by someone. You will move down to camp one and gather the information that the others send back. Boris and Dovka, you will go into Kiev with three others and gather what intelligence you can. In the meantime, I and my group will plan the actual mission which will depend on the information you return to us."

Solomon's first project was to get the proper papers made up by the three men of letters for those who were going to Kiev: identification papers, food coupons, work papers, all that were needed to pass a sidewalk interrogation at any soldier's whim.

The intelligence team went into Kiev with Ivan, where he had arranged for them to stay with the Gregor Kirtzof family. Ivan had met Gregor once through Father Peter. At that meeting, he did not tell Gregor of his activities with the partisans, but Gregor had let Ivan know in no uncertain terms of his displeasure with the occupation. He had also let Ivan know that if there was any way in which he and his family could help in a struggle against the Nazis, they would be only too happy to take part. Gregor obviously found the courage to speak so candidly before Ivan because Father Peter let him know that it would be safe to do so. Even with Father Peter's confidence in Gregor, Ivan said nothing at that time to encourage Gregor further. Now an opportunity had arisen to use Gregor. It was not a step taken lightly. This was the first time these Jewish partisans ever entrusted their lives to any gentiles other than Ivan and Sosha or Father Peter.

Once in the city, the Jews spread out into various crowded sections to watch and listen. Before they parted, Gregor warned, "If military vehicles come, get off of the street immediately. Go into a building, down an alley, up a side street—somehow vanish. It could be a roundup." He paused a moment. "And be off the streets by the six-thirty curfew every night or you may well be shot on sight."

Dovka went into the marketplace with Ivan, where they split up. She double-checked her newly forged papers. They were indistinguishable from Ivan's real documents: identity papers, a few food-ration coupons, and a work permit—all necessary for survival. She had a little money—*that* was real. The partisans had considerable amounts of currency taken from Germans they had killed. Compared with the citizens of Kiev, they were well off.

Dovka moved about the marketplace. There was hardly anything to buy. People sat about hawking their belongings to buy food. But little food was available, even if one did have money. Long lines huddled in front of the few food stores open. Dovka happened by a bakery at the moment the baker was trying to close and lock his door. The line in front of his shop was very long, and the people had been waiting for hours. The people nearest the door, who had been waiting the longest, protested loudly. "What do you mean you're out of bread?" cried the closest man. "It's not yet two o'clock. We've waited three hours, and now you tell us you're out of bread!"

"Don't complain to me," the baker shouted back. "I only have what I can make. Complain to the commandant; maybe *he'll* listen! We've had our supplies cut for the next eight days because of those pilots. We're rationed so they can have their damned party! So tell the Germans! Maybe they'll invite you to the affair." He laughed in the man's face as he slammed and locked the door.

"Eight days," said Dovka under her breath.

She was filled with excitement. At about four forty-five she met Ivan again. She could hardly wait to tell him what she'd heard, but he spoke first.

"A week from tomorrow," Ivan said.

"Yes," she said, surprised. "Eight days."

"How do you know?" After hearing her story, Ivan added. "That is much the same way I found out. I overheard two women complaining of a cut in their flour supply. Everyone in town seems to know the day. Now if we can just piece together the other details as easily."

They returned to Gregor's home. Comparing stories that evening, each confirmed that the Goering Squadron would arrive in Kiev in eight days. Ivan went back to Solomon while the rest stayed in the city.

For four days, the Jews risked their lives on the streets of Kiev but found out nothing new. On the evening of the fourth day, they were depressed and frustrated. It was then that Gregor's father came in with a newspaper. "I have it!" He was waving the newspaper excitedly over his head. "It's right here!"

"What? Let's see," Gregor said.

"A soldier threw it away and I picked it up," Gregor's father explained.

"Goering Squadron in Warsaw," Gregor read aloud. It took a few seconds to sink in: the Goering Squadron had been sent by way of Warsaw to boost morale in that area. They were being wined and dined in the officers' club there and would soon leave for the front. The paper was one day old. "Now we know the route," Gregor announced. "There is only one railway that runs directly from Warsaw."

"Now we know the day and the track," Dovka said. "I don't think we should stay to discover the exact time. We can assume they'll arrive in the early morning if they leave Warsaw in the evening or arrive here in the late afternoon if they leave Warsaw in the morning. It's narrowed down to a twelve-hour period. The mission will be a little more risky, but I don't think we have time to waste getting more accurate information."

The Jews thanked Gregor and his father. It was early morning by the time they arrived at the second camp. That morning, after the partisans had left Kiev, all the local papers carried news of the Goering Squadron in Warsaw.

30

The morning the Squadron was to leave Warsaw, Major Hans Oberman awaited his Colonel's call to give his report. He remembered how uneasy he'd felt at their last meeting, but today would be different. He would give his report, put his plan into action, accomplish his task, and in a few days things would be pleasant again. The call came, and Oberman strode into the Colonel's office.

"Well, I assume you have a plan to trap those partisans!" the Colonel said expectantly.

"Yes, Colonel, I have a trap, part of which has already been implemented. The wheels are in motion," Oberman said with satisfaction.

"Don't you think you should have cleared it with me first?" There was anger in his voice.

"You can stop it if you like, but I had to take care of preliminaries. There was no time to check with you. If you like the plan," said Oberman neutrally, "and if it works, I will gladly let it be known that you were instrumental in it. If you don't like it, we'll scrap it." The colonel's tense face slowly relaxed. He motioned to Oberman to go on. "As you know, sir, there has been a security leak regarding the Goering Squadron."

"I am aware of that—painfully so." He squinted and sourly pursed his lips.

"Colonel—I am that leak."

"What?" The Colonel flew to his feet. "Are you crazy? Are

you trying to get us all demoted?"

"I hope not, sir," Oberman said, a smug smile on his face.

The Colonel sputtered and growled, "Explain yourself! This had better be good!"

"As of now, they are not coming," said Oberman quietly. "Instead—and unless I change the orders in twenty minutes, a trainload of Jews will leave Warsaw."

"Jews?" cried the Colonel in disbelief. "We're receiving a trainload of *Jews*?"

"I doubt we'll ever get them this far. When the Goering Squadron's coming became public, I thought surely every partisan within a hundred kilometers would be after the train's route and schedule. So I rerouted them, but not their train. My guess is that the partisans will sabotage the train, and when they do we will have the partisans too. Now," he remarked acidly, "if you think the partisans will not try something, we can let the squadron come by the original route."

The Colonel disliked Oberman's sarcasm, but he liked his plan. "Go on, Major."

"Well, these partisans have always worked a fifty-kilometer area north of Kiev. There are five excellent places there to sabotage the train. Right now we have lookouts at each of those places, and as soon as one of them reports partisan activity, we will converge and wait. The partisans will either kill a trainload of Jews, in which case we'll take them, or the train will get through and add a few more bodies to the ravine at Babi Yar."

The Colonel was smiling now but still had questions. "What about the train crew?"

"All Poles," Oberman answered, returning the smile. "Even the guards are Polish collaborators. We can afford to sacrifice three dozen Poles for this plan."

"But what if the partisans have spies in Warsaw? What if they're warned?"

"They may well have a spy system to Warsaw," the Major conceded. "But the spies will see what they *think* are pilots boarding the train. The Jews have been on the train twenty hours already; they were put on before the train entered the station." Oberman looked at his watch. "Right now, thirty Polish collaborators in Luftwaffe uniforms are boarding that train to guard it enroute. We will have our party tonight." Oberman chuckled with satisfaction. "But we will be celebrating something more than the Goring Squadron!"

And the Colonel joined him in laughter.

31

While Major Hans Oberman and his Colonel were toasting their plan, the partisans were leaving camp one led by Boris who had been chosen to command this important mission. They headed for the spot they had picked to sabotage the train, a trestle about thirty kilometers north of Kiev. If the explosion didn't kill the squadron, they reasoned, the long fall would. Traveling with caution through the area took several hours. As soon as they arrived at the appointed spot, they set the charges on the trestle. They had no idea they were being carefully watched.

Just before dusk, an ear-shattering explosion shook the earth. The trestle and train which had just steamed onto it fell into the deep, narrow ravine. When the dust finally settled, there was silence. Each witness was momentarily transfixed. Then Boris's voice broke the spell. "Down to the train! Let's finish our job. Gather weapons and anything else we can use." The partisans came out of their hiding places. It was a difficult climb down into the ravine. It took several minutes, yet the watching Germans did not reveal themselves.

When the first men reached the bottom and looked into the broken rail cars at the carnage, they realized something was wrong. "Boris," one called. "There are no weapons here. And these men are tied into their seats—those who have not been torn loose by the fall."

Then another voice called out. "Halt! Do not move! You are

surrounded! Lay down your weapons!''

Boris and his men looked up from the bottom and sides of the ravine to where the command came from. Confusion gripped them as they looked into the muzzles of fifty-two automatic weapons trained down on them.

A long second passed. Then one partisan yelled, "Run for cover!''

But there was little cover to run for. Most of the partisans still on the walls of the ravine were caught climbing down when the Germans opened fire. Most were unable to return a single shot. The few men who reached the bottom were able to duck into the wreckage of the train for momentary protection, but when their comrades had all been shot, they found themselves—four men and one woman—facing ten times their number. For the next few minutes, high-caliber ammunition showered remnants of the train. When the partisans tried to return fire, they only disclosed their positions and invited a new barrage. Finally, no gunfire was returned. There were nineteen dead partisans and one severely wounded. Then a single shot rang out: Boris Spovinski had finished what four German bullets had not quite accomplished.

That evening in the officer's club, the Germans celebrated, not the Goering Squadron, but the deaths of one thousand Jews from Warsaw, thirty-six unfortunate Polish collaborators, and twenty partisans. No one yet knew that all were Jewish partisans.

32

The facts did not get back to the family camp until Gregor took a newspaper from Kiev to Father Peter, who took it to Ivan, who carried it to the family camp. Until then the partisans knew only that the mission participants had not yet returned to the second camp.

Moshe Pinsker, Uri Bolnik, Solomon Shalensky, Dovka, Rachel, Ivan and several other of the partisans sat dejected in the main meeting hut. Twenty of their friends were dead— among them, Boris Spovinski.

"God has given us good fortune until now," Uri said.

"Yes." Moshe agreed. "That makes this all the more painful. We've had few injuries and only seven deaths. I guess this was bound to happen sooner or later."

"But how did it happen?" Dovka asked. "They were waiting. We stepped right into their trap. Do you suppose Gregor informed them?"

Ivan had dreaded this question, though he'd asked it himself. After all, it was *he* who persuaded the partisans to take another gentile into their confidence.

"But how did they know where we would strike?" Solomon asked. "That decision wasn't made until after our people returned from Kiev, and Gregor wasn't there. No, this was more than simple betrayal. We betrayed ourselves by forgetting that our enemies aren't fools. If it wasn't a trap from the first, why did the train have only Jews on board?"

"They could have changed their plans after finding us out," Dovka argued. "And Gregor could still have been in on it."

"I know how you feel about gentiles," Ivan said, "and especially Gregor. But I think he was not involved. Gregor has no idea of how many of us there are or that we have more than one camp; but if he did, and if he'd betrayed us, the Germans would have hunted us *all* down. Father Peter and I would have been arrested already. The Germans were clever, yes; but I think they acted without Gregor's help."

The others were not convinced.

After a short silence, Solomon spoke. "We were not victims of Goering's ego, but of our own. Our motives were stupid. This was a mission of vengeance, not of necessity."

"In these times vengeance *is* a necessity," Rachel angrily interjected. "Besides, would we feel any better if our brothers and sisters had died for another reason? We have to grieve, but let's keep a proper perspective. The world has condemned our people for not fighting back; now you would condemn us for retaliation. You have no right to add guilt to our grief!"

"And what of the Jews on that train? Are we to feel no guilt over them?" Solomon asked.

"And may I ask you, Solomon," Rachel replied, "where do you think they were headed. Yes, I grieve for them. But we did not kill them. The Nazis could have trapped us without filling the train with Jews. That was their little joke! They probably bet on whether their cattle would make it to Babi Yar. No! Think of the terror and pain we saved them. Solomon, you know what that trip to the ravine would have been for them. Would you wish that for anyone? Would you go through that again for an extra few hours of life? Do you have any doubt that they were headed for the same thing?" Rachel was being purposely brutal. Everyone in the room was headed in the same depression as Solomon. They had been shocked into it . . . they would have to be shocked out of it. Rachel was sensitive to the complications of grief, but they could not afford the luxury. She'd had to forego it herself when her father and fiance were killed.

Dovka went around the room pouring fresh coffee.

Solomon sat looking into his cup. The perplexing, haunting thought returned to Solomon as it had frequently in the past: Why me? Why me? Why was I chosen for life while all of those other tens of thousands of Jews were murdered? Why me? Why me instead of the twenty who went on that ill-fated mission? Why me instead of the thousand on that train? Dovka poured coffee into his cup and snapped him back from his thoughts. He looked up at her. "Thank you, Dovka." She smiled back at him briefly and went on to pour for others. Solomon's eyes scanned the room. Did anyone else feel guilty? he wondered. As his gaze traveled the room, he realized that almost everyone here was a remnant. With the exception of two who had their immediate family with them in the camp, no one in that room had any family left. All of their pasts had been annihilated, murdered, buried or burned by the Nazis. Not because they had been enemies. Not because they had been hostile to the Germans. Only because they had been Jewish.

Why have we been spared? Why has God done this to us? Solomon had no answer. Where is God? Can it be that *He* doesn't know? No answer. His thoughts rambled. And as usual with ·such thoughts, some were logical and some not; some were realistic and some not; some made sense, some did not. . . . Are we survivors the fortunate or the unfortunate ones? No answer. Have the ones who died *earned* the right to die? Is *that* God's plan? The faithful would say we have to earn a better world. Yet how hard it is to keep faith in these times! Perhaps God is testing our faith. Will we pass the test? My parents, my grandfather, my brothers and sister, did they pass or fail the test? Why them and not me? No answer. If the reward is after death, why does the *Torah* tell us, "Choose Life"? God tells us in the Law, "Choose Life." Is that why we cling? Are we too obedient to die, or do we lack the faith to die well?

He had no answer.

Solomon came back to the present and reality and the room for a moment. Everyone was silent—looking into cups, drinking coffee, gazing into space. All were with their own thoughts, asking themselves their own questions. Were they being answered?

Why do we choose this life? But I *didn't* choose; it was chosen for me. Some of these people are here because they chose and acted; they escaped by their own cunning and action. But all I did was slip. They were killing all of us, and only I slipped. Was it pure luck? To be one in tens of thousands . . . was it chance, or was I chosen? The thought overwhelmed him. How presumptuous! He had no right to think that—but the thought was there.

33

It was an overcast day. A constant, chilling wind blew through the ravine at Babi Yar, bit hard at the naked bodies of the "enemies of the Reich" who were still being marched to the pit. The same wind carried the sound of the gunfire out of the ravine, over the woods to the church of Father Peter. He, too, sat in deep depression, distraught over the catastrophic partisan mission. He wondered whether the partisans would think they had been betrayed. He had faith that neither Gregor nor his family had betrayed them, but how could the partisans be expected to believe? He had come to understand why the Jews doubted the good will of Christians. He could not escape the sound of gunfire that drifted to his ears daily.

"Dear God. Let that sound drift to the ears of the Holy See. Let the Vatican hear, Dear God. They are silent enough so they should be able to hear. Let them hear too. Then perhaps they will not be so *silent*," he muttered through clenched teeth toward the icon that hung on his chamber wall.

He could hold back no longer. Again he wrote to his superiors.

34

The same wind that plagued Father Peter brought a violent storm to the area. It was nearly the end of the winter, but thirteen inches of snow dropped on the family camp, and the wind in places drifted it to several feet in depth. It made travel between the second and the family camps impossible. Ivan was stranded at the family camp, where the total isolation further depressed the partisans. A mission would have diverted their thoughts, but the weather kept them confined with their torment.

Solomon was preoccupied with the ghosts of all whom he had lost. They drove him deeper and deeper into thoughts of death. *Perhaps I have not given the Angel of Death a fair chance to reach me. Have I unconsciously avoided hazardous situations?* True, he hadn't often volunteered, but he never hesitated when he was asked to go. Moshe never sent him on a terribly hazardous mission, but there was risk in all their operations. He'd been lucky. Or was it more than just luck? Death seemed to ignore him. Death wanted only those he loved.

Rachel hated his melancholia, his total immersion in guilt and torment.

"Solomon, we have an obligation," she said one day. "An obligation to those whose lives were stolen from them. I do not believe God has forgotten them, and *we* must never forget them. We must survive to make sure the rest of the world never forgets them. And believe me, if we are not there to remind the world, the world will forget as quickly as possible. We must survive to be the conscience of the world. Our lives have gained meaning by their deaths. We cannot shirk our responsibility now." Solomon heard but did not answer. There was sadness in Rachel's eyes. She put her head on Solomon's shoulder, her arms about him. "Poor Solomon. My poor Solomon. It's all hitting you at once. You have put it out of your mind all these months, and now it is pouring over you."

The storm came and went. Solomon's depression persisted. Three days later, a path was finally cleared to the second camp. They had to wait two more days before a mission could be sent out; it would have been too easy for the enemy to follow tracks in the snow.

Solomon volunteered for that first mission, and for as many missions after that as he could stand. By April of 1942, he was a seasoned guerrilla, having gone on two to three missions a week. At times he would not reach the family camp for two weeks, coming in from one mission and volunteering for the next one, sometimes in the same day. At first Rachel and Moshe and the others were concerned. They feared that he didn't care whether he survived but saw that he always acted with caution. On the fifth mission after the storm, he killed for the first time. It had been a routine mission. He and two others had been out on reconnaissance when they were surprised by a German on a motorcycle. He was alone, the sidecar empty. Leaning around a curve, he almost ran into the three. The German swerved and ran his cycle into a ditch. His reflex action proved to be his last. Solomon leaped into the ditch and onto the German before either realized what had happened. On top of the cyclist, pistol in hand, Solomon pulled the trigger. Afterwards, Solomon trembled at himself; he had done it without hesitation! After that he killed several times, always disturbed that he felt nothing. Do others kill so coldly? he wondered. Or am I alone?

35

By the end of April, much of the snow had started to melt in the woods. The weather was much warmer. It was easier to move about now. Missions were easier to carry out. The partisans attacked supply convoys, sabotaged troop trains, plundered and burned warehouses; they attacked small German patrols whenever and wherever they found them. They also took heavy losses themselves. Losing ten to twenty percent of their forces became common. But the partisans took comfort in the motto, "At least we die fighting the Nazis." They didn't think of the future. The Germans were winning in Europe and Russia, and if the Germans were the victors, there would be no future for them. It was only a matter of time until the Jews were wiped out completely. At least these Jews had the opportunity to strike back on behalf of themselves and the millions who had no chance to resist. As the missions became more frequent and more hazardous, Solomon and many others began avoiding close relationships. The injury or death of a partisan was painful enough; the injury or death of a close friend was devastating.

Rachel recognized Solomon's withdrawal and fought against it. When he tried to get off by himself, she forced her company on him. "I'll not let you go off and brood alone, Solomon. You have no special claim on tragedy, so stop feeling sorry for yourself." At first her behavior angered Solomon, but she was wise and knew that even hostility was better than self-pity. Though only a few months had passed since Rachel lost her father and fiance to the Nazis and the anti-Semitic Ukrainians, it had seemed an eternity.

Rachel needed close relationships. In many ways Solomon was similar to her fiance. Perhaps that is what attracted her to him in the beginning. As her fiance had been, Solomon was sensitive, warm, considerate and respectful. Now he was trying to suppress these characteristics to protect himself from further hurt, but Rachel still recognized them in him, and she was determined to keep them alive. Solomon did not have the formal education that her fiance had had, but he was well read on his own. He also had a practical "street education" so necessary for surviving the poverty of Kiev's Podol. Physically, Solomon was taller and slimmer and not as handsome, but his facial features were more distinctive. Solomon was less impulsive and more thoughtful of his actions, but both had a determination to see things through to completion once started. Both were highly principled and intolerant of injustice. As was the old custom, Rachel's betrothal had been prearranged by his and her parents, but she had fallen in love with her selected fiance. That love had now very naturally transferred to Solomon.

When Solomon was away from the family camp, Rachel was busy in the infirmary. They had limited medical supplies, no trained medical personnel, and a growing number of patients. Rachel did the best she could for the injured and sick of the camp. With the help of God and her nursing care, many survived; those who did not survive at least did not die alone.

When Solomon was in the family camp, she spent as much time with him as she could.

Solomon, for his part, never pursued her aggressively. Not only had she recently lost her father and fiance, but she was orthodox in her upbringing, the daughter of a rabbi.

Solomon was not experienced in the ways of love. Having turned eighteen shortly before the invasion, there had been no real opportunity. And now in his depression, Rachel realized that if their love was to develop, she would have to be the aggressor. Her physical and emotional needs were strong and awake. His needed awakening.

It was now mid-May. For the first time since the Germans had occupied the Ukraine, the weather was becoming warm. The long and dreadful winter was over. The forest life was renewed. A freshness was in the air—a wonderful fragrance. During the days the partisans could abandon their heavy clothes and greatcoats; at night it was still quite cool. During the days they could bathe in a nearby lake. Until the spring thaw they hadn't known the lake was there but had thought the white expanse a snow-covered clearing to be avoided at all costs. The lake's discovery was a pleasant surprise to all, not only for its beauty, but for its abundance of fish, which added variety to the otherwise boring diet of the partisans. The depression which had been suffocating the partisans melted away with the winter snows.

36

Sudden excitement spread through the family camp, excitement tinged with panic. Ivan had come from the second camp with news that he had Father Peter, Gregor and his entire family and seven other Kievites hidden in the forest. He wanted permission to take them to camp two. All were gentiles.

The catastrophic events of the Goering Squadron mission came to mind. Many still wondered whether the goyim had betrayed the Jews. How could the partisans be sure this was not another Nazi ploy?

A command meeting was immediately called. Ivan began, "Let me bring you up on all of the facts. Father Peter came to me in the middle of the night—three nights ago. He had the others hidden in the woods. He told me he and the others were being sought for arrest by the Nazis. I had no choice but to help them. For two days I kept to the woods. I think that if we had been followed, I would have found it out. I ask your permission to bring them in. By the way, they have brought with them some valuable equipment and supplies: three radios! For a change we won't be cut off from the rest of the world."

"Radios!" Moshe exclaimed. "That is a Godsend. How did they get radios?"

"Yes. How did they get radios?" Dovka asked suspiciously. "How can we be sure that they are not working for the Germans. It would be a small price for the Nazis to pay for our lives. Just give a collaborator a radio to gain our confidence, follow the goyim to our camp, and carry out the slaughter. I believe Father Peter is safe, but how do we know that they have not fooled him, too?"

"We can't be too sure," Moshe said. "That is why we must watch them closely and be on our guard. They could be a great asset to us if loyal. If not . . ."

"If it will add a little confidence," Ivan said, "I must tell you Gregor warned that we could listen to the radios anywhere but that we must never send messages from within proximity of our camp. He warned me that the Germans could locate us by our signals with a method called triangulation. He insisted that I be aware that any messages we send had to be transmitted from points distant from our encampment and never from the same point twice. Now does that sound like a warning of a Nazi collaborator? If he wanted to give our location to the Germans, the radio messages from our headquarters would have been an ideal way to get the job done."

Most agreed it was a favorable point, but skepticism still ran high in the group.

"Why are the Germans after them? How did they get the equipment and supplies? How did they get the radios? There is much we still have to know," Dovka cautioned.

Father Peter told me he recently wrote to his superiors of the German atrocities," Ivan replied. "Especially those at Babi Yar. He pointed out that mass murder is going on there and that the Church in its silence is condoning the crime. He wrote that he could no longer sit by as if deaf and blind. Not to condemn the Nazis, he told them, is a sin of omission. He closed his letter by asking direction."

Looking about, Ivan saw the still-skeptical faces of the Jews.

"Well, his reply came, opened by the Germans. Father Peter knew then that *his* letter had also been opened. But the Germans had not yet made a move against him! Possibly they also were awaiting the reply. Because of the reply—which pleased them, I'm sure—the Germans probably decided to hold off a little longer. After all, the priest's arrest would incite the members of his congregation."

"What was the reply?" Solomon asked, hoping to get Ivan

back on the subject.

"The gist of the letter is that Father Peter had already been informed of Church policy," Ivan continued. "They reminded him that his job concerned the religious needs of his parishioners, not the nation's political problems. As a crowning blow, it pointed out that deviation from policy might lead to German retaliation, from which the Church could not protect him. Also, his superiors threatened that if he deviated sufficiently from Church policy, he might be subject to punishment by the Church—even excommunication, if his actions warranted it."

The Jews understood what excommunication meant to a priest, or to any devout Catholic. Ivan could see that the hard expressions of doubt were beginning to soften. He pressed his argument.

"I'm sure the reply satisfied the Nazis. I'm sure they decided just to watch Father Peter more closely, perhaps avoiding the problems that his arrest might initiate. Anyway, Sunday the die was cast. In his sermon, Father Peter condemned the Nazis as murderers, not only of human beings, but of civilization. He condemned the Church and the Holy See for disassociating themselves from morality and humanity. He called the Vatican 'the seat of world hypocrisy.' He called on his parishioners to strike out against the Nazis or be damned with them, for to be silent was to condone the horror."

Ivan's conviction was felt by the listeners, and one by one they were swayed from their fears.

"Father Peter told me that he was awaiting his arrest after the service, when suddenly Gregor and several others of his parish came to his chambers. They had met after the service, waited until the rest of the congregation left—and most left in one hell of a hurry!—then decided to spirit him away before the Nazis returned to arrest him. Without waiting for his consent, they took him from the premises and hid him in the forest. It was then that Gregor, his family and the others decided that they would try to find a partisan group to join. Each went to get what things he had that might be of value. They met back in the woods with their things and began their new life. Two days later, Father Peter contacted me to see if I would lead them to you."

"How did they get the radios?" Dovka questioned again, to keep the partisans from lowering their defenses.

"Yes," Moshe asked, "how did they come by those radios?"

"Gregor and his father have the biggest blacksmith shop and foundry in Kiev. The Germans have taken their heavy equipment there for repairs since the beginning of the occupation. When they decided to leave for the forests, Gregor and his brothers stripped the radios out of three half-track trucks that were in for welding. When they took all that they could carry, they put the torch to their home and their facilities. A lot of German equipment and everything they owned went up in flames."

"Well, what do we do?" Moshe asked.

"I am not convinced," Dovka announced. "We must be very careful."

"I trust them," Solomon said. "But I agree we must be very careful. I would bring in Father Peter. I would bring in all of their equipment and supplies. I would keep them in the woods under close surveillance. Supply them with what they need to live in the woods while we establish a *new* camp for them. Then, as they win our confidence, we bring them into camp two and from there to the family camp as we have always done with newcomers in the past."

It seemed a safe and reasonable plan, and the partisans agreed upon it.

37

Solomon believed the newcomers were what they claimed, but he still longed for a plan to prove them safe. It was a frustrating dilemma that troubled him all day. After their evening meal, Rachel tried to distract Solomon. "You are trying too hard," she told him. "The solution will come to you if you relax and let it. It's a beautiful night for a walk. Why don't you take me down to the lake? Let's forget the war and the Germans and those other people for a while. Please, Solomon."

He agreed. She picked up a blanket and they went.

The night was cool. A light breeze ruffled the small lake. There was neither moon nor clouds in the sky. Stars shone brightly. Solomon pointed out the various constellations. He had learned them as a boy from his oldest brother. "I guess as long as I can recall the stars and their names, a little of my brother will live on."

"Solomon, all of our past lives on in our memories," Rachel said softly. "It's an age-old proverb that as long as you are remembered by someone, you have a little immortality."

"I guess that's so."

He lay flat on his back looking up, recalling nights many years past when his brother would show him the stars. He could always see the big and little dippers, but he could never even imagine all the other constellations. He distinguished the grouping that was said to represent a bowman; he could find the stars, but no bowman. Rachel lay on her side watching him. Then impulsively she raised up on her elbow, leaned over to him, and kissed him on the lips. Surprised, Solomon lay rigid a moment before responding.

"There," she said. "I think that was long overdue!"

"Very long overdue." He kissed her and held her to him for a very long time. "Rachel, Rachel. It is possible that you feel as I do?"

"Only if you love me," she said almost teasingly. Again there was a long silence as they held each other and kissed.

"Solomon, these are unusual times," Rachel finally said. "It isn't good that we keep our feelings to ourselves. In our lives where there is so much tragedy and terror, we *need* to express our love. We cannot live on vengeance alone. And when everything is so indefinite, we need to hold on to our love. It gives us one more thing to hope for. We mustn't suppress our desires. The times do not allow us the luxury of long courtship. Time is too precious! We must express ourselves fully and without inhibition."

Solomon wanted her very much, but he was shy. He pulled her very close again and held her. She sensed his uneasiness. She took his hand and put it to her breast. Solomon felt helpless, almost terrified. He felt the fool. He had heard other men talk boastfully of their exploits with women, but he had never had any experience like this himself. He had always felt self-conscious about it when among more experienced men; now he felt almost ashamed. What would she think of him?

"Solomon, please don't be nervous. You're so tense! Do I offend you? Don't you want me?"

"Oh God, Rachel. Yes, I want you. And I love you. I just don't want to do the wrong thing. I'll be clumsy. I'll disappoint you."

"I assure you, Solomon, I'm no expert. I have no sordid past to judge you by. We will learn together. Solomon, I love you. Please be at ease with me."

For the first time he relaxed enough to feel the warmth and smoothness of her breast, the nipple erect and firm. He moved his fingers slowly over the breast, exploring all of its contours.

"You'll tell me if I hurt you. I've heard that it can be very sensitive."

"It? I have two of them, Solomon." She giggled at him. He slid his hand to the other, his own embarrassed chuckle smothered by a warm and tender kiss. "Oh, Solomon. I do love you. More than I've ever loved anyone." She felt suddenly very sexual. Having discovered and explored her sensitive parts at an early age, Rachel knew her needs well. But never had those needs been stronger than right here and now with Solomon. "Have you ever had a woman, Solomon?"

"Do you mean made love to a woman? No. I've never even kissed anyone outside my family before. I'm afraid I'll be a disappointment to you."

"Don't you think I have fears? After all, I'm a rabbi's daughter. My courtship was very proper."

His excitement rose. Bravely he started to move his hand downward. He reached her smooth, slim stomach. There he froze. His courage failed him. When it did not return, he started slowly to move his hand back.

"No," Rachel whispered. "Please go on. I want you to. Please." Solomon was terrified. "Please, please, Solomon." She took his hand and moved it slowly and gently down. She felt that she had awaited this moment all her life.

"Please make love to me. Make love to me now."

38

Father Peter and much of the equipment were brought into the family camp the next day. Two radios were brought up, the third left in camp two. Gregor's tools were brought up. If only the blacksmiths themselves would check out as *safe*, they would be invaluable to the partisans.

"Kiev is an unbearable place to live," Father Peter told the news-starved group that first evening after dinner. "Starvation, looting, disease, reprisal roundups, shortages of everything— people are shot on the streets like dogs for being out after curfew! There is no fuel, not even wood. People sell everything they own to buy a little food, and they have little to sell. If you have something a German wants, you might get a few kopeks."

The partisans were not very impressed. True, they ate well, but they knew cold and the threat of discovery and death. And they knew that much of what was being sold and traded in the marketplace had been stolen from the hundred thousand Jews that had lived in Kiev. Still, no one interrupted the priest. "People had to destroy all of their books under threat of death. Most used them for fuel to heat their houses. All the books from the public library were thrown out of its windows to be burned. Schools are closed."

Finally someone asked about the ravine—Babi Yar.

"Babi Yar." He hung his head. "Babi Yar is the shame of the world." It obviously pained him to talk of the ravine. He spoke, eyes to the floor. "It is inconceivable what the Germans do at Babi Yar, but I know they do it. It is inconceivable that no one speaks out against them, but I know that the world is silent. Babi Yar is everyone's sin. In just two days at Babi Yar, over thirty thousand people were murdered—all Jews. Perhaps a few escaped. But they had no chance! Those who tried were shot on the spot. Many invited death by running just to end the torture of waiting."

The room remained hushed as the priest paused. Even Solomon, who had lived through it all at Babi Yar, found the tale crushing when told by someone else.

"By the end of the week, no Jews could be found in Kiev. There had been a hundred thousand! No one raised a protest. It is a sin shared by all the world."

The priest was still for a few moments, gazing at the floor. Then he continued. "But the ravine is not full yet. The gunfire continues. From dawn to dusk I hear the deadly report of the guns. Trains come with thousands of new victims. I cannot recall a day when I've not heard the terrible staccato from Babi Yar. I've prayed for the winds to blow *toward* the ravine, and a few times my prayer has been answered; but even then, the wind would die down and I would hear it again! And several times each day, I've heard enormous explosions. What they mean, I don't know. I fear to think what new device the Germans have come up with." Again he fell silent. Rachel handed him a cup of coffee. He thanked her and continued his morbid account.

"Only the efficient Germans could invent the 'gaswagon.' I first heard of it when one of my parishioners came to me distraught over the death of her mother. The mother had been a patient at the Pavlov Psychiatric Hospital. In mid-October of 1941, a German doctor came there and announced that the patients would be sent to another facility to free up the Pavlov Hospital space for 'more important needs.' The patients were put into the back of the truck, the doors were closed, and the truck was driven off. Only the Germans knew that the truck's exhaust was piped into the sealed compartment, that their only destination was a pit at Babi Yar. Since that time, one can see the gaswagons daily driving toward Babi Yar. They save the

Germans time. And even with the gaswagons, the sound of the machine guns continues from dawn to dusk!"

Father Peter took a long drink from his coffee cup. His throat and mouth were dry. No one among the partisans in the room spoke. Dovka refilled his cup which he acknowledged with a nod.

"Sadly, the German character rubs off. The people of Kiev—too many of them—have learned from the Germans. Or perhaps they have not learned anything from the Germans. Perhaps they *were* the way they *are*. Perhaps they just needed the German occupation to show their true character. Perhaps the Germans will show us the true character of the whole world.

"Yes, perhaps the Germans will show us what *we* really are. Our own people turn in their neighbors to the Gestapo for an extra ration of food, or worse, for money. In the blackmarket, our own people prey and profit on the need of their neighbors. They hoard and cheat. And no one protests. No one. No one."

The Jews in the room didn't think about the Vatican or the rest of the world. They had long since learned to expect inhumanity from the non-Jewish world. The only difference now was that they were fighting back.

"Is our effort being felt?" Dovka asked. "Do our activities hurt the Germans?"

"I am sure it hurts the Germans," Father Peter answered. "There is no way to know how much. We get no news of the actual acts, but only of Nazi reprisals carried out because of them. There are several partisan groups around Kiev, I think, and no way for us to know which group is doing what. One thing is certain: No one knows there are Jewish partisans at work in the area. The Germans might, of course, but they do not let that information out if they do know it. Their propaganda would not allow it. They would never let it be known that the Jews would do anything but go to their deaths like sheep."

"Do they really take reprisals for every act against them?" Solomon asked.

"They have reprisal roundups almost daily. People are

picked up at random, usually. Hundreds every day. They just pick up the first one, two, or three hundred people they find on the street. Men, women, children, it doesn't matter. They are executed either in the street or at Babi Yar."

"Then our acts cause the deaths of innocent people," Solomon said almost inaudibly.

Rachel retaliated with fury in her voice. "Solomon you are not going to carry the burden of the Nazis' guilt! If the Germans were to take reprisals, which they may well do someday, when the Russian army stages its counter-offensive to rid this land of the German scourge, do you think they would or should call off their war so that the Germans would not execute civilians? We are fighting a war, too. Maybe if the Germans take enough reprisals, the citizens of Kiev also will rise up against the Nazis! If we curtail our missions because of their inhumanity, then we justify it! And at least it is not our Jewish brethren being slaughtered in reprisal. They are already dead. Now they slaughter those who cheered openly and in their hearts when the Jews were rounded up. Those who were glad the Jews went to their deaths like sheep can now go to *their* deaths because *we* resist! Father Peter is right when he says that the German atrocities are the sin of the world. Anyone who does not resist in some other way must share the guilt. That is a course we must refuse."

There was a long silence until Moshe said, "She sounds more like a rabbi than a rabbi's daughter." A chuckle passed through the room.

39

Days passed. Father Peter operated the radio having been taught how by one of the other newcomers still in the second camp. No messages were sent; they had no one to send to. Heeding Gregor's warning, they didn't send between the camps. All day long, partisans would drop in to the radio room which had quickly been added to the main headquarters and listened to the signals, dispatches and newscasts that the priest continually monitored. Of course, all messages of importance were sent in code. But the partisans had been starved for news. Now they could hear not only the local transmissions but also broadcasts beamed into the area from unoccupied Russia. The news from Russia was not good. The Germans were beating the Russians with superior equipment and crack troops. But the Russians were fighting hard. The thing that most heartened the partisans was that the Russian broadcasts often referred to the damage that was being done to the German war effort by guerrilla activities. It meant that the partisans were not alone.

By June of 1942, the Germans were moving troops and supplies at a feverish pace. They were making every effort to advance on the Russian front before the hard winter returned. On the radio came appeals from Russia for the partisans to sabotage the German effort. After the first broadcast that Father Peter monitored, Moshe sent out scouts to determine which roads and rails carried the most military traffic. They would disrupt as many of those routes as they could. The new gentile arrivals were relied on heavily in the scouting missions; it was an opportunity to test further their loyalty.

On their return from one of these surveillance missions, six of the gentiles came upon three German soldiers grazing horses in a field. Two trucks were parked on the road to Kiev that bordered the field on one side. A fourth German was in one of the vehicles. He was skillfully and silently killed by a knife-wielding partisan, and his weapon, ammunition, papers and money were taken. The other three Germans sat near a fence at the edge of the woods. They were in full view of the truck, so the partisans had to crawl along a ditch on the far side of the road. They crawled until they were opposite the woods and out of sight of the three relaxing Germans. Then they crossed the road, entered the woods, and came through the trees to where the soldiers sat. Their weapons had been leaned against the fence, and the three were talking and laughing. At a signal, two of the partisans went for the weapons while the other four went at the unwary Germans. Before they died, one of them got out a horrified scream, but there was no one who could help to hear him. Each had met death at the sharp end of a blade. It took them a while to round up the horses. Only one of the six was experienced with the animals.

Once rounded up, they tied the horses in tandem. They made a quick search of the trucks and found saddles and other equipment. Papers in the truck showed that the horses were being brought to Kiev for the pleasure of the officers.

They took their booty through the woods to the second camp. Two of the men covered the tracks the horses left.

The horses would make it possible for the partisans to expand their area of operations. The animals were kept at either camp one or two and never the family camp. Horses would leave too distinct a trail, and if camp two were discovered by the Germans, it was feared they could too easily get to the family camp by tracking them.

By the end of the first week in June, Gregor and all of his companions had been approved for residence in the family camp.

40

Exhaustion overtook Yorgi Tzarof. Sleep claimed him right there on the dusty ground where his German captors threw him. He was unconscious of the search of his clothes by other prisoners. He had nothing of value on him except his shoes, which were quickly removed while he slept. Once he'd been searched and stripped of his shoes, he was completely ignored by the other prisoners who wandered or just sat around in the vast compound.

Yorgi awoke after two and a half hours of motionless sleep. He had to think a moment before he could recall where he was: Darnitsa. He opened his eyes slowly, but still did not move. Finally he raised his head cautiously and looked around. There were thousands of prisoners in the compound, and to Yorgi's relief none seemed the least concerned with him. He had been in prisoner-of-war camps before. He knew that other prisoners could be as dangerous as the guards. He sat up. That was when he realized his shoes had been stolen. He made no outward sign of emotion or recognition of the fact. He knew he would have to get the shoes back, or another pair at least as good. All in its time, he thought to himself.

Darnitsa was across the Dnieper River from Kiev, a suburb made up mostly of working-class people. During World War I the area had hosted an enormous prisoner-of-war camp. At that time it was the Germans who died there by the thousands. Now, the Germans had turned the tables on their former keepers. These Russian prisoners could not complain that they were being treated any worse than they had treated the German prisoners nearly a quarter of a century earlier. In those days, hundreds of Germans died daily in Darnitsa from hunger, exhaustion, exposure, and disease. If more Russians died now, it was only because there were more of them detained in the same area. As Yorgi looked about him, he saw a mass of wretched humanity. Some wandered aimlessly; most just sat or lay on the ground. All had dull, unseeing, emotionless expressions. They'd be reduced to spiritless animals. Draining them of all their hope and ambition made control of them easy. Yorgi wondered whether any even cared if they took another breath. He had been in other prisoner camps, but none like this. Sixty or seventy thousand prisoners of war were enclosed by barbed wire in this place. The ground was hard, dry and dusty. There had been an abundance of plant life here before it had been reclaimed as a prison compound, but all of that had been picked and eaten by starving men, picked clean and down to the last blade of grass. As soon as they were discovered inside the camp, officers, political prisoners, and Jews were put into a separate enclosure where their life expectancy was even shorter than in the main camp. Yorgi had made every effort to keep two facts to himself since the Germans had occupied the Ukraine: that he was an officer and a Jew. There had been a fairly large number of Jews conscripted into the Russian army. It was a method by which the Russians had tried to assimilate the Jews out of existence. Few of these Jews had become officers, but Yorgi was an exceptional Jew. He had an aptitude for survival. Even now, as he looked around the Darnitsa compound for the first time, he was thinking of escape.

He got up. The warm dusty ground felt good to his feet. From past experience he knew that it would not be too hard to get another pair of shoes. The death rate in such camps was sufficiently high that many pairs of shoes would become available every day. Right now he enjoyed the feel of the warm earth against his feet. He was a little concerned about the night when it would cool off, but that was several hours off, according to the sun. He started to walk around the Darnitsa camp. He knew that in a few days he, too, would be like the other prisoners—unable to help himself and not caring. He knew that if he were able to escape, it would have to be before his strength and will were systematically drained.

Walking around the camp he memorized everything. The entire enclosure was barbed wired. At intervals of about two hundred meters, there were guard towers, but surprisingly most of them were unarmed. Instead, the Germans and Ukrainian guards were walking around outside the wire, more often laughing and joking with each other rather than attending to their business. Obviously, they expected no escape effort from those broken-spirited creatures. The guards were bored. It was an ideal situation for escape, but Yorgi wondered whether he would be able to find anyone else to help him in the effort. He walked on and observed.

There were two single fences around the camp; no electric barrier, no mine fields that he could see, not even large clearings to cross. Along one area, a road passed right along the barbed wire. Lines of women stood there on the chance that they might catch sight of a husband, brother, father, or son who might be a prisoner. They knew that if a loved one were there, he'd be dead in a week or two. Many carried baskets or small bags from which they would take potatoes, turnips, or onions to throw over the fence as people throw food to animals in the zoo. When the camp first opened, the Germans had shot at the women for throwing food, but in time they stopped; they'd come to find it entertaining to watch the starving men fight each other to get at the food. Often, one would kill another for a morsel. It was one of the few times that anyone in the camp showed signs of life.

It was along this fence that Yorgi might find a few comrades still interested in and capable of escape. He also knew that he would probably have to join the scramble for food to maintain his strength. There were no buildings in the compound. Men slept, relieved themselves, lived and died wherever they happened to be at the time. There were a few trees, but their bark had been picked off as high as men could reach—picked off to be eaten. Starvation was everywhere. Here and there Yorgi saw men chewing leather belts and shoes. Men picked lice from their own bodies and popped them into their mouths. If a mouse or rat or squirrel or rabbit happened into Darnitsa, it would be captured instantly and eaten raw—bones, entrails, skin, but not before it had caused a near riot. It was so entertaining that often the Germans would catch them and throw them in. Even stray cats or small dogs had been thrown in, but now there were few of them left because the hunger in the city had made them a delicacy there, too. Disease was rampant, especially dysentery—everywhere the smell of urine and excrement. In another part of the camp was a rubbish heap. It was near the Germans' kitchen, and they would throw their garbage into the compound. Here, also, there was always a large number of prisoners rummaging through the refuse, picking out anything edible. Onion and potato peels, apple cores, orange rind—delicacies all—could be found.

Yorgi continued his walk. At the back of the compound an area was fenced off and under guard. Inside the wire were building materials. The Germans planned to build barracks in which to keep some of the healthier prisoners. They would be worked while they still had some strength left. But the work program would come too late for Yorgi; if he stayed in Darnitsa, he would be dead long before the program was to start.

He continued around until he was back in the approximate area where he had started. After dark he would make another round of the camp to see what the nighttime security was like. Also at that time he would find a new pair of shoes. He lay down and went to sleep.

Yorgi slept longer than he'd intended. When he awoke, a quarter moon hung high in the sky, but a layer of clouds diminished its light. Without sitting up, Yorgi carefully looked about, scanning the camp while his eyes got used to the darkness. There was no movement, only a few moans and snores to be heard. Several search lights intermittently swept the entire compound, but they covered it sloppily. Yorgi correctly assumed that the night guards were as bored with their work as those on the daytime shifts.

Quietly, he got to his feet and started around the compound.

As a sweep of a floodlight approached him, he would lie down and feign sleep until it passed, then he would get up and go on. An important difference between the day and the night was that now the watchtowers were manned, and each had a light that swept the area between the two lines of barbed wire. Slowly, carefully, he continued on until he reached the building materials. Not many prisoners were sleeping in this area. Three German guards were stationed inside the wire around the supplies. Yorgi lay down so that he could study the area a little longer in safety. One of the lights swept over him without a pause and went on. Now Yorgi focused his attention on the lights from the towers that swept between the two lines of barbed wire. It took about fifteen seconds for the lights to make a complete sweep, too short a period for him to dig under a wire, run across the alley between the two lines and dig under the second. He moved on.

About fifty meters beyond the building materials, Yorgi came to a sudden stop and fell to his stomach among some sleeping prisoners. Something had caught his eye, and he had to check it further. He watched a sweep of light between the wires at this area. He watched a second and a third time. It was the same each time. Each light swept the area between it and the next tower to its left, but the light at the tower directly in front of him didn't make a complete sweep. It swept out to the next tower, but when the beam came back, it was three meters short of where the light from the tower to the right reached. Yorgi watched the lights through several more sweeps. In each sweep there was an area of at least three meters which was never illuminated. Yorgi crawled to that area on his stomach. When he got to the spot, he dug at the earth under the first line of wire. It was loose. It came away easily. Before he knew what he had done, there was an opening in the earth under that wire large enough to pass his body through. In a completely unplanned and spontaneous move, Yorgi slid his body under the first line of fencing. Suddenly he found himself in the alley between the two fences, looking up at the base of the guard tower. The two searchlights were converging on him, one from the right, one from the left. He held his breath. They stopped at the end of their sweep, leaving Yorgi still in darkness. He bounded across the alley to the second fence. The earth was loose there, too. He dug in panic. Two more sweeps of the light passed and a third, and Yorgi remained in the dark.

And suddenly he was out. He started to run. His heart pounded feverishly as a kettle drum. In the protection of some woods, he fell to the ground. It was a miracle! He was out almost by accident. Then he realized he was still barefoot. But Yorgi got up on his bare feet and ran some more. He wanted to put as much distance between himself and Darnitsa as he could before morning.

41

All night Yorgi forced a rapid march on himself. He first headed due north until he reached another suburb of Kiev, Sotsgorodok. Keeping to the outskirts of that district, he turned northwest to the Dnieper River. Reaching the eastern bank of the river, he headed south in search of a crossing. In a short distance he found a road with a bridge. It was guarded by two Germans. A sign near the bridge disclosed to Yorgi that this was not yet the Dnieper, but the Kesenka, a tributary that paralled it. The water was low at this time, and to avoid the guards, Yorgi crossed the tributary in its shallows, keeping to sand bars. He stayed at the edge of the sand bars, in the water so as not to leave footprints or scent to be followed by men with dogs. He crossed the narrow landstrip between the Kesenka and the Dnieper and found himself due east of another subdivision of Kiev, a district called Kurenevka. Now he had the Dnieper to cross. There were no narrows or shallows on the Dnieper, and all of the main bridges crossing it were heavily guarded against saboteurs. Yorgi hoped to find a deserted boat along the bank, but there was none. He contemplated swimming for a while, but decided the risk was too great. He continued his search upriver. The bank offered him no solution. His search took him several kilometers above the city.

It will be dawn in less than two hours, Yorgi thought desperately. I want to put the rivers between myself and Darnitsa. If the Germans search for me in the morning, it will be east of the rivers. He was about to change his mind and make a swim for his life when he came across a log floating with the current of the river. His decision was almost reflex. He plunged after it, fearing the rapid current might carry the log beyond his reach. I've got it!

He let the log carry him along for a few moments. Then he started a slow but steady side stroke, forcing the log and himself out into the center of the river. He furnished the power to take himself and the log across the river, while the current furnished the force to carry them back toward Kiev. He stroked, rested, stroked again.

Though not attempting to fight the current, Yorgi was very fatigued a half-hour later when he found himself less than thirty meters from the west bank of the Dnieper River. It was still dark, though the eastern horizon held a hint of daylight. Yorgi rested briefly, clinging to his log. Now he could see the outline of the bridge crossing into Kiev, perhaps two hundred meters ahead. He wanted to be out of the river before reaching it. Gathering together what strength he had, he began stroking vigorously. By the time he had stroked twenty meters closer to the bank, he was less than a hundred meters from the bridge. He let go of his log and swam the last of the distance. It took him only a few seconds, but it also took all of the strength he had left.

Yorgi Tzarof pulled himself up onto the western bank about fifty meters from the bridge. Drenched and breathing painfully, he lay there trying to regain his strength and his bearings. He figured that he had to be northeast of the city. Directly west of him was a totally unpopulated area. After a short rest, he started across it. Five minutes later, he came to another body of water, which struck fear into his heart. He didn't have the strength to cross another river! Despairing, he began to follow the edge of the water. After a few hundred yards the bank turned due east, and Yorgi realized he'd only come across a cove in the Dnieper River that extended a finger of water inland.

Continuing west, the water fell away behind him. In fifteen more minutes he was within fifty meters of the first buildings of Kiev's Kurenevka district. Aware of the curfew, Yorgi hesitated to enter the city before daylight. He was still barefoot. His ragged clothes would not raise too much suspicion in the city where the German occupation had brought poverty to a majority of the citizens. But the bare feet bothered him. That might draw some attention which, along with his lack of identity papers, would be fatal. Finally, he decided that it would be better to try to get through the city as soon as possible. With caution, he might get through before the day had advanced too far.

Looking in every direction, he entered the city, trying to avoid the main thoroughfare. He had not gone far when he stumbled upon a body in the street, shot through the neck and chest. "Poor bastard," Yorgi said under his breath. "Caught out after the curfew." The man's misfortune was Yorgi's good luck, for the corpse still wore shoes. Not only that, but a threadbare suitcoat with which Yorgi covered his ragged shirt. He also had papers that, though they would not withstand close scrutiny, might increase Yorgi's chances a little. The shoes were tight on Yorgi and hurt his feet, but they would do until a better pair was available. "Thank you," Yorgi mumbled solemnly to the corpse. Then he hurried on his way.

As Yorgi made his way through the back streets, he became aware of the risk he was taking. In the brief time he had been in the streets of Kiev, he'd seen no less than three bodies—all, he presumed, shot for curfew violations. After sighting the third, Yorgi decided not to force his luck. He hid in an alleyway behind some trash containers to await the rapidly approaching daylight which would usher in the end of the lethal curfew. He rested but could not sleep. Soon the sun was up, and with it the activity on the streets increased. He hoped that he would be able to lose himself in the gathering crowds. By six in the morning there were a good number of people on the streets, and Yorgi fell in with them, continuing constantly westward. As he walked, he was aware of a constant, repeating sound of gunfire.

It took him only twenty minutes to go to the west edge of the city, which led him to the cover of woods—the same woods that had hidden Solomon Shalensky almost ten months earlier on the day he'd escaped the death pits of Babi Yar.

42

In the weeks that followed the acquisition of the radios, horses, and first non-Jewish partisans, Moshe and Solomon's group carried out numerous raids on German troop movements and supply lines. Roads and rail lines were being sabotaged and blown up daily. The favorite method of the partisans was to place mines under roads and railroad bridges. These would detonate when the weight of a train or convoy passed over. In the case of a train, the entire string of cars would derail and crash. Then the partisans waiting in the vicinity would fire on the personnel as they ran from the damaged railcars. When the enemy was finally silenced, the partisans would scavenge the car and bodies for equipment and supplies. These raids were not without casualties to the partisans; in their attacks on the trains, the guerrillas lost an average of ten percent of their comrades. When attacking a truck convoy, their losses were usually greater. The entire convoy was not damaged with the first explosion. At best, the first three vehicles were damaged. The rest of the convoy would have to be attacked, and the Germans had a better chance to defend themselves. The battles were longer, and more fire was returned. Losses were at times double the casualties of a train raid. In addition, the partisans struck at supply depots, taking away what they could and destroying the rest. Whatever the losses to the partisans, they always were greater for the Germans, and that justified the missions for the attackers.

Dovka was returning to the family camp. She had been out for nearly a week on daily missions. It was not unusual for the groups to go out that frequently now. The Germans were sending troops and supplies to the Russian front at a feverish pace. Another winter would follow this summer, and the Germans knew they had to have their troops supplied and at full strength before the snows fell. The partisans knew this too, and they felt that every convoy or train that got through meant a lengthening of the war. They were receiving radio broadcasts now, and they felt there would eventually be a Russian counteroffensive. Each time they destroyed a convoy, they felt it would be that much sooner. But the pace was exhausting.

No one thought much about Dovka's exhaustion. Everyone in the group was exhausted. It was the normal state of the returning participants. They would all take a few days of rest in the family camp before going out again.

She went to bed with a chill despite the warm summer temperature. She complained to Rachel of feeling cold but was fast asleep, unrousable, before her friend returned with a blanket. Rachel covered Dovka. As she did, she noticed her skin was hot. She wondered whether it would be better not to cover her, but Dovka shivered as she slept, and Rachel placed the cover on her loosely. She wanted to give Dovka some fluids to drink and some aspirin, but she would not be awakened. Still concerned, Rachel decided to let her sleep. Maybe in an hour or two fatigue would relinquish its grip.

Rachel checked on Dovka several times over the next two hours. Her body would not cool. She woke Solomon, who had returned to the family camp with Dovka. Together they tried to rouse her. Dovka was a little more responsive now and tried to resist their attempts. Together they moved her to the infirmary. There were a few injured partisans there. Because of the fever and fear that Dovka had something contagious, they put her in a separate room, usually used by Rachel when there were overnight patients in the primitive hospital. With Solomon's help, Rachel got Dovka's clothing off and covered her. Dovka was moaning and mumbling now, and her fever remained high. Rachel started to sponge her hot skin. After about half an hour, Dovka felt a little cooler to their touch. The shivering stopped. She responded more. She seemed dazed, and Rachel doubted that Dovka really knew what was being done for her. They did get her to take three crushed aspirin tablets dissovled in some water. They also got a little tea down her before she again lapsed into slumber. After another hour Dovka felt a little cooler and Rachel felt relieved.

Rachel asked Solomon to go to each of the other partisans who had returned to the family camp with them that morning. If anyone else had such a fever, she wanted to know it. When Solomon returned, he reported that no one else showed any symptoms. Most of the returnees had napped an hour or two, but by lunch time most had gotten up again, many still tired but none of them ill. One thought he might be getting a cold, but there was nothing unusual about that. It appeared that only Dovka came back sick. Probably her resistance was just down from all the stress and strain of her missions. She would have several days to get over it.

43

Yorgi struggled through underbrush, crawled across fields of wheat, and sloshed through irrigation ditches. He traveled any route that offered him cover. In spite of aching muscles and blistering feet, rubbed raw by his tight shoes, he refused to stop. Distance—that was the key to his survival. He maintained a pace that he knew he could keep up steadily. Until dusk, he continued his torturous, self-disciplined trek.

During that quarter hour between day and dark when the eyes adapt and visual acuity is poorest, Yorgi rested. He had come out of the woods and found himself near a road. Across the road was a small farm. The house was well back from the road. A dim light shone through the farmhouse window. Someone had just lit a coaloil lantern. I wonder whether they're friend or foe, Yorgi thought. I'd love a warm meal, some fresh clothing, a chance to clean myself up, to rest—oh, just to rest!

It was no time to cast aside caution. Yorgi decided to cross over and see what he could glean from the field. It wouldn't be a warm meal, but it would fill the emptiness that gnawed at his gut. How long had it been since he ate a warm meal? He could not remember. Would he ever have another except in his fantasies? He couldn't imagine it. He crossed over the road and climbed the rail fence fronting the property.

The greater part of the land was planted in grain, probably wheat. He crept over the property looking for the vegetable garden that most farmers planted for their personal use. As usual, it was near the home. If I can get to it without arousing the chickens, he thought. If only they don't have a dog! Hunger drove him. He was only a few feet from the house now. Circumventing it quiety, he found a surprisingly large garden at the rear. This garden must raise more than one family can eat, he thought. Staying to the edges farthest from the house, he started to dig at the plants. First he found potatoes. Pulling up a plant, he started to eat, dirt and all. As he ate, he slipped two into his coat pocket, all the time moving on to find some other food to vary his diet. He did not see the man quietly approaching him, rifle cocked, finger poised on the trigger.

"Fall flat to your stomach or I'll blow off your head," Ivan Igonovitch barked at the trespasser.

Yorgi Tzarof fell flat to his stomach, the cool soft dirt in his face. "I'm unarmed! I mean you no harm. I'm taking only what I need not to starve. Let me go, I'll move on!" Yorgi exclaimed rapidly.

"Who are you? Where do you come from? Where are you going?"

Yorgi's intuition prompted him to try the truth. "My name is Yorgi Tzarof. I am escaped from Darnitsa last night. I have no destination but to get as far from the Germans as I can."

Sosha had now come up behind Ivan. She, too, held a gun, though it was not pointed at the captive. Ivan's weapon was pointed directly at the base of Yorgi's neck, between the shoulders. Yorgi sensed it, and the hair at the back of his neck bristled.

"Sosha, hand me your pistol and search him. Make sure you don't get between him and the end of my gun. If he as much as takes a deep breath, his head's coming off!"

Sosha approached Yorgi from the side opposite Ivan. Keeping away from his extended arms, she swept her hands skillfully over his body. Her search disclosed only the papers he'd stolen from the corpse that morning. Handing them to Ivan, she lit a match to reveal their message. "These papers do not say you are anyone named Yorgi Tzarof."

"Those papers came with these shoes and this coat. I took

them off of a dead man in the city this morning. I tell you I am Yorgi Tzarof! I am what I said I am."

Ivan was satisfied with the answer. Had the man intended to deceive, he would have given the name on the papers. But he kept the gun trained on Yorgi. Handing the pistol back to Sosha, he told her to keep the man covered. He stepped back a few paces and told Sosha to do the same and move to her left a few meters so the prisoner could not lunge at them both at the same time. "All right, get up very slowly and move toward that storage cellar—that mound outlined by the moon to the left of the house."

Yorgi did as he was told. When Sosha opened the door, she lit the lantern that hung just inside and went down the stairs ahead of the two men. Inside, the captors and captive got their first good look at each other.

After considerable interrogation, both Sosha and Ivan were satisfied that this man was a safe guest. Yorgi's fantasies were to be realized. He had a warm meal, a bath, and received a pair of shoes. They were at least too large rather than too small. They gave him fresh clothing. Best of all, he slept that night on a cot. It was the nearest he had come to sleeping in a bed in the ten months since the German occupation. He slept free of fear for the first time in as many months, on a little cot in a secret room under the stairs of a storage cellar.

44

Dovka's fever started to climb again. She turned from sleep to delirium. She thrashed and threw off her covers. They tried to force fluids down her. It was impossible. Again they dissolved aspirin, but she spit them out. They tried again with better success. Her temperature dropped a little and she settled down. Her breathing was noisy, as if she had fluid in her chest. They wanted to make her cough but could not. Her fever spiked again and her breathing became labored. Then she was dead.

Before the sun set, she was dead. Dovka was dead. The whole course of her illness had taken less than six hours.

Dovka was dead and no one knew why. These partisans were prepared for sudden death in battle; *that* they could understand and accept. But this unseen enemy . . .

Was Dovka's illness contagious? Would there be an epidemic? If so, how could they fight it—defend against it? If only they had a doctor.

Solomon decided to do several things immediately. Dovka would have to be buried. Two men were sent out to dig the grave. Since he and Rachel had already been in close contact with the body, they alone would have to take Dovka to the grave and bury her. It was a horrible task, but they could not risk anyone else contacting the disease. Secondly, everyone else was moved out of the infirmary into another building where they would be kept isolated for a week, and everything in the infirmary itself would be burned. Since the infirmary was a dugout, everything in it was piled at its center, doused with coal oil and ignited. Dovka's bedding was buried with her. Her belongings were buried with her.

Then Solomon and Rachel quarantined themselves by going together to a dugout apart from the others where they would stay for a week. They could leave the hut and go to the woods or walk outside the camp, but they dared not mingle. Each day, supplies were brought to them. Rachel cooked their meals. They were isolated and they mourned.

The days passed. No one became ill. Ivan brought a new man into the camp—a soldier, a Jew, an escapee from several German prisoner-of-war camps. Solomon wrote in his diary, trying to bring it up to date. Rachel was grief-stricken. She kept wondering what she should have done differently for her friend. For a change, it was she who had to rely on Solomon's strength and comfort.

45

When the period of isolation was over, Yorgi had already been indoctrinated. Daily he was regaining his strength. He was becoming eager to go out on missions. It would feel good to strike back at the Germans again. Vengeance burned in him. Meanwhile, he had been put on the general staff to replace Dovka. His military background was invaluable.

Dovka's death had had as devastating an effect as the Goering Squadron incident. Being an outsider, Yorgi recognized the seriousness of the situation first, and he knew that something had to be done right away to take everyone's mind off the matter. Something spectacular, something all-consuming had to happen: a mission that would hurt the German effort beyond anything they'd yet carried out. To Yorgi, nothing was impossible. That was why he was still alive. When others wrote off an idea as impossible, Yorgi started to look for a way to make it possible. When others resigned themselves to imprisonment, Yorgi started to look for the weaknesses in the prison. Now those same qualities would be turned to offensive instead of defensive efforts. No sooner had he decided what was necessary to change the self-destructive mood of these battle-weary guerrillas than he was planning the operation.

Yorgi was the first to refer to this group as a community of guerrilla fighters. It was only a name, but Yorgi made an important implication with it. Heretofore, Yorgi pointed out, the partisans had been opportunists. They had attacked the enemy when the enemy came through their territory. Many of their actions were spontaneous, such as the time they'd found the horses. The opportunity presented itself and they acted.

"If you needed horses," Yorgi said, "you should have planned a mission to get them. As it turned out, you were lucky and got them accidentally. But I think that you will have less casualties and do more damage to the Germans if your missions are planned specifically to their purpose. I am amazed that you have had such good fortune.

"One of the best ways we have of hurting the enemy is to disrupt their supply lines," Yorgi went on, speaking to the crowd of partisans that had gathered around him in the community hut. "Now you've been hitting as many trains and convoys as possible, using anywhere between twenty and sixty people on those missions, and you've taken ten to twenty percent losses. No doubt the enemy has felt the sting of your efforts, but they have been more annoyances than crippling blows. What I have in mind should make the Germans sit up and take notice. With about the same risk as a raid on the convoy, I think we can have the effect of hitting a hundred convoys! Let me tell you my plan."

Everyone in the room listened to Yorgi. He was a big man and he spoke with authority. "We know one thing, and that is that the traffic *beyond* Kiev is not as great as it is going *to* Kiev. That can mean only one thing. The Nazis are storing their supplies somewhere in the vicinity. It makes sense. Kiev is near enough to the front to get supplies to the fighting forces, yet far enough away to protect them if there were to be a brief counteroffensive. Now we must find out where these storage depots are. We need only to follow the convoys. Once we know their whereabouts, we'll destroy these depots! One depot must contain the supplies from a hundred convoys and trains."

There was skepticism, but no one voiced it. They had never considered themselves important enough to take on such a mission; such a target seemed a major military objective. Yorgi saw it that way too, but the difference was that Yorgi saw the partisans as a major military unit. They still saw themselves as refugee Jews who were fortunate enough to be able to carry on some sabotage against the Germans. They did not realize that their experiences of the past ten months had molded them into a top-caliber fighting force.

"Do you honestly think we can carry out such a mission?" Moshe asked.

"And why not?" Yorgi replied. "If I had my old army unit here, I would not hesitate to pick such an objective, and you are better equipped and far more experienced than they ever were. Our war against the Germans was a catastrophe and lasted only a few days before we were routed. We didn't have half the arms you do. We were using outdated Russian arms. You are equipped with German weapons—the best in the world today. With careful preparation we will deal the Germans a blow that will set them back months!"

Renewed enthusiasm in the room soon spread throughout the encampment.

The next day the partisans had scouts out on all the major roads to Kiev. They found out that the major traffic was not even entering Kiev, so they tracked back on the roads and found a large percentage of the trucks were turning toward the city of Zhitomir directly west of Kiev at a little more than a hundred kilometers distance.

The day after that, the partisans coverged on the Zhitomir area. There they discovered that the trucks turned east toward Kiev again. Now they followed that road. At some distance, they came to a small town called Rozvazhev. It was little more than a village, but the Germans had turned it into a major storage depot. Its warehouses were being filled with supplies and equipment. Trucks stood in long lines waiting to discharge their loads into the storage buildings. It seemed that the entire German army was there too, but on closer observation it was clear that most of the military personnel were truck drivers and crews. Obviously, they didn't trust the Ukrainians with these supplies, for only German soldiers unloaded the convoys.

The majority of the partisans left Rozvazhev to take their information back to their headquarters. Two of them stayed at the village to get more detailed information that they would need for the success of the raid. They spent the rest of that day memorizing everything they could about the town, and that evening they drew a detailed map of the entire area. That evening they also discovered the majority of the Germans were gone with the trucks. The Germans who worked to unload the trucks were barracked at the edge of the town. The warehouses were well guarded, but not overwhelmingly so. They estimated the guard force to be no greater than fifty, with several dogs inside the electrified fences. Ten kilometers from the town, the last two partisans turned for the long trip home. They had their horses hidden in the forest. Even by horseback, the trip back took them all of the night and most of the next day.

46

The news from the scouts created excitement. All information was put before the general staff, and planning began. As it turned out, this was a major supply depot for the Germans. Yorgi was ecstatic over the thought of what a crippling blow this might be to the German war effort. "My friends," he started, "this mission should stagger the Nazis, and I see no reason why it should not be a tremendous success."

"When shall we hit them?" Uri Bolnik asked.

"Not until we are ready," Yorgi answered. "Everything must be right. We can afford to take our time with this mission. If we louse it up, we will have missed our best chance. It must be right on the first try."

Then Solomon interjected, "The longer we wait, the better. We do not want to strike too soon and give them a chance to resupply."

"What do you mean?" Moshe asked.

"Just this. The Germans have been bringing in those supplies for months now. It is just the first week of July. The longer we wait, the more of their equipment we will destroy. Those warehouses were far from full. They will bring in much more equipment over the next several weeks. The nearer our raid is to the winter, the more it will hurt them. That is obviously when they will need that equipment. If we hit them now, they will have three to four months to resupply. If we strike in September, they will have no time to resupply before the winter, and all they do bring in between now and then will also go up in smoke. It will be hard to wait, but I think it would be foolish not to."

Disappointment spread through the group. Yorgi was most disappointed of all, but he was the first to admit that Solomon was right. Silently, everyone tried to think of an argument to hasten the mission, but no one could come up with one.

"Well," Yorgi finally said, "we will have to keep observers around that town. If they change their routines, we will have to know it. They are bound to make changes in the next few months. We will have to work out an intelligence system— specifically for the Rozvazhev mission, I mean."

Solomon felt he had thrown cold water on the enthusiasm of his friends, and he sought something more immediate to take the raid's place.

"These summer days make it easy to repress the memory of the past winter and all of its sufferings. Now is the time to plan ahead for next winter. We have over two hundred people now to be thought of. To keep them fed and clothed and sheltered will be far more difficult than last winter."

The more they discussed the matter, the more they realized that they had little time to prepare.

47

September came and September passed. This first week in October, the eve of the raid on Rozvazhev, was already unseasonably cold. In the months between the conception of the mission and its execution, the guerrillas had prepared for winter. They carried out only those missions that would supply them with food and shelter. Others prepared for the Rozvazhev action.

Yorgi's philosophy was proving sound. Instead of hitting convoys randomly, the partisans planned each mission with specific aims. If food was needed, they went where the food was. If weapons were to be obtained, they planned a raid that would get them. If by luck other supplies and equipment fell into their possession, it was a bonus. Sabotage became a secondary motive for the time being. It was carried out whenever the opportunity arose, but it was not now the primary objective. Now they were primarily concerned with supplying themselves for the approaching winter and preparing for Rozvazhev.

To make this change in their mode of operation, they had to develop a superior intelligence-gathering system. The radios were monitored twenty-four hours a day. Partisans with false papers were in all of the towns, villages, and cities of the area. The money they had taken from their victims and hoarded for the past year now became extremely valuable. With money, one could buy remarkable things in the blackmarket, and information was no exception. In fact, blackmarketeers survived and supplied themselves with goods by using the same information that the partisans needed.

The blackmarket knew schedules of convoys, what they carried, where they were going, and how they were defended. Once the guerrillas made contact with the proper people, they could buy almost any information they needed. At first, money, and large amounts of it, was the tool of exchange, but after mutual trust was developed—the relationship between the guerrillas and the blackmarketeers—barter became mutually beneficial. The guerrillas took only what they needed out of a mission. Now, instead of destroying what was left so the Germans could not use it, they left it intact for the blackmarketeers who waited like buzzards to scavenge the remains. The blackmarketeers, of course, bought their information and protection from the Nazis themselves, so in effect the Germans were selling to the guerrillas. Everyone seemed satisfied with the arrangement. It was risky, but everyone had much to lose, so the partisans took their chances.

The raids that grew out of the information they gathered and bought turned out to be excellent practice missions for the upcoming Rozvazhev action. Because of their new methods, the guerrillas didn't attack convoys and trains as often. With their information they could strike at points in the chain of supply that would offer greater rewards at less risk. It was far safer to get food where and when the shops were being supplied; it was easier to obtain equipment at a rural transfer point less populated with military personnel; it was more efficient to obtain weapons at small-arms depots than to take them from randomly ambushed soldiers.

The new method supplied the partisans richly with food and equipment for the winter and for the impending mission. It also turned them into a top-notch fighting force—a fine army—and reduced their casualties to about seven to twelve percent on a raid. Still, they anticipated much higher losses on the Rozvazhev mission.

48

Never before had so many of the partisans been committed to a single action. Ninety-three made up the total of the force. Even at that, they expected to be outnumbered four to one. The number of Germans stationed permanently in Rozvazhev had increased since the warehouses had been filled to near capacity. The guards, however, had only been increased to sixty at each shift; the rest were inventory personnel. All were potential adversaries, and the partisans would have to keep as many as possible out of the battle.

For the first time the guerrilla force would battle in style. They had a convoy of stolen German trucks and military vehicles. They would drive to the vicinity of Rozvazhev and then separate into groups, each with its own objectives. The three men of letters had worked diligently to prepare the proper orders and papers. The drivers and those visible from the vehicles wore captured German coats and caps. The four-hour trip to the separation point went without incident. It was 11:30 p.m., just ten minutes before the first shot in the twenty-five minute raid would be fired. The first group to go into action cut telegraph and telephone lines at two designated places, isolating the town except for the wireless-transmission station, which two dynamite blasts destroyed thirty seconds later.

The second group had stationed machine guns around the barracks. When the transmission station exploded, the partisans threw dynamite into each of the four buildings, blowing them to pieces. A huge fire erupted and lit the entire sky. The few Germans who escaped through windows or doors were cut down by gunfire. In the first seconds of the battle, more than a hundred and thirty Germans died.

Almost simultaneously, the police station housed in an old church and the few Ukrainian policemen inside met the same fate. An officers' club and one for enlisted men were also leveled. After the first two minutes of battle, other than those on duty, all the Germans in the town were dead or dying. This left the sixty or seventy guards at the warehouses without replacements or reinforcements.

Two groups carried the main attack to the warehouses. One was to attack the main entrance first, drawing as much fire as possible; the second would then attack the rail gate. At several points near the main entrance, dynamite blasted out large sections of electric fencing. The attackers immediately cut down a number of guards with machine gun fire. The remaining guards took cover and trained their guns on the gaps in the fence, waiting for the attackers to rush through the breach. None came. The Germans were puzzled: the attackers would *have* to come through there to reach the warehouse! Suddenly a gigantic explosion behind them brought the front wall of the warehouse down, crushing twenty sequestered Germans. Then another explosion rolled flames into the sky. The Germans scattered into gunfire as they broke into the open. More explosions followed, and flames licked at the stars from several areas in the building. Now there were secondary concussions as volatile material stored in the buildings exploded.

As planned, many of the guards were drawn to the action at the front of the building. But minutes later, at the rear, the partisans blew the fence and fired on any exposed Germans. Then they set up their secret weapon.

They had made giant slingshots out of forks of small trees and rubber from truck inner tubes. Two men held each trunk firmly while a third drew the sling which cradled a packet of six dynamite sticks. A fourth man lit the short fuse, and at the first sign of sparks, they let go the payload. The device lobbed dynamite nearly a hundred meters. The first two or three charges dropped onto the warehouse roofs, where they blew gaping holes. The payloads that followed destroyed the stored supplies.

While all was going as planned at the main entrance, the remaining group of guerrillas led by Moshe Pinsker drove toward the rear of the compound. Crossing a cleared field, the truck passed into a minefield. A sudden blast tossed the truck onto its side, igniting its fuel. Before the stunned passengers could crawl free, the extra dynamite they carried exploded. When the smoke cleared, little was left of Moshe Pinsker and his group.

Finally, secondary explosions and wind-driven flames destroyed the whole warehouse complex. The surviving partisans withdrew. The entire operation took fifteen minutes. It was not yet midnight when the survivors raced their vehicles out of Rozvazhev. They had not yet counted their casualties.

49

Major Hans Oberman was livid with rage, but only because his superiors were livid with rage, and that created unpleasantness for Oberman. As did his superiors, he passed the unpleasantness down to his subordinates.

"I want a complete report on Rozvazhev!" he screamed as he stomped through the outer office. "I want facts and figures— and quickly!" The lieutenant cowered and nodded.

All day long, bits and pieces of information filtered into Oberman's office. "Total destruction of the warehouses. Total destruction of all barracks. Destruction of the communications center. Destruction of the Ukrainian police facility. Two hundred seven German military personnel known dead, seventy-nine injured, most serious to critical, and ninety-six unaccounted for." The figures changed as the day drew on, the injured joining the dead, the unaccounted uncovered in the rubble. The one figure that remained the same all day was "twenty-three enemy dead, no wounded."

The next morning, Oberman reported to his superiors. "Gentlemen, it appears our troops were the victims of a very well-planned raid. They obviously knew our entire routine and layout at the Rozvazhev complex. How they came by their information is yet to be discovered."

"And who are 'they'?" one of his superiors demanded.

"Partisans," Oberman stalled. "An army of partisans. Our estimates indicate a minimum of five hundred."

"An army of five hundred partisans?" the Colonel sputtered. "How can that be? Where would they operate from?"

"Perhaps this force was made up of several groups who joined for this specific action. We know that several groups operate throughout the Ukraine. We would be naive to think they could not work together on major projects. Until now, they've carried out only minor raids on trains, convoys, isolated patrols, and small storage depots. Never before have they ventured a major military action." He paused. "We think this was directed and organized out of Russia."

"Out of Russia?" the Colonel barked in surprise.

"Yes. We have monitored almost daily broadcasts into the occupied territories from the Russians. They encourage resistance. They could have sent leadership, even troops, to participate in this action."

"You have evidence to support these ideas?" one of the officers asked.

Major Oberman looked down at his hands. "We have no hard evidence yet. It is evident, however, that this raid two days ago was a superb military effort—not what we expect from loosely disciplined guerrilla gangsters."

"Well, let us hear some facts now," the Colonel insisted, pointing impatiently toward Oberman's papers. "Continue."

"Very well," the Major said with a shrug. "Our latest figures, and these are still not final, indicate that of our total military force of three hundred eighty-two men assigned to Rozvazhev that night, three hundred forty-eight have died, twenty-three are on the injured list, and eleven are still unaccounted for."

"And what price did the enemy pay?" inquired one of the officers.

"Oberman's eyes dropped to the desk. His voice weakened. "Twenty-three of their dead have been found. But we do not know how many wounded or dead they took with them."

"I have heard enough!" the Colonel exploded. "I want no more speculation! I want no more excuses! Oberman," he said, voice dangerously quiet, "I want action. I want the forests of the Ukraine purged of all partisans. I want every guerrilla rotting in Babi Yar!'' He sprang to his feet and stomped out of the room. During the silence that followed, while each officer digested his commander's orders, each gaze turned to Oberman.

50

It looked as though the entire town of Rozvazhev were going up in flames as the partisans drove out after the raid, each group making its individual escape. They drove to a predetermined point on the road out of Rozvazhev, and there they abandoned their vehicles in a jam to slow what help would eventually be coming from Zhitomir. They waited for the last truck, Moshe's, to come. When it did not appear as scheduled, they grew concerned.

"They should be here by now," Father Peter said anxiously. "Even allowing for the extra time it would take them to come from the back of the depot . . ."

"I'm afraid they've had trouble," Rachel interrupted, "maybe we should send someone back . . ."

"No one goes back!" Solomon insisted. "We can't risk more lives to their unknown fate. We have agreed to that from the very beginning of our existence as a fighting unit."

"But it is Moshe—his whole group," Rachel protested as more and more of the concerned partisans gathered, awaiting a decision.

"I know it is Moshe's group. No one loves Moshe more than I." Solomon paused. The entire group was looking to him to make the decision. *How has this come to fall on my shoulders?* Then he said with all the conviction he could muster, "It is not my decision that we not go back; it is Moshe's. He made the rule, wisely. We all agreed long ago! And each of us knew we might one day be the ones left behind."

"How much longer can we wait?" another partisan asked.

"Not long," Yorgi Tzarof answered, stepping into the group. "Solomon is right. We have no choice but to go on, and very soon." He looked back down the road toward Rozvazhev. They could all see the sky brilliantly lit where the town had been. "I'm afraid the illumination can be seen clear to Zhitomir. Even with communications down, that glow will bring Germans."

"But surely we can wait a little longer," Rachel pleaded.

Yorgi looked at his watch, a fine German timepiece captured several weeks earlier on another mission. He thought a moment. He too was fond of Moshe and the others, but as a soldier and a commander he could not let emotion cloud judgment.

"Rachel, I understand how you feel, but I could send none of you back on such a foolish venture. If they are trapped, more than likely our rescue group would meet with the same end. By now the Germans in the town have regrouped. If Moshe and his men are dead, we cannot help; we would only be adding to our casualties. If they are well, I'm confident they will make good their own escape. After all, they were some of our best seasoned fighters. Our only alternative is to make good our own escape. Now."

Yorgi turned his attention to the next command: "Set off two dynamite charges in those vehicles after you jam them together in the center of the road." Then they plunged into the forest with their wounded. The journey by foot to their base was expected to take them two days. With them they carried seven seriously wounded comrades; twelve others with minor injuries traveled without help. Before the night was over, four of the seriously wounded died. Their friends could not stop to bury them—that had been understood before the mission began.

"It is difficult to leave friends alone, even in death. Final farewells are not meant to be so abrupt and unceremonious," Solomon said.

Father Peter and Rachel were in charge of the wounded.

They had become close friends since Dovka's death. Along with Solomon, the young priest had helped Rachel regain her strength and objectivity. In turn, Rachel understood better than anyone else the torment and personal anguish that plagued Father Peter. When he was not busy with the radios, and she not occupied with the hospital or alone with Solomon, she and the priest spent many hours together, trying to fathom their ungodly world.

As each vehicle came to the meeting point, Rachel and Father Peter assigned all to help with the wounded. Makeshift bandages were checked and changed, but little more could be done for the seriously wounded. They continued to bleed and writhe in delirium with nothing to reduce their pain. They knew that their efforts with most of the critically injured were futile and that carrying them was a tremendous expenditure of energy, but it was difficult enough to leave their dead behind— and impossible to leave their wounded.

By noon of the next morning, the last of the seven critically wounded had died. The partisans had traveled many kilometers but could not stop to rest. They knew that at dawn the Germans would start out with dogs from the point where the trucks had been destroyed, giving the partisans only a five-hour lead. Hampered by their wounded, that lead would be reduced to three hours. The first six hours of their journey had not led them toward home; instead, they'd headed west past Zhitomir, about five kilometers south of that city. By dawn they had passed the city, and they continued twenty kilometers due west until noon when they came to the Teterev River.

The river flowed northeast at that point. There the partisans entered the river and doubled back, walking in the water to confuse the dogs. They waded for three or four kilometers—a slow and dangerous route because the Germans were searching by air as well as by ground. Every so often a plane would drone in the distance, and the party would scatter for cover along the bank until the aircraft passed, almost skimming the water. When they finally left the river, they headed north toward home.

They plodded in silence, each partisan weighing in his mind

success and loss. Five had died in battle, seven more since, and eighteen were missing and probably dead—among them Moshe, their leader. If the worst were true, they'd lost nearly a third of their original force. Except for those lost with Moshe's truck, their comrades had been felled by small-arms fire. What targets they'd made, silhouetted against the fires! They'd probably been shot by Germans roused from the beds of their mistresses when the dynamite blasts shook them.

After reaching camp two, the partisans waited two days for their missing comrades. The lookouts saw no signs of either their friends or Germans. Finally, the survivors started back to the family camp.

51

Asked by his superiors who the attackers had been, Major Hans Oberman had kept his knowledge to himself, knowing it would only have added to their rage. Now that he was sure, he himself didn't want to believe it. The seven additional dead found in the woods the day after the raid had convinced him. Do I dare insult my superiors with this? he wondered. A band of Jewish partisans were operating under his nose! More insulting would be the reports that showed these Jews had probably been operating for more than a year in the area—had been responsible, in fact, for most of the resistance activities in and around Kiev. To be outsmarted by these subhuman Jews! Oberman did not want the responsibility of suppressing this new information; so, knowing his colonel would share the brunt of the wrath if the facts came to light, he decided to share with him also the responsibility.

"What do you mean, Jews?" the Colonel exclaimed. "Jews are not capable of such bravery. Are you mad? We will be committed as lunatics if we expound such a theory!"

"It is not a theory," Oberman said. "I have substantial proof."

"Proof? What proof?"

"Their dead—my proof is their dead. Whenever dead partisans have been left behind, it was clear at once they were Jews."

"How do you know?"

"Because, Colonel, only Jews mutilate their penises."

"You mean to tell me that all those dead were cut?"

"Circumcized, yes. Almost a majority. In certain actions all the dead have been cut; in others, none. There are non-Jewish groups at work, of course. But at least one very active group is Jewish."

The Colonel was silent a moment, his face scarlet. "Who have you told of this, Oberman?"

"You."

The Colonel took a large, shaky breath. "For the time being, keep it that way." He pondered a moment, then continued. "Have any ideas of how to wipe out these Jews? Before your information gets out?"

"I have some ideas. If you will come to my apartment tonight, I will show you what I've gathered."

"Your apartment?"

"Yes, Colonel. I want no one around here to see what data I've brought together."

"I see your point, Major. I will be there."

The Colonel had never been to the Major's apartment before. The Major greeted him at the door dressed in a smoking jacket. The Colonel was disturbed. He owned no civilian clothes.

"Come in, sir," said Oberman graciously.

"Thank you," the Colonel replied uncomfortably. In the Colonel's office, Oberman was a subordinate to be belittled at whim. Here, the Colonel felt ill at ease and off balance.

"May I offer you a drink?" Oberman asked with a smile. He'd registered the Colonel's discomfort and knew he would now be listened to with greater respect.

"Schnaps, thank you."

"Excellent! I will have the same." He poured the drinks slowly, giving the Colonel plenty of time to take in the opulence of the room.

The apartment reflected both Oberman's flamboyant private life and his family's wealth. In one corner of the living room was a large credenza, which served as Oberman's bar. Other fine furnishings, those he had not confiscated from previous owners, he had bought at a fraction of their value or traded for favors. Several fine oils hung about the room, and there was a beautiful floor-to-ceiling window that overlooked a park across the street below. The parquet floors were covered with fine oriental rugs. Nowhere in the Ukraine, under the Bolsheviks, could rugs such as those have been found. The Colonel noticed a woman's coat hanging up in the corner on the large brass coat stand. He wondered whether it had been forgotten there—or whether the owner was behind the closed door at the far end of the room. Ordinarily, it would have bothered the Colonel that his subordinate lived so much more luxuriously than himself, but he was too overwhelmed to brood upon it now.

Bringing the drinks, Oberman asked, "Cigar? They are fine Dutch imports. In my opinion, no one makes better cigars than the Dutch."

The Colonel helped himself. He rolled the cigar between his fingers and sniffed its fragrance. He was impressed with the freshness and scent, but not nearly as impressed as when he looked at the black-and-gold cigar ring which displayed a family crest and the words, "Major Hans Oberman."

Oberman grinned with satisfaction, struck a match, and held it under the Colonel's cigar. "I think you will enjoy that. I have them specially selected, wrapped, and sent directly from Holland. If you like, I will take the liberty of ordering some for you."

The Colonel nodded his approval as he drew in the first mild wisps of smoke.

"Well, shall we get down to work?" Oberman asked.

"Yes. What do you have to show me?"

Oberman brought a map over and rolled it out on the coffee table in front of the Colonel. Taking a seat on the sofa next to his superior, something he could never have done in the office, Oberman began.

"This is a map of Kiev and the countryside surrounding it within a hundred-kilometer radius. I have made three separate markings on this overlay, you will notice. The "X" marks represent acts of hostility against the occupation. Where there is a circle about the "X" mark, like this one, there were circumcized dead found. Now *that* information was not reported in the accounts of the guerrilla actions; I had to go to the individual medical reports for that information. Those two groups of information were never filed together by action. But when I *brought* them together, these facts appeared." He pointed to a cluster of circled X's on the map overlay.

"And what do these circles without the 'X's' mean?" the Colonel asked.

"Those are points we have been fortunate enough to triangulate in on radio transmissions. Oh, they're smart, Colonel! They seldom broadcast for long, leaving us no time to fix a location. But in a few instances, we have been able to pinpoint them. They are never there when we search the area, of course, because they're too clever to transmit from their camps. Still, we have collected the information—and now it will tell us part of what we want to know!"

The Colonel studied the markings on the overlay in silence. Finally, he said, "This is quite impressive, Oberman. Now just what do you conclude from this information?"

Major Hans Oberman smiled and raised one index finger. "First of all, if we take into account the dates of the actions, which are represented by circled X's, then we must conclude that these Jews have been active against us since almost the beginning of our occupation here. I have to admit I find it difficult to believe that the Jews are capable of such actions, but I cannot come to any other conclusion. I fear that we have become victims of our own propaganda. Secondly, there are many guerrilla groups in the forests around Kiev. The wide range of territory in which these activities have taken place precludes there being only a few. They could not travel freely enough to cover such vast areas. I think there are many groups which work independently, perhaps within a radius of fifty kilometers of their camps. If that is true, these vast forests around Kiev could easily hide twenty to thirty guerrilla groups."

The Colonel was stunned. "Twenty? Thirty?"

"Easily, Colonel. Our best hope is to totally overpower them. We would by risking many lives and even then they might escape. But to go into those woods blindly with less than a hundred well-armed men—well, that would be inviting disaster! Now, a second method might be more productive, but it would require knowing their exact locations."

The Colonel pondered Oberman's assessment of the situation.

"If we concentrate on the circled X's," Oberman continued, "we see that they are concentrated in this area to the west and north of the city. They occur outside it a few times, but seldom to the east of Kiev, and seldom beyond this radius. The Rozvazhev raid and a few others are exceptions. I'm sure they're encamped in this large forest northeast of us. Of course, that area covers two-thousand square kilometers. We must narrow it far more than that. If we assume that the radio transmissions in that same area are from them, then that will narrow it some more. Admittedly, we have few circles in that area, but if we assume that they would travel a much shorter distance to transmit, then we can assume that their camp is within perhaps five kilometers of the transmissions. These three circles are all we have to go by, but it narrows the area to less than fifty square kilometers. Still a large area, but much less than the original twenty-five hundred."

A pleased expression appeared on the Colonel's face.

"Now Colonel, let me pose a question to you. Do we want to go after those Jews, or shall we go after one of the other guerrilla groups?"

The question took the Colonel completely by surprise. "I do not understand you, Oberman. One minute you are brilliant, and the next you ask a question like that and I am convinced you are completely mad! Why would we spare those Jew bastards, especially since they are responsible for Rozvazhev."

"Not only Rozvazhev, but many other major actions," Oberman added. "But remember, you and I are the only ones who know that, and since I have these files it is unlikely that anyone else will find it out—unless we make it known."

"Oberman, I still don't understand."

"Let me pour you another drink, Colonel, and I will explain." He filled both glasses. "Prost!"

The Colonel raised his glass in a silent salute. "Please

explain yourself, Oberman."

"As I see it, Colonel, there will be great repercussions if it becomes known that Jews have been operating under our noses in Kiev. You and I will bear the brunt. The high command will not be pleased to hear that the Jewish subhumans have been carrying on a guerrilla war against the finest army in the world for over a year—and undetected! Who do you think they will lay the blame on for such humiliation? Colonel, you and I will be made out to be fools. I hate to think what our reward for such stupidity will be."

The Colonel saw Oberman's point. The wrath of the Reich would be upon them. "What shall we do?" His voice was edged with fear.

Oberman was calm. He drew on his cigar and savored the smoke, which he exhaled slowly through pursed lips. "It is simple. If we keep all of this to ourselves, we can still be the heroes. I will see to it—with your permission, of course—that these medical reports never reappear. Without the corpse descriptions, no one will ever know what they were. Germany's propaganda will go unquestioned. The Jews will be remembered as cowards who went like lambs to slaughter! And we will not be seen as fools and failures."

"How? How can we save the situation? What must we do?"

"As I said, it is simple. All our superiors want is to get the guerrillas. With this information, all we have to do is go after one of the other groups—from another area, where dead Jews have not been found. In fact, it will be easier to go after a group that's been careless about its activities and that resides in a smaller, more accessible forest."

Again there was silence as Oberman let the Colonel ponder his words. Finally, a smile crept onto the Colonel's face—a smile where strain had been moments before.

"Fate plays many strange tricks, but none of those partisans would ever believe that they're being saved because they are Jewish!" Oberman grinned.

"Major!" said the Colonel in mock surprise. "Say not 'saved,' but only 'reprieved.' "

Oberman staged a raid on a small wooded area south of Kiev. His calculations indicated that a small guerrilla band was working in that area. He sent an overpowering force which annihilated the entire group. He ordered no prisoners taken—they might prove uninvolved in the Rozvazhev action. The ruse worked, and his and the Colonel's superiors were satisfied.

For Major Hans Oberman, however, the matter was not closed. He knew that Jews were operating in the area and that eventually they would come back to haunt him. As far as he was concerned, the decoy operation only bought him time. Sooner or later, he would have to destroy the Jewish guerrillas. Now he could take his time and do it quietly. He set about developing a plan to accomplish his own final solution.

52

After the Rozvazhev mission, the partisans had to reorganize. Moshe, their leader, was dead, and they had suffered more casualties than anticipated. Solomon and Yorgi became joint heads of the general command—Yorgi as leader of all military matters and Solomon as head of all non-military matters. The rest of the general command was made up of Rachel, Father Peter, Ivan, Gregor, and Uri Bolnik. During this reorganization Solomon realized that Rachel, Uri, Ivan and he himself were among the few survivors of the original partisan group. Time and battle had taken their toll, and again Solomon found himself asking, "Why? Why me? Why *not* me?"

PART IV
LIBERATION

53

The winter of 1943 made an abrupt and ferocious debut. Autumn of 1942 had hardly arrived when snow began to fall on Russia. By the end of October, the forest floor was carpeted in white. The partisans' attention narrowed to problems of food and shelter.

Elsewhere in the Soviet Union, nature was about to play a decisive role in history. A year earlier she had saved a nation under siege; now she would strike the blow that would eventually bring down the aggressor nation.

"Operation Barbarossa" began on June 22, 1941, when Hitler hurled the most powerful army the world had ever seen against Stalin's ill-equipped, poorly trained, and ineptly led troops. He attacked the Russians on a front that spread from the Black Sea to the Arctic Ocean. An enormous force of more than two hundred and fifty divisions was set in motion to race for Moscow, Leningrad, Kiev, Stalingrad, and all territories between. Barbarossa's objective was not just to gain these territories, but to destroy totally the Red Army. Had nature not sided with the Soviets, Barbarossa would have succeeded.

It was Hitler's idea that Barbarossa would accomplish all its objectives within eight months, putting the Soviet Union at the mercy of the German Reich. His timetable was delayed from the beginning. Barbarossa was to be launched in May of 1941, but because of misfortunes on other fronts—especially Mussolini's problems in Greece and at Belgrade—the starting date was postponed. Kiev fell, and with it the Ukraine. But when the Germans began their assault on Moscow and Leningrad, winter entered the battle on the side of the Russians. The first snows of the Russian winter were falling.

The modern and ferocious German war machine bogged down in snowdrifts. Men and animals froze. Supplies could not keep up with the advancing armies, and men and machines became stranded without fuel, ammunitions, warm clothes, and sufficient food. For the first time, the Germans found themselves at a disadvantage. German losses became heavier and harder to replace. By the time winter had set in at the end of 1941, Hitler had lost more than three-quarters of a million men to the Russian campaign. That was only about a fourth of the original force he had thrown into the campaign. Seven hundred and fifty thousand Germans dead, and the fury of the Russian winter brought the momentum of the Nazi advance to a standstill. An age-old Russian strategy was to work again. They had traded space for time, strategically retreating over vast wastelands while they equipped and trained men for the eventual counterattack in their heartland.

Now the Russians could start trading lives with the Germans, and they were willing to do it because they knew they were fighting for their very survival and in their own homeland. Under these circumstances, the Germans stood no chance. They had difficulty getting replacements to the front now, while the Russians had endless replacements, taking them right out of the population when necessary. The Russians could trade five lives for every German if need be and still outnumber them.

While the German mechanized divisions stood with their radiators frozen and their fuel tanks empty, the Russian cavalry, six hundred thousand strong, galloped out of the forests to surprise and slaughter the Germans, paralyzed by the weather.

By the third week of October in 1941, the German Army was within one hundred kilometers of Moscow. It was probably the worst moment of the war for the Russians. Stalin himself would direct the battle for the defense of Moscow from the Kremlin. It was Russia's moment of truth. If Moscow fell, the Kremlin would fall, and with it the entire Soviet Union. Barbarossa would be realized. The retreat of the Russians would have to end at Moscow's doorstep.

Every war has many miracles—events decisive in their timeliness. Such was the first heavy snow of the winter which began to fall when the Germans were preparing to make their final assault at the heart of the Soviet Union. First the snow came, then a melt and a rain which left the Germans wallowing in mud. Then came a freeze and ice and then more snow. Suddenly, the great German army found itself frozen in its tracks to the west, north and southeast of Moscow. Through the long and cold month of November, the German army tried to regroup and salvage what it could. The generals wanted to withdraw to a point where they could dig in and resupply, but Hitler would not hear of it.

The Russians spent this time productively, building forces and supplies at the points where they would be needed. And they waited for their ally, winter, to unleash its full force against the Germans. Now the Russians would decide when and where the next offensive would take place . . . the Russian offensive. On December 6, 1941, General Georgi Zhukov dispatched his one hundred divisions in a counteroffensive that shattered the German lines. The myth of German invincibility was destroyed.

To the north of Leningrad, the Germans were also stopped before they could enter that city, but there the story was quite different. The Germans were stopped, but the city was surrounded on three sides with its back against the Baltic Sea. And across that sea was Finland, a small but determined enemy of Russia and an ally of the Germans against the Soviets. When Leningrad was first cut off, surrounded, there were only a few days' food supply in that city. It led to a ghastly siege. By the height of that winter of 1941-42, up to five thousand people were dying daily of starvation. That blockade lasted until 1943. Never did the Germans or Finnish armies penetrate the boundaries of Leningrad, but they shelled and bombed the city to rubble. A few supplies were smuggled in or dropped by parachute, but they were a mere pittance to what was needed.

Still, those people of Leningrad held on. By the time the blockade was broken in 1943, more than six hundred thousand men, women and children had died there.

As the summer of 1942 approached, it became increasingly clear that the German takeover of Russia had ended. It was obvious to everyone but Hitler and a few of his closest confidants who shared his madness and unshaken belief in their own propaganda.

Hitler issued his directive that Stalingrad and the Caucasus were to be the objectives of the 1942 German offensive. On September 13, 1942, a German division broke through the defenses of Stalingrad and entered that city. What they found was a bombed-out city, but not a relinquished city. Every foot of that city cost the Germans dearly in lives. Every deserted building was mined, almost room by room. Snipers were everywhere. Each overhead window was an opening through which death could be hurled in the form of a Molotov cocktail. The German advance was no longer measured in kilometers, blocks, or even in meters. It was measured in corpses.

Miraculously, General Vasili Chuikov and his troops, reinforced by civilians of Stalingrad, held the besieged city. For more than two months they dealt death to the Germans who shared their city with them, while they themselves suffered terrible casualties.

Then, on November 19, 1942, Zhukov, the General who saved Moscow, launched a counterattack at Stalingrad. In four days he had the Germans trapped. Hitler would not allow his generals to surrender when they realized the struggle was hopeless. They continued their futile effort until January 13, 1943. By that time, General Freidrich Paulus had no choice. He was forced to surrender his German 6th army to the Russians. He and ninety thousand emaciated, ragged, half-frozen men were all that was left of the once-proud three hundred thousand men who planned to take Stalingrad. The series of defeats that started at Moscow continued to plague the Germans along the entire Russian front. What the winter of 1941-42 started, the winter of 1943 finished.

54

As hard as the winter of 1941-42 was on the partisans, the winter of 1943 was far more difficult—even though they were better prepared for the second winter in their family camp.

This winter, the partisans had sufficient fuel for heating their dugouts; there was plenty of warm clothing; like Ivan, the Zionists had grown vegetables, and they had adequate stores of other food taken in missions.

This winter of 1943, the snowfall was heavier, and the zero winds made going out impossible for days at a time. The very first storm dropped on the family camp more than a meter of snow, which fierce winds drifted here and there to three meters in depth. An elderly woman who'd led a young child to the latrine lost her way in the blizzard; disoriented by the blinding snow, they froze to death not twenty meters from their dugout. When it was over, the dugouts looked like white burial mounds among the trees. No sooner did the partisans clear out their huts and chimneys than the snow began once more. The second storm brought no high winds but added another half meter of snow to the partisans' worry.

Fortunately, Ivan and Sosha had been at their farm when the first storm broke, and the only partisans caught in it were five at the second camp. When the blizzard ended, the five made their difficult way to the cave Solomon had found the year before. It was still used as a warehouse and emergency hideaway.

There was sufficient food both at the family camp and at the cave, but feed for horses was a real problem. The five partisans from the second camp had led their horses to the ravine where the cave was, but once there they found no hay, and the animals could not graze the snow-covered ground. There was not enough grain stored to last the horses even two days. The partisans knew they could either shoot the horses or let them go free in hopes they would be claimed by someone who could care for them. But merely to let them loose would not work; the animals would starve among the deep drifts. They decided to try to get the horses to the vicinity of Irpen and let them go there, though they'd probably fall into German hands. Still, the Germans treated animals well; it was not like turning over Jews to the Nazis.

The day after the partisans reached the cave, the second snow started. The horses were tied together, and under the cover of the snowfall one man led the animals out of the ravine to the road that led to Irpen. Two kilometers from the village, he let the animals loose, and he returned to the cave, letting the new snowfall cover the fresh tracks.

In the family camp, the partisans remained snowbound. The days turned to weeks, the weeks to months. The many kilometers of waist-to-shoulder-deep snow they'd have to struggle through made guerrilla actions impossible. And if they could make it out, the deep tracks they would leave would never be entirely erased by snow. The Germans would surely find them, and slaughter the partisans they found. So the partisans became prisoners in their family camp from November 1942 through most of February 1943.

The radios were the only link to the outside world. Without them, their morale would dwindle. They could not get far enough from camp to transmit safely, but the news coming in was tremendously uplifting. Each day brought news of more and greater disasters befalling the Nazis. The Russians beamed news of their victories over the now-starving German army into the occupied territories, so that in the midst of their white prison the partisans gathered hope for the future.

When Father Peter was not busy with the radios, or helping Rachel with the sick, or in philosophic conversations with his other new comrades, he sat brooding on his own future: What does it hold for me? Will the Church accept me when this is all over? I've rebelled on behalf of my conscience, but did the Church really condone the acts of the Nazis? Each time Father Peter asked the question the answer wounded him: if the Church didn't condemn the Nazi atrocities, it condoned them. Anyone who did not cry out against the crimes was guilty of the sin of omission. Father Peter wondered, in fact, whether, he could in clear conscience return to the pulpit, even should the Church accept him back. The Vatican had lost its purity, its mystique, its holiness.

But why did it take the Nazis to make me see? I'm a historian. Did I simply close my eyes to the facts? Yes, this has been my own sin of omission.

He knew his Church's history of torture, anti-Semitism, war—but had never questioned it . . . never questioned the hypocrisy of it. He could no longer deny one shattering fact— that the Nazi success was the outcome of nearly two thousand years of Christian ideology and hatred of the Jews.

When Paul of Tarsus could not convert the Jews of his time, he introduced anti-Semitism into his teachings for those who *would* listen. In the Gospels of Matthew and John, two major anti-Semitic themes appeared: that the Jews killed Christ and should therefore be identified with the powers of evil. Father Peter recalled that early Christians had renounced the Jewish rebellion against Rome, had minimized the role of Pilate in the crucifixion to pacify the Roman authorities. He recalled the two centuries of Crusades in the Middle Ages, during which hundreds of thousands of Jews were raped and murdered with the Church's blessing. Why have these facts never disturbed me before? Father Peter asked himself. In more recent years there had been the pogroms. How many churchmen had preached hatred of Jews, encouraging their flocks to kill and maim, plunder and burn Jewish villages? So much anti-Semitism was so deeply ingrained in parochial education, it was no wonder the Germans had found it so easy to slaughter Jews without Christian resistance.

That winter was one of anguish for Father Peter. He felt the weight of his own and his Church's sins building up on all sides like the snow.

55

That winter, Solomon and Rachel, for the first time since the occupation, allowed themselves to think of the future. Since the news of the Russian victories and the changing tide of the war, many of the partisans were starting to think that there might be a future for them after all. The group of young Zionists that had joined earlier in 1942 spoke constantly of their plans to continue on to Palestine after the war. Their plans influenced many other partisans, including Solomon and Rachel.

"There is no place left in Russia or Europe for the Jews," was the contention of the young Zionists. "The survival of our people depends on a homeland for the Jews. Now is the time to re-establish our State of Israel in the promised land!" It had been recognized almost a century earlier that for the Jews to ever have their just dignity and freedom, they would have to have their own nation. The Jews were a nation in Diaspora. That fact, and Christianity's refusal to allow Jews equal status in any nation under its influence, made Europe and Russia no homeland for the Jews. These young Zionist partisans, under the influence of Theodor Herzl, had organized before the war with the intention of settling on land in Palestine purchased by the Jewish Agency. There they would form a settlement, a kibbutz. They would be one of the many settlments with the dream of joining to become a new Jewish State—the State of Israel. The training for the hardships they would face in

Palestine stood them well here in the forests of the Ukraine. But all the time they fought against the German occupation, they kept alive their dream. For the Zionists, this was just one of the difficult steps to the Promised Land. Rachel and Solomon decided they would make their way to Palestine with the young Zionists and start a new life after the war. Their families had been exterminated; there was not even a grave marker to visit anywhere in Europe.

56

Major Hans Oberman spent much of that winter seeking out and destroying guerrilla groups. Using his clever map and tracks left in the snow, he established an impressive record for his superiors. In a few short months he rid the Kiev area of a dozen partisan groups, not as well supplied as the Jews. Forced to move out of their camps to obtain supplies, most groups were easily stalked by the Germans. Oberman still suspected Jewish partisans of headquartering in the vast forest but was unable to detect movement.

Frustrated, Oberman decided to fly over the forest personally with an experienced reconnaissance pilot. For two days they flew over the area northwest of Kiev and found nothing. On the third day, they spotted deep tracks in the snow. They followed them from the air for several kilometers to a small herd of deer. Oberman swore at the animals and cursed the pilot. "Damn it, find me some tracks or some smoke or some lodges! Those bastards are down there someplace. Why the hell can't you find them? You're supposed to be the best we have!"

The pilot answered meekly, "I'm sorry, sir. That is an enormous area down there. We could fly over it for a week and not find them. They're probably smart enough to put out their fires on windless days; when it is windy, the smoke dissipates before it clears the trees. And to see tracks among the trees from this altitude is impossible. We only found those deer because they crossed a clearing. I doubt the guerrillas ever get out from the cover of the trees."

Oberman fumed in silence. When they landed back at Kiev, he canceled any further overflights. He would find another way.

57

When spring arrived in 1943, everyone was ready.

Major Hans Oberman was disgruntled that he had not yet pinpointed the location of the Jews. The advent of spring would allow partisans all over Eastern Europe and the Ukraine to move about freely and resume their activities. Oberman had been unable to track the Jews in the snow; perhaps he could get at them through their activities now.

The German army was, of course, overjoyed at the end of winter. Winter had been their mightiest foe so far. Now they could retrench, resupply, and reinforce their starved and frozen troops. But what they did not realize was that during the long winter the Russians had built up their forces and supplies and had modernized their equipment. The Russians were also ready for spring.

During the long winter, while Father Peter monitored the radio, he began to suspect that another partisan group had moved into the area. They did not broadcast often, but when they did their transmissions were always clear. Also, though most of what they transmitted was brief and in coded conversation, they occasionally made references to familiar things—to a fierce blizzard, for example. A few other transmissions had raised Father Peter's suspicion—also his fears. He had maintained radio silence to avoid detection by the Germans, and now another group was sending messages that might bring the Nazis down on them all.

The rest of the group was also concerned, and they considered breaking radio silence to warn the others not to transmit, but they feared the others might want to make contact and join forces.

"How can we arrange a meeting without inviting the Germans also?" Solomon asked the General staff. "And what if this other group is hostile to Jews? With all our equipment and supplies, the new group might just decide to attack us."

"A definite possibility," Yorgi agreed. "If only we could locate the new group without revealing ourselves. That would give us a chance to look them over before risking our own security."

Everyone feared too long a wait. If the group increased their transmissions or did something else to bring on the Germans, the Jews might also be found. They didn't just want to transmit a warning, but almost everyone agreed it was the wisest move. Just before the vote, Rachel asked, "Just how do the Germans locate a radio transmission?"

Yorgi explained. "Most radios have directional aerials. They receive the best when the aerials are trained in the direction of the transmission. That being the case, all the Germans need do is draw a line on a map from their receiver in the direction of the signals. Then they know the transmitter is somewhere along that line. To pinpoint the spot, they have another listener at a different location draw a second line from his receiver to the signal's point of origin. Where those two lines intersect on the map, they will find the transmitter. That's why we go far from the camp to transmit and why we never transmit from the same spot twice."

"We have two radios. Can't we do the same thing to locate the other camp?" Rachel asked.

"If we had a map," Yorgi conceded. "But then we would only be locating the point they transmitted from. By the time we got there, we'd find only empty woods—if we were lucky— Germans with the same idea if we were unlucky."

"I'm not so sure," Solomon said. "I have an idea. It has some problems, but I think we can work it out. Wait a few minutes while I get Ilya."

He jumped to his feet and ran out of the room, leaving all there wondering what he had in mind.

Ilya Chuikov was a small man in his early thirties. He wore thick glasses; one lens was cracked and the metal frame held it precariously. The crack caused him to squint—and to remember. The lens had been cracked by Nazis when they broke into his home months earlier. They'd arrested him, his wife, and his two children—a boy of three and a girl two months old. They were immediately separated and he never saw his family again. He cherished no illusions about their survival.

The Nazis took him to the school building where he had been a mathematics teacher and threw him into the basement lunchroom. There he was detained with about a hundred others—all men, all Jews. He never found out why he had been spared his family's fate. None in that room knew why they were there.

They'd remained in the room for about an hour. There were no windows, only a ventilator shaft on one wall about three meters up from the floor. It had no windows and only one door, and rather than risk being rushed by the prisoners, the Germans guarded from the outside. After a while, a few of the men started talking about the possibilities of escape. It seemed hopeless until someone suggested the vent.

"It's too small," one noted.

"Perhaps some of us could get out," countered another, not wanting to give up all hope.

"The only one who could get through there is that little man," said a third, pointing at Ilya, who was totally preoccupied with worry about his family.

"Hey you. You with the broken glasses," the same man called, trying to get Ilya's attention. "You, there. Come here."

"Ilya looked up, squinting through his newly-broken lens. Without the glasses, he was as good as blind. The man who had called to him was motioning for him to join the group.

"What do you want of me?" Ilya asked.

"If we can get that screen off that vent up there, you think you could get through it?"

"Where does it go?"

"Who knows? But what do we have to lose? Maybe it leads outside. Maybe you can get out and figure a way to help us. On the other hand, you may get caught in there." He paused, then shrugged. "Will you try?"

Ilya agreed without hesitation. If he got out, he might also help his own family. He realized his chances of even fitting through the ventilator shaft were slim, that he was probably crawling into his death. But what choice was there?

Two of the larger men lifted his frail body easily. He tugged at the screen covering the vent, which came loose, bringing dust down on himself and those below. He handed the screen down, and the two men all but heaved him into the small opening. After he was in, they lifted another man and snapped the screen back into place.

It was cramped and dark in the shaft. As he slid along, dust flew into his nostrils. Struggling to stifle a sneeze, Ilya Chuikov snaked his way on. Then he came to an elbow turn in the duct. He could get his head far enough into the elbow to see the shaft's outside screen. Daylight shone through the screen, and Ilya felt sure he could force his way through, but he could not get his shoulders past the elbow turn. With escape only two meters away, Ilya was forced to return to the basement room.

As he started to back down the duct, he raised more dust. It penetrated his nostrils and he found himself sneezing before he could stifle it. He was over a seam in the duct, at a point where the thin sheet metal was poorly supported, and the convulsing motion of his body was more than the duct could withstand. The seam gave way and dumped Ilya into a shallow crawl space.

Stunned and sore, Ilya found himself in darkness pierced only by a sliver of light off to his left; it came from an opening a few meters away. He crawled in the loose, cool dirt under the building. The light was coming through a crack between two boards in what felt like a small, wooden access door. He put his eye up to the crack. Beyond it was a German standing by a car, probably its chauffeur waiting for his officer. Ilya knew right away where he was. The little door was one he had often seen from the outside as he walked to and from school. He had never paid much attention to it; now it was his doorway to escape. It opened, he knew, onto an alley at the side of the building, next to the faculty entrance to the school. The stairway to the faculty entrance would give Ilya protection from the view of anyone on the street. On the other side, he would be kept from view by trash bins. Now if only that damn German would leave!

For six hours that German remained at his spot. He kept getting in and out of his car, yawning and talking to himself, but never did he leave. Finally, after dark, Ilya heard the officer return to his car. After exchanging a few words with someone in German (which Ilya couldn't understand), the officer started the car and drove away. Alone with his thumping heart, Ilya waited several minutes before trying the door. It moved easily. He slowly and carefully opened it. The alley was empty. Ilya slipped out and followed the shadows to where the trash bins stood in the alley. He saw no Germans.

Now he paused. How could he possibly help his fellow Jews? No sooner had he started to ponder the problem than he heard a commotion at the rear of the building. The Germans were moving the Jews he had been imprisoned with into trucks. If there had been any chance to help them, it was too late now.

Ilya escaped to the countryside. He could not help his family either. He had no idea of where they might be. He made his way into the forest, like a ghost, empty and in despair. Three weeks later, his path crossed that of the partisans, and he joined their ranks.

Solomon explained the problem to Ilya when they got back to the room where the general staff was trying to chart their actions.

"Ilya, what information would we have to give you to locate another group of partisans in these woods? We can pick up their transmissions from two different locations and can tell you the directions from which the transmission comes, but we have no map to plot their locations."

Ilya didn't even have to think. "That's a simple trigonometry problem. If you can give me the directions, I can convert them into the degrees of two sides of a triangle. Then if you can give me the exact distance between the two receiving sets, I will have two angles and one side of a triangle. Given that, I can easily construct the rest of the triangle and tell you exactly how far you have to go and in what direction to find them."

"There is the answer," Solomon said to the group.

"There are still a few problems with that," Yorgi pointed out. "First we will not find their camp, only a transmission point from which they will have fled by the time we get there."

"I have figured that out, too!" Solomon smiled triumphantly. "We will send out two men with the radios. At a known distance, the men will then send an emergency message to the other group, which they hopefully will return. That will give Ilya his two angles. Then our men will come home. Meanwhile, Ilya will point us in the right direction and tell us how far to go. Our reconnaissance group will intercept the other partisans. If they look safe, we will bring them back here. If not, we will just warn them to get the hell out of the area before the Germans get them!"

"But do you think they'll be foolish enough to transmit back to us from their camp?" Yorgi challenged.

"I have a theory about that group," Solomon explained. "I don't think they have a permanent camp like this one. I think they are mobile and move about every few days. That would explain why they are less cautious about their transmissions. If their camp is permanent, I don't think they will transmit. Anyway, that decision will be theirs. At least then they will know we want to contact them. I think we have nothing to lose by trying it."

Without maps, the most difficult problem was measuring the exact distance between the two radios. Finally, the partisans measured off two hundred meters of rope. One man walked with one end of the rope until it was fully extended; then the second walked until he reached the first, who then walked until the rope was once more fully extended. They repeated this tedious operation twenty times, making the distance four kilometers. The forest snow had melted to a depth that was easy to travel in, and large areas were completely free of snow, so they made good time without the fear of being tracked. When they reached their destination, the two partisans set up their radio and transmitted, using the other group's coded name, picked up from previous transmissions.

"White Rabbit . . . White Rabbit . . . please respond, White Rabbit . . . brothers in arms share your woods . . . please reply, White Rabbit." They transmitted the same message five times, once every minute. Then suddenly a reply came.

"Brothers in arms . . . this is White Rabbit . . . this is White Rabbit . . . Transmit your message . . . We hear you . . . Please transmit . . ."

"White Rabbit . . . brothers in arms need to make contact with you . . . Can you make transmission appointment for tomorrow? Please give time and frequency . . . We will stand by . . ."

The Jews were not interested in really establishing a time for the other group to transmit to them the next day; they just wanted them to transmit an answer that they could aim for. The reply came.

"White Rabbit . . . Will transmit on this frequency tomorrow at 14:00 hours . . . repeat . . . White Rabbit will transmit on this frequency tomorrow at 14:00 . . . Will stand by for one minute now if there is any further message."

As soon as the message started to come in, the Jews at both receivers moved their aerials to determine the direction of best reception. Two minutes after the transmission from the other partisans ended, the Jews at the family camp changed to another prearranged frequency and received the exact directions by the other radio. Ilya took less than one minute to figure. "They are exactly thirty-one kilometers due north of here."

In minutes a contingent of five Jews set out in that direction. It would be a torturous journey through virgin forest, with no roads or trails to make travel easier. In thirty kilometers, an error of one or two degrees could cause them to miss the other camp completely. They took one of the radios with them. If they had not made contact by transmission time tomorrow, they could use that broadcast to give them a new fix.

The trip proved more difficult than anticipated. It took more than twenty hours to travel what they estimated to be the proper distance. It was three hours before White Rabbit was scheduled to transmit again. The Jews decided to rest for the remainder of the time rather than go on searching blindly through the woods. When the transmission came, they would get a new direction.

Of course, the Germans had monitored the transmissions of the day before and had pinpointed both parties. Their locations were marked on a map for Major Hans Oberman.

58

While four of the Jewish partisans rested, one got up to explore the immediate area. He went in one direction and then another. He found nothing, nor did he expect to, but he could not sleep and this kept him occupied. He had been doing this for about twenty minutes when he found himself looking down the barrel of a German machine pistol. It was in the hands of a bearded man in civilian clothes. He had crossed the path of one of the sentries posted by the other partisan group.

It had been the intention of the Jewish partisans to observe the other group before they made contact. Now as he looked down the barrel of his captor's guns, the Jew wondered what he should do next. He assumed the man he faced was a partisan, but he made a split-second decision not to reveal his four comrades. Certainly he was not about to reveal himself as a Jew.

"Who are you? What do you do here?" the captor demanded.

"I am a refugee. I escaped arrest in Irpen," the Jew answered, making up what he thought would be a believable story.

"Irpen? That is a long way from here. How long have you been in this forest?"

"Five days, I think. I am no longer sure."

"Why are the Germans after you?"

"They suspect that I was involved in partisan activities."

"Were you?"

"Nothing organized."

"Why are you in this part of the forest?"

Now the Jew wondered whether he should say he was lost
and just wandered here or test this man. "I heard in Irpen that a
guerrilla group was active in these woods," he said at last. "I
was hoping that I could join and fight the Nazis properly."

The captor said nothing for a moment but looked his captive
over carefully. Then he motioned with his weapon and
said, "Lie down flat on your belly."

The Jew went down.

"Now spread your legs and arms to their full reach."

The Jew stretched.

"Make one move and you're dead."

The Jew froze. Carefully the captor searched him. Inside the
Jew's shirt, he found a German pistol. "How did you come by
this?"

"It's a long story. It has to do with why the Germans are after
me."

"Okay. Get to your feet. Put your hands behind your back
and grasp your wrists. If I see you let go of either wrist, you will
have taken your last breath. Now walk." The captor pointed
the direction with his gun.

The Jew walked.

One of the other Jews awoke and noticed his comrade was
gone. He had gotten up and looked for him. Hearing the
captor and captive talking, he followed the sounds until he
saw what was transpiring. He, too, assumed that the captor
was a partisan and did not reveal his own presence. When the
Jew and his captor started away from the spot where the
confrontation took place, the observer followed unnoticed.
They only had to go about two kilometers before they came to
the temporary encampment. As soon as the follower saw where
the camp was, he returned to his three remaining companions
and led them back to their objective. To their surprise, they
found the captive Jew coming out of the encampment with
three of the other partisans. They were returning to get his
companions.

They could not understand what could have gained his
confidence so rapidly. They had no chance to duck for cover.

"Don't be afraid," the Jew called to them as soon as he saw them. "They are Jews. This is the group of the famous Diadia Misha."

59

Diadia Misha was a name well known over the partisan radio transmissions in Eastern Europe and the Ukraine. The exploits of his guerrilla group were transmitted into the occupied areas by Russian radio as a morale booster and as an encouragement for other partisan groups. What radio Russia did not publicize was that Diadia Misha's band was made up mostly of Jews.

Misha Gildenman was the name he was known by when he was an engineer in the town of Koretz. He'd been a peaceful man—a family man. He'd never been a leader, nor had he ever been inclined toward military matters. He would have been only too happy to live out his life as an average citizen in his town. Life in Koretz could have been described as simple, and Diadia Misha was content with his wife, son and daughter. He was approaching his middle years with satisfaction and looked forward to the future.

As had been the case in Kiev and most of the towns and cities where the Germans came, they were greeted as liberators when they entered Koretz. The welcome was short-lived. Almost immediately after occupying Koretz, the Germans rounded up all the Jews in the area. The elderly, children, women, the weak and the ill were taken to a pit twenty meters long, twenty meters wide, and three meters deep, undressed and thrown in, six at a time. The Germans found great sport in shooting those stunned by the fall or the others who made futile attempts to climb out. The Nazis had set up picnic tables laden with food and drink to make a holiday atmosphere. By the end of the day, the Germans had slaughtered two thousand two hundred Jews. Misha's wife and thirteen-year-old daughter were among them.

The Jews not murdered were herded into a ghetto. There was a synagogue where many went to say the *Kaddish* for their dead. Often, grief was oblivious; it had happened so fast! So fantastic were the horrible events of the day that many of the survivors felt mainly disbelief. Some time after the Kaddish, what happened began to sink into Misha's mind. Those who did not die today would surely be chosen for death tomorrow. He looked at his eldest son Simcha, who sat staring into space. Misha concluded that to prevent his murder there was but one course of action: to get away from the Nazis, escape to the forests.

"We must go, Simcha. We must get out right away. Tomorrow might be too late."

"Go? Go where?" Simcha asked, still in shock.

"To the forest," he answered as he was getting up to face the others in the Synagogue. "Listen! Listen to me, all of you! You condemned Jews! Be assured that we have no hope but escape to the forest. From there we'll take our vengeance on these Nazi pigs! Who is with me?"

Most of the unfortunate Jews in the Synagogue were still too stunned to understand what Misha was saying. Most probably did not even hear him. Misha was, after all, one of the luckier in the sanctuary; he still had his son. Almost all others had seen entire families butchered. Suddenly alone in the world, it was too much.

Sixteen men fled the ghetto in small groups under the shelter of darkness. They decided to meet at the house of a friendly gentile at the outskirts of town where they would regroup and make for the forest. Between them they had one pistol and five rounds of ammunition.

"Our most immediate problem is weapons," Misha said. "We now live in a world where the currency is bullets."

"I know where we can get more weapons," Simcha interjected. "There is a house not far from here, at the edge of the forest, where the district forester lives with his wife. I know he has several guns. He used to burst with pride showing them off to us when we played in the woods near his home. I don't know if he ever used one, but he always carried one under his arm as he inspected the woods for traps and poachers."

"He still lives there?" Misha asked.

"I suppose so," Simcha shrugged. "Unless he also has fled from the Germans."

"Or the Nazis may have confiscated his guns," interjected a third.

"Let's go and see," Misha said.

It was past midnight when the band of Jews got to the forester's hut. Misha—in possession of the one pistol they had, its clip short one bullet—knocked at the door of the little house. Guns were completely foreign to Misha. He had never fired one before, and now he was about to threaten a man with his pistol.

The dim glow of a kerosene lamp came on and shone through a window at the front of the house. A voice came through the bolted wooden door. "Yes, who is it? What do you want?"

"I am told you are the forester in this district," Misha answered. "I was sent to report a fire to you. It is burning in the forest about three kilometers from here."

They could hear the bolt of the door slide back. Misha's throat tightened and his heart pounded. As the door swung open, Misha thrust the pistol forward. In his excitement he miscalculated the distance to the man, who stood closer than he had expected. The barrel of the pistol jammed right into the left nostril of the flabbergasted forester. "Don't move!" And seeing what he had just done, Misha added, "This is a gun I have in your nose!" The error in judgment was quite effective, and the poor man stood speechless, looking down with crossed eyes at the pistol barrel.

One of the other Jews shouldered past the terrified forester and in a moment brought the forester's wife out from the only other room in the house. Both were clad in nightshirts, speechless with fear. Simcha and two others went in and searched the premises.

"You have guns and ammunition?" Misha finally said, overcoming his own anxiety sufficiently to get the words out.

"Yes . . . yes . . . Please don't hurt us! I will give you anything you want. Please trust me! Please!"

Misha began to feel sorry for the poor devil, but he was struggling for his own survival and that of his band. "Get them. All of them. No tricks. And all of the ammunition, too."

The forester went to a locked cupboard in a corner of the room and took down a key hidden above the door. He unlocked and opened it, and before he could do more, one of the men shoved him aside and emptied the cabinet: three rifles, a shotgun, and enough ammunition to last quite a while.

Simcha and the other searchers found a few other supplies that would be helpful in the forests.

The guerrillas abandoned the house as quickly as they'd come, leaving the forester and his wife safe inside. Their first action was a success. But as they left the hut, Misha felt pangs of guilt. He was not yet used to bullying his fellow human beings.

Diadia Misha was the name by which Misha Gildenman became known. His group grew and remained predominantly Jewish. They were mobile, in spite of the fact that they had families and elderly Jews with them. Their activities against the Germans from the forests of the Ukraine soon became legend.

60

The five Jewish partisans who had come to make the rendezvous were welcomed into the camp, where they were introduced to Diadia Misha, his son, Simcha, and his entire general staff. They told of their own group and some of their activities, some of which the Russians credited to Diadia's men for lack of information.

It was decided at that meeting that Diadia Misha would move his group to the vicinity of the family camp. They had no intention of merging the groups, but perhaps they could exchange supplies, equipment and weapons; perhaps they could also coordinate a few missions. So mobile was this guerrilla group that they broke camp and were on the way in less than two hours, in spite of the fact that they were nearly two hundred people. At the prearranged time, they transmitted a brief message: "Brothers in arms . . . White Rabbit coming in. Brothers in arms . . . White Rabbit coming in." And then, just as a teaser which they knew the recipients of the message would not fully understand, they signed off: "*Shalom*, brothers in arms. *Shalom* from White Rabbit."

It took three days for the large group to migrate to the family camp. They had to move slowly because their pace was set by the elderly and the children. Two of the five partisans who had come to Misha's camp stayed with the group to show the way. The other three went ahead with a small contingent, Simcha among them, to announce the group's arrival.

Fittingly, the meeting of the two Jewish groups took place just before the beginning of Passover. On April 18, 1943, the two Jewish partisan groups celebrated the first night of Passover together. While the Jews had their Seder, the gentiles monitored the radios and took care of all the chores of the camps. Father Peter was at his favorite post in the radio hut. He was the first to hear a message relayed from an underground transmitter in the Jewish Ghetto of Warsaw, Poland: "Please send help. All resistance forces in Warsaw area, please send help. All resistance forces in Warsaw area, please send help. Siege of our ghetto is imminent. Please send help. . . ."

61

Messages from or about the Jewish ghetto at Warsaw were not unusual. They came over the radios in the Ukraine and Eastern Europe intermittently, and with increasing frequency, during the days of 1943. Actual signals from within the ghetto were too weak to be heard in the Ukrainian partisan camps, but the messages were relayed by others who could receive them. Most messages were reports of the inhuman treatment of the Jews in the ghetto. They told of roundups, starvation, deportations, disease, overcrowding. They also asked for help from nearby partisan groups, from governments of the free world, from the people of Warsaw. Help never came.

But this new series of messages that came around the 18th of April of 1943 were different. They indicated that the ghetto's destruction was imminent, and they asked for supplies, weapons, ammunition. The Jews of the ghetto were going to fight. They also asked that the freedom-loving people of Poland rise up against the Nazis simultaneously outside the ghetto. They suggested that while the Germans were occupied with the attempted elimination of those Jews left inside the Warsaw Ghetto, the guerrilla and partisan groups take the opportunity to attack the Germans at other points to divide their attention and forces. The suggestion went unheeded. After all, there had never been a major uprising against the Germans since the beginning of the war; why expect these surrounded, half-starved, relatively unarmed Jews to cause the

Germans any problems? Once the Germans started their destruction of the ghetto, it would only be a matter of hours, maybe a day or two, before all the Jews would be eliminated. To many of the Poles, that thought was not disturbing anyway. Let the Germans do what many of them had wanted to do themselves—rid Poland of the Jews.

On the night of April 18, the Jews of the Warsaw Ghetto were totally alone. They awaited the German attack, which they knew would come early the next morning. There were secret routes of escape from the ghetto, difficult and dangerous, but not as difficult and hopeless as the coming days would be in the ghetto. Only a few of the ghetto Jews chose to escape. In fact, many Jews who by some good fortune and deception were able to continue living outside, chose this time to enter the ghetto. Many of those Jews entered the ghetto through the secret escape routes so they could fight the Germans with their brothers. That night ⌐f April 18, 1943, Jews from outside the Warsaw Ghetto celebrated the first night of Passover with the Jews inside the Warsaw Ghetto. All knew that this would probably be their last Passover. They chose to die fighting the Nazis.

While the world watched in silence, Himmler himself decided to destroy the Warsaw Ghetto. The Germans feared that if the Jews resisted, others might be encouraged. Better raze the entire ghetto and kill every Jew in it. Himmler intended to accomplish this in one day, so he could give Hitler a birthday present on April 20: The message, *"Warsaw ist Judenrein* . . . Warsaw is clean of Jews."

To do the job, the Germans mobilized two thousand SS men and officers, three detachments of Wehrmacht artillery and mine experts, two battalions of German police, more than three hundred fifty Polish police, and a battalion of turncoat Ukrainians who chose collaboration over prisoner of war camps. In addition, a massive force of seven thousand men was brought into the Warsaw area in case reinforcements were needed. The weapons of war to be used against the poorly armed Jews were the most modern and sophisticated in the world. After all, the world is watching, and Himmler did not want to be embarrassed on the Fuhrer's birthday.

62

On the morning of April 19, Father Peter monitored the radio: "The Jews of the Warsaw Ghetto are fighting. Armed uprising against the Germans. . . ." There was no more news than that. The same message was transmitted throughout the day. No details were given. The same message was received and relayed throughout occupied Europe and Russia. "The Jews of the Warsaw Ghetto are fighting."

63

On the evening of April 19, Father Peter heard another message relayed to the radio receivers of the Ukraine. "Warsaw Ghetto Jews still hold the ghetto . . . Germans beaten today. . . . Fellow freedom fighters join the revolt. . . ."

There were messages the night of the 20th and 21st, and for many more nights. Each night the listeners thought it would be the last. Each night they were surprised and elated that the Jews still held the ghetto. Each night there was an appeal for help; each night the appeal fell on deaf ears. The partisans in the Ukraine were too far away; those who were near enough didn't help. Then the ghetto fighters appealed to the Allied forces to bomb the Germans, to drop supplies, to help in any way they could. No one seemed to care. But the Warsaw Jews were determined to fight to the end, alone if need be.

The days and nights turned into a week, the single week into a miraculous two. Each day the Jews fought heroically against staggering odds. They suffered savage casualties but fought back with unbelievable determination. Even the German officers developed a silent, unspoken respect for them. The German soldiers dreaded every time they had to enter the ghetto. There was merciless shelling and mortar barraging of the area. If the Jews had given up at any time, they would still have the respect of those who watched—those who watched but would not help. But the Jews refused to give up. They knew surrender meant death. So did continuing the battle, but they preferred to die with weapons in hand, even when those weapons were only sticks and clubs. And each day their broadcast said they still had control of their ghetto.

On May 8, the resistance in its twentieth day, the Germans came across the headquarters of the Jewish Fighting Organization, a large underground bunker at Mila 18. At the time it hid about three hundred noncombatants and just under a hundred ghetto fighters. There were five outside entrances to that bunker, and the Germans surrounded it.

The fighters chose to stay behind and hope for some slim chance that they might still be able to fight. They pointed out to the civilian noncombatants that death faced them surely in the bunker, and most probably if they gave themselves up, but that the choice was theirs. The bunker was terribly over-crowded, and if there were any chance to make a fight of it, it would have to be emptied of some people. Under the circumstances, a majority of noncombatants gave themselves up to the Germans. Those who stayed received what weapons were available. The remaining fighters in the bunker prepared themselves for a war literally underground, but the Germans did not come in. They sealed the five entrances and piped lethal gas down into the bunker. With the exception of a few who were by accident near an air source, the fighters died either of suicide or the horrible choking gas.

That night there was no message to the outside world. Mila 18 had been the communication point from which news of the actions was transmitted. It had been the coordination center of the Jewish Fighting Organization. But even though the communication and nerve center of the revolt was struck down, the Warsaw Ghetto was still not in the hands of the Germans.

On May 16, after four weeks of fighting, there was still enough resistance from the ghetto that Germans could not enter it without risk. It was rubble. A continuous black smoke rose from smoldering buildings. The resistance was no longer organized, but death greeted any German who dared enter. There had been no surrender. Nevertheless, SS General Jurgen von Stroop sent a message to his superiors that the Warsaw Ghetto no longer existed.

64

The Warsaw Ghetto Uprising was a tremendous encouragement to all partisans in the occupied territories. The myth of the German super race was shattered forever. That, along with the daily reports of Russian victories, gave guerrilla fighters all the courage they needed to take on the enemy.

Sabotage, ambushes, raids, harassments, and reprisals were going on all over the occupied territories. In the Kiev area, the joint coordinated actions of the two Jewish partisan groups became intolerable to the Nazis.

Because of the permanence of the family camp, the partisans still kept relative radio silence. Diadia Misha's group encamped themselves about fifteen kilometers from the family camp, and Solomon frequently acted as a courier between the two bases. He enjoyed the trips through the forest during the spring and summer months. Often he would be accompanied by Rachel, and then the journey would be especially wonderful. They would pretend it was a summer picnic outing, that there was no war, that they were free to pursue normal lives. With the increasing number of reports coming in of Nazi retreats on the Russian front, they began to talk more and more of their future.

On one such occasion, Solomon was particularly optimistic. The day was warm and beautiful and his mood was reflected in the brisk pace he set for Rachel as they walked. She loved it when he felt uplifted like this, but his buoyancy was wearing her out.

"Solomon, darling. Please slow down. It's so lovely in the woods. Let's sit down a while and just enjoy it. Smell how fresh and sweet the air is." She grabbed at his hand and slowed him down, then led him to a fallen tree and made him sit on its trunk.

"It really is a wonderful day, Rachel."

"It's a day when you could almost put the past out of your mind. It's a day to think only of now."

"It's better than that, Rachel." Solomon had an almost dreamy look in his eyes as he stared off into the little bit of blue sky that was allowed through the treetops. "It is a day to think about a future."

Rachel rested her head on Solomon's shoulder and hugged him gently. "Oh, Solomon. There really will be a future for us. It makes me so happy to know you realize it too. I do love you so."

Solomon was still caught up in his daydreams. "Can you imagine, Rachel, what it will be like in Palestine? The Zionists tell me it is like nowhere else in the world for a Jew. Our history began there; it is our heritage. They say it will someday be our nation again. Imagine it! Our own country, a place where we will be free, one place in this damned world where we will feel welcome, where we will be among our own people. Can you imagine it?"

"What do you mean, the Zionists tell you? Solomon, you *are* a Zionist! You know, it's all you ever talk about anymore. I think you've persuaded more of our group to go there than anyone else has."

"I guess you're right. But what else is there to do after the war? There is no place for us anywhere else in the world, except maybe America, and there is an ocean between us. To Palestine we can walk if necessary!"

"Are you sure there will not be a place for the Jews in Europe or Russia after the war? Don't you think the world will be wiser for the tragedy it has witnessed now?"

"Did the world lift a finger for the ghetto Jews of Warsaw? The same apathy that let the Warsaw Ghetto Jews die will let the anti-Semites run rampant with their pogroms again. Whenever there will be problems in a country, the Jew will again be the scapegoat. We will only live in freedom if we have our own country."

"When will we go?"

"As soon as the way is clear."

"That might be a long time, Solomon."

"If what the radio broadcasts is true, it may not be as long as we think. The German defenses are breaking down everywhere now. And with England and American becoming more of a threat, and the losses in Africa, Hitler's attentions are being divided. While Russia becomes stronger, the Nazi is weakening. And we must do everything we can to weaken him further!"

In the months after the two groups joined forces, their coordinated effort took a devastating toll of the German supplies and troops. Together they attacked trains, convoys, struck at factories, fuel depots, warehouses, small German outposts, whatever appeared to them as an important target. The partisans lost many of their own fighters, but now with the tide of the war turning and the Germans becoming more intolerable as occupiers of the Ukraine, more and more people wanted to join the resistance.

In all of the cities and towns in the occupied areas, the Germans were now rounding up civilians for forced-labor camps. People who were willing to outlast quietly the occupation were now being threatened with deportation to German labor camps to the west. People would leave their homes in the morning and never return. And no one ever returned from a labor camp. The only way to avoid deportation was to bribe someone, and few had anything to bribe with. Many of the young and able who remained in the occupied lands, who were the prime targets of roundups, preferred escape into the woods to join partisan groups.

65

Major Hans Oberman over the months had turned partisan-hunting into a science. More groups were forming, and at the same time it was becoming easier to run them down. Oberman was not capturing groups faster than they were organizing, but he made sure that only he knew that. He released to his superiors only the numbers he'd captured and destroyed; statistics favorable to the partisans he kept strictly to himself. Oberman's only frustration was that he could not pinpoint the "Jewish group"—did not even know that now there were two. By midsummer, "getting those Jews" obsessed him.

He pondered his problem for hours at a time. He would go into rages if someone disturbed his thoughts. It insulted his intelligence to think the "subhumans" could outsmart him. He was determined. He would get them. He had to get them. Each week that passed deepened his obsession. He had the map of those woods memorized. There were hundreds of locations that could hide a large contingent of Jews. How can I isolate them? he asked himself. Where would I hide *my* troops in those forests? There had to be an answer. And when he found it, it would probably be a simple answer.

66

I've been working too hard on this, Oberman finally decided. I must get away for a while and come back to it when I'm fresh. A new approach is what I need!

He called one of his many women companions, Eva Kromer, and arranged to go with her to a resort area that the Germans had established for their officers. Eva was perfect for his needs. If anyone could take his mind off of his problems, it would be Eva. She was a perfect distraction. She had beautiful long red hair, when it was let down, and she let it down often. She was a little taller than Oberman, but that didn't bother him. She had long legs, well curved and gracefully joined to her slim body by perfectly shaped buttocks. Nature had sculptured her breasts to go ideally with the rest of her body. She considered her freckles a flaw, but Oberman thought they made her even more attractive, contrasting and setting off a sparkle in her blue eyes. Her looks alone were enough to distract most men from their problems, even if they didn't know that the only thing more fiery than her flaming hair was her insatiable passion.

The ride to the resort took them through heavily wooded hills. In the chauffeur-driven staff car, the beautiful Eva at his side, Oberman started to unwind.

The resort was old and posh, established nearly a century earlier to host aristocracy in the days of the Tsars. Now it was a favorite German hideaway. The palatial lodge had hundreds of rooms. It boasted seven elegant dining rooms, three ballrooms, billiard rooms, a library which had been emptied of most of its good books under Communists, and three kitchens. There were several cocktail lounges and even more sitting rooms. A long porch graced the back of the building and overlooked formal gardens that led down to a large lake where the Germans swam, sunned, and went boating. The stables housed finely bred riding horses. About half the rooms were available to the officers; the others housed a rotating complement of prostitutes, some imported from Germany, some brought in from the occupied countries. The rest of the sizable staff lived in special servants' quarters. It was the type of building the Communists loved to destroy or cut up into apartments for the masses. Only because it was secluded, and a place the Communist Party also used for high-ranking officials, did it survive.

Oberman loved this place. It fit his self-image. By the time he and Eva had dinner and drinks and a walk in the garden, they were ready to retire. With the drive up, it had been a full and tiring day, and Oberman wanted to use what energies he had left for a prolonged evening of sexual pleasures. His holiday was already a success. Kiev, the war, the Jews—they were the furthest things from his mind.

Eva knew her part well, but for her it was not an act. She loved what she did best, and if she could do it the way that excited her companion the most, it heightened her own pleasure. She had a knack for discovering what each of her suitors liked and no inhibitions to prevent her pleasing them. She even had a masochistic side to her that pleased many of the sadistic tastes of the German officers she knew.

Oberman sat down in an easy chair and lifted his leg toward Eva, her cue to start the ritual. She took his boot by the heel and with a giggle swung her own leg over his, showing as much thigh as she could in the move. This left her straddling Oberman's boot, holding the heel in her hand, her shapely posterior swaying before his eyes. Oberman placed his other foot on her backside and pushed until the boot came off, sending her sprawling onto the big bed nearby. This brought a roar of laughter from Oberman and more giggles from Eva.

She repeated the procedure with the other boot, this time showing off as much of her inner thighs as she could when she fell. Again laughter. "And what do you see that is so interesting, you rascal," she asked, displaying the fact that she wore no undergarment.

Oberman roared with laughter and drew his pistol and took aim at his ultimate target. "Bang, bang. Now you have a big hole there."

"The better to engulf you with," she said in a low, wolfish voice.

Then she got up and unbuttoned his tunic, belts, and shirt, and removed them all. She pulled off his socks and left him sitting only in his trousers. "Now I feel self-conscious with all of my clothes on. What can I do about that?" and without waiting for an answer, she moved about the room dropping her garments in the most seductive ways she could think up, ending up directly before him in a full display of her beauty.

"Eva, you are one of the few women I've ever known who is more beautiful naked than partially dressed."

"Oh Hans, you say such sweet things. I'm happy you like what you see," and she giggled again.

"Do what I like to see!"

He became increasingly aroused as she performed every autoerotic act she could think of for him, pleasuring herself with every variety of stimulation. When she sensed that he was eager for her touch, she removed the remainder of his clothing and stimulated him both manually and orally. It was quite some time before they fondled and manipulated their way to the bed, and there they tried every contortion imaginable. By 10:00 that night, all his pleasures fulfilled, he and his companion were deep in slumber.

Oberman began to stir about 6 a.m. It took him a few moments to realize where he was. He didn't have to get up. He rolled over, resting his naked thigh against the soft, warm buttocks of his sleeping bed partner, then he dozed off again.

"Water!" Oberman came to a sitting position as he shouted the word.

"My God! What is it, Hans?"

"That's the answer! The water! Damn if it didn't come to me in my sleep. I'll get those bastards because they need water. My God, it's so obvious! How could I have missed it?" He jumped out of bed with no further explanation to the woman. "Go back to sleep. I'm going to take a ride around the lake and think. It's a military problem and does not concern you. Sleep a few more hours. When I return, we will go to breakfast."

Oberman was at the stables in fifteen minutes. He was given a fine animal—spirited and sleek. He was an excellent rider, having been taught as a child by his grandfather who had been a cavalry officer.

It was early, and he had the bridle path to himself. Spririted as it was, the horse knew that the man on its back would not be intimidated, and it settled down to accepting Oberman's every subtle command. There was a chill and mist in the air; it would be the better part of an hour before the sun would burn it off. Oberman's mind was free.

He mentally went over the maps he had so thoroughly memorized, seeing them as if they were spread before him. "It has to work. It can't miss," he said to himself aloud. "Those Jews have to live near water, and it must be a sizable source. Let me see," he said, visualizing the maps. "There are one, two, three . . . four, five . . . and there is a lake . . . six, seven . . . eight and another lake . . . yes, that's it. I'm sure, two lakes and eight streams or rivers large enough to support a large band. They have to be along one of them. I've got them now!" He thought it through again, smiling broadly. "Yes, by damn, I have them!"

67

As soon as he returned to his office, Oberman rechecked his maps. They were just as he had recalled them. Then he sent for one of his lieutenants. In a few minutes a young, ruddy-faced, blue-eyed German entered the office. He snapped his heels smartly, extended his arm in the proper, "Heil Hitler! Lieutenant Meinhart reporting as ordered sir."

"Heil Hitler. At ease, Meinhart." Oberman paused."Please sit down, Lieutenant. I have heard much about you. You are a very conscientious officer. I have an important project, and I need a man with your qualifications."

"Thank you, sir. I try my best to do my duty to the Fuhrer."

"Meinhart, I want you to put together a mission for me and carry it out to the letter. There can be no blunders. If it is carried out properly, there will be a citation for you." Meinhart's eyes lit up. Oberman knew they would. "This operation is in two stages. The first stage will require ten small detachments, perhaps five men each. They should be made up of Ukranian or Polish collaborators. The second stage will depend on a large detachment of our finest men, battle-seasoned men if possible; perhaps two hundred, well armed."

Meinhart's eagerness could not be disguised, "I am honored, Major Oberman. I have been hoping for a chance like this, to serve my Fuhrer. I will not let you down!"

"I know I have picked the best man for this important job."

Oberman rolled out a map on his desk. He motioned Meinhart over. "Our objective is somewhere in this vast forested area. It is the headquarters of the most dangerous guerrilla group in the Kiev area. They have caused us more losses in men and equipment than all the other groups together. I estimate them to be at least two to three hundred strong."

Looking over the map, Meinhart asked, "What is your plan, sir?"

"The first stage is to locate them. That is where the non-German personnel will be used. To find the guerrillas, we will have to sacrifice some of the men from the first detachments. Once we've located them, the German troops must move in immediately before the partisans can escape." Oberman took a pencil from his desk top. He motioned Meinhart to bend closer. "For a group as large as the one we are after, there must be a large water supply. We know they have been operating in the area for a long time, and to me that means they have a permanent camp. That camp has to be near one of ten water sources." With a broad motion, Oberman circled the area showing the potential sites. "You will note that in this area there are eight streams and two lakes that could support such a large group."

Meinhart leaned even closer to the map as Oberman paused to let him study each of the water sources. "Yes. They must be on one of those water supplies. But which one? And how will we send our troops there before they move out?"

"Ah, that is the beauty of my plan." Oberman grinned. "We send one detachment of collaborators up each of the streams and one to each lake. We have our troops ready for instant mobilization. Each reconnaissance unit will carry a field radio on which it will transmit a password every fifteen minutes. Each will have its own codeword. They will transmit only that codeword, so if the partisans are monitoring us, they will not know what we are up to."

Meinhart straightened up. "I think I understand. When one of them stops transmitting, we will know that the guerillas have taken them."

I knew I had the right man in you," Oberman replied. "If a detachment is killed or captured by the guerillas, they will miss a code transmission. We'll know immediately which area to send our troops to, and within a quarter of an hour, they'll be mobilized."

"You realize the partrol won't have a chance to survive."

"That is why we use the Slavs."

"When do we do this?"

"As soon as the details are worked out. First of all, we have to determine the best way to transport the attack force. We must assume those—I mean, those guerillas—are going to be in the most difficult area to reach. We'll have to move a lot of men and equipment through difficult terrain in a hurry. And one thing for sure: I want every one of them wiped out. No prisoners!"

"To set an example?"

"Yes. They'll be destroyed and buried in a mass grave right in their camp, and the camp will be leveled. Do you understand?"

"I'll work out every detail."

"Meinhart—take your time. Make sure there is no room for error. Take a whole week if you must."

Meinhart left Oberman's office, his assignment under his arm. Oberman looked out of his window and saw what a sunny day it was.

Enough work for today. Then he turned and headed out the door. As he passed his aide's desk, he said, "Give me a blank sheet of paper." The aide handed him a sheet of official letterhead, and Oberman signed it on the bottom.

"There, now type up an order for a roundup in retribution for the train derailment last night. Pick a place where we can get about two hundred of these Ukrainian dogs. Just type it up above my signature and get the roundup taken care of today. Dispose of them in the usual manner."

He left the building to spend the rest of his day at leisure.

68

Ivan and Sosha were enjoying the lovely day as they made their way into town. They made the trip about once a week by horse cart to keep abreast of what was new in the occupation.

"One would almost think there was no war on a day like this," Ivan said.

"It is beautiful today," she agreed as she looked up at the cloudless sky. The sun warmed her face, and she remembered how it used to be to enjoy carefree days. A bird flew through her field of vision. "I wonder if birds know there is a war?"

Ivan looked at her and chuckled.

"I really mean it, Ivan. Do you think they know or sense a difference? After all, we share this place with them. We live in a hell on earth. Could they be indifferent to it? Are they disturbed by what we do to each other? Or are they in a world apart? If so, I wish I could be a bird." Frivolous thoughts were a luxury, and Sosha wanted to savor the mood.

Ivan remained silent, holding the reins out of habit, the horse making all of the important decisions of the morning. How much longer? he wondered. When will this horrible time pass? It seems an eternity since Solomon came into our lives and brought the war with him. How will it all end?

A squirrel ran across the road ahead of the horse. The animals seemed to ignore each other completely.

"Why can't people be like that?" Ivan said, nodding toward the squirrel as it vanished into the brush. "They just live and let live. They only attack for survival, while man attacks for the sake of destruction—pure destruction."

"What?" Sosha asked. "I'm sorry. What did you say?"

"Nothing. It's not important."

It was midmorning when they approached Kiev. There didn't seem to be the usual turmoil as they let their horse take them to the marketplace by the route it knew so well. Everyone seemed affected by the weather. It was like that first day of sunshine after a dismal week of rain.

"We picked a good day to come to the city," Sosha said. "It was a lovely ride, and the people will be in a mood for gossip."

Ivan was about to agree when he heard a commotion behind him. He turned to look over his shoulder as a truck crossed the street and stopped in the intersection just ahead of them. Soldiers with machine guns jumped from its tailgate. Then he realized what the commotion behind them must be.

"It's a roundup! Jump off the wagon and run back the way we came." But he looked over his shoulder as he'd started to do a second earlier and lost all heart. "Dear God, we're caught!"

The street behind them was cordoned off. All around them people were screaming, running for doorways that were barricaded and boarded up. The Germans, as usual, had chosen the site of the roundup well. The only escape was to charge the barricade and be shot. Some did just that, and gunners obligingly shot them down. As things settled down, Ivan estimated that there were perhaps seventy people in the area. At precisely the same time, roundups were taking place in two other places just a block apart.

"Ivan, what can we do?"

"Stay with me, Sosha. If you see any chance at all for escape, tell me. But don't let us get separated and don't do anything to draw their fire. Maybe they will interrogate us and let us go. Just keep your eyes open and be cautious."

The Germans were advancing from both ends of the street. Ivan and Sosha climbed from the wagon. The people were being herded into a compact group for easier control.

"Look, they're taking our wagon and horse!" Sosha exclaimed, watching a soldier lead the nag by his reins.

"Shh! There is nothing we can do about that. If all we lose today is our horse and wagon, I'll consider it a bargain."

The group was tightly crowded together. Two Germans guarded them, as two trucks pulled up. "Get in. *Schnell. Hinein!* Hurry, get in!" one of the Germans commanded gruffly. The crowd was divided into the two trucks. Ivan and Sosha remained together.

69

It was only a few minutes by truck to Gestapo headquarters in the old Palace of Labor building at Vladimirskaya Street 33. It was an enormous, dark gray, almost black building. An ominous building. People were known to walk blocks out of their way not to have to pass near that structure. Its facade was almost majestic, but it fooled no one. Inside were a multitude of interrogation rooms, detention cells, torture chambers, and, for lack of a better word, dungeons. The trucks pulled into a courtyard in the rear of the Gestapo building and unloaded their terrified cargo. The trucks from the other roundups were already there, and the poor souls that had disembarked were lined up in three rows along one wall of the yards. The newcomers, Ivan and Sosha among them, were shoved into three more lines in front of the original three. An SS captain walked in front of the rows of captives, a riding whip in his right hand. As he walked past each person in the front row, he pointed the whip at that row and counted by sixes as he went. Ivan thought it remarkable that he knew his multiplication tables of sixes so fluently. How often he must do this. Ivan wondered bitterly. When he got to the end there were only five in that row. He had thirty-four rows of six and one row of five deep.

"Two hundred and nine of you is what I count," he said. "My orders call for two hundred." With his whip, he tapped nine of the prisoners in the first row on the shoulders. Ivan and

Sosha were ten and eleven in that row. "You nine I have tapped, get out of here—fast!" He waved his whip toward an iron door in the wall of the courtyard. The fortunate nine wasted no time in getting out the portal that was opened for them by a guard.

"All right," the Captain started. "Last night a train was derailed by partisans. You are the price for that act." Then he said what Ivan had feared he would hear. "Sergeant, separate the men and women and take them into the male and female detention rooms." He went on into the building, and Ivan was separated from Sosha.

The women were taken into the building first while the men were kept standing in the new lines they had formed. After about twenty minutes a door opened, and an officer called to the sergeant who had been put in charge to bring in the men.

"Get going. The first two lines through that door. The second two lines follow next, then the last two lines. Go. *Schnell!*"

As they entered the building, they were immediately redivided. An officer stood where he could quickly see each man as he entered. Most he sent down a hall to the right. Every once in a while he directed someone out of the line and had him held in a new line that was forming along a wall of a hallway to the left. When everyone was inside the building, Ivan found himself standing in the left hall along with about thirty other men, all particularly strong and healthy looking. Ivan was among the oldest in that group. All of the elderly, sickly, and those younger than their late teens had been sent on. Ivan immediately determined that they had been separated out for work details. He feared for the others. He hoped that the same division was being made among the women. Sosha was, after all, a strong and healthy woman. Oh God, please let her be safe, he prayed.

There had been fewer women than men in the roundup—only fifty-seven of them. They, too, had been divided into two groups. Out of the entire group, nine had been pulled out for further evaluation, all in their late teens or early twenties and all attractive. Sosha and the others had been sent down the hall to the right. At the end of that hall they were put into a large, windowless room.

There were two doors on one wall—a small one for people and next to it an opening with two swinging doors, large enough to let in supplies off trucks. The floor was concrete, the walls bare brick. The room was illuminated from overhead lights. It had obviously been built as a large storage room. As the women entered the room, a woman in a German uniform handed each of them a large envelope and a pencil and directed them to one wall of the room, the one opposite the two doors.

When everyone was in, she announced, "Each of you has an envelope and pencil. First of all, write your name and your home address on the front. Then put all of your belongings into the envelope. Everything! Papers, money, jewelry, rings, bracelets, necklaces. Your name on the envelope will insure that you get it back after you are either released from custody here or when you reach your destination, if it is decided that you are to be sent to a factory for work."

"What about our husbands, our families?" one woman asked.

"If you were picked up together, you will be reunited at your destination, or you will be released together if all of your papers are in order. Those of you who are sent to work in a factory will have a chance to tell your families after processing. Now all of you do as you're told. Bring up your envelopes as soon as you've followed instructions. And be sure, you will be searched later. If you hold out anything, it will go hard for you."

One by one, the women handed in their envelopes.

"Very well, is that everyone?" She paused and looked at the women. "Good. Now line up in two rows by the double doors here. When they open, you will be asked to get on a truck that will drive you the short distance to the old school a few blocks from here. There you will be taken into the building for further processing. Be prepared to tell them what skills you have. Also, you will have the opportunity to request that the rest of your family be notified where you are. Those of you who are to be released will get your belongings back then, also. Those of you who were picked up with husbands or family will be reunited there—as long as all papers are in order. When the doors open, hurry along. Those who loiter will have the last choices for the good jobs.''

As soon as her speech was ended, the doors swung open.

The women rushed forward. No one wanted to be last. No sooner were they in the van of the truck than the truck doors were slammed shut, plunging the women into pitch darkness. The darkness brought terror. The truck lurched, and in the blackness most of the women fell over each other. There was screaming and swearing. It was so noisy that no one heard the hissing. The smell of engine fumes started to fill the darkness. Suddenly Sosha realized and cried, "It's a gassing van! They are killing us!"

For an instant it became quiet . . . quiet enough to hear the hissing. And then pandemonium.

"Oh Ivan! I want to be with you, Ivan!" Tears burned in Sosha's eyes. She lay on the floor where she'd fallen when the truck started, oblivious to the panic about her. "Oh dear Ivan, why?" She became nauseated and dizzy. She wanted not to vomit. Then her head began to throb. When the headache became unbearable, she screamed. She screamed once, twice . . . then passed into unconsciousness. One by one, the screams from inside the van died out. And then there was only the hiss.

The truck bumped and bounced down a rough dirt road into the ravine of Babi Yar. It came to a stop at the front of a sand and clay cliff about five meters high. The van doors were opened. A stench of human waste and carbon monoxide fumes poured out as daylight poured in to reveal a limp tangle of female corpses, their lips all strangely red from the gas.

Four Ukrainians jumped into the van and started to throw out the bodies. A few still lived, but that didn't matter; they were thrown off with the others. Once empty, the truck was driven off. It would be hosed out and cleaned up for its next load. The four Ukrainians joined two others who were already taking shoes and other garments off the dead, placing them on piles of coats, blouses, skirts, socks, even underwear. One Ukrainian checked each mouth and pulled out with pliers what valuable teeth he found, tossing them into buckets. His work was easy. Death by gas left the mouths gaping. Another Ukrainian pressed a finger into each anus and vagina to make sure no valuables had been smuggled that way: it was an exercise that often produced rings, diamonds, gold coins, and other small valuables.

They were an efficient crew, and in just a few minutes the bodies were being layed out neatly next to each other at the foot of the cliff. A German supervised the entire operation. He passed by the bodies, and any one that didn't seem dead he shot in the head with his pistol. Sometimes he did it just out of boredom. The Ukrainians were ready for the next truck, which would be along soon.

After several trucks, when there were a few hundred bodies, German ingenuity was again demonstrated. To expedite the burial, a large charge of dynamite would be set off in the cliff, bringing down just the right portion of it to cover the dead. Over several months this procedure had terraced the ravine in this section of Babi Yar.

70

Ivan and the group of men he was with were taken to another large room where they too turned over all their possessions. No pretense was made that they would ever get anything back. Good clothing was exchanged for rags; their hair was cut away, and they were told that if they didn't cooperate they would be shot on the spot. They were taken back out to the courtyard by another door and herded onto open trucks under heavy guard. As they pulled out of the courtyard, a gas van waited to enter. Seeing it, Ivan's fear for Sosha became despair.

After a few moments of driving, Ivan saw that they were being taken in the direction of Babi Yar. At the entrance to the ravine the road forked, just inside the gate. The road to the right wound downward into the ravine. The fork to the left, which their truck took, led around the top of the ravine's southern rim. Shortly, the truck came upon a double set of barbed wire gates. An armed guard opened the first, which was situated at the foot of a machine gun tower. As soon as the truck passed through, the gate behind it was closed, and another guard opened the second one. On both of the gates, as well as on the barbed wire fences in which the gates were situated, there were signs in German, Ukrainian and Russian: "Lethal Electric Charge . . . Danger!" Once inside the second gate, the truck drove on for a short distance and then came to a stop in what seemed to be a camp. Ivan and his companions were ordered to disembark.

Immediately they were met by a harsh command to line up and stand at attention. They were left standing that way for what seemed an eternity. Three Germans kept them covered with machine guns, while a junior officer silently walked up and down, as if he had something on his mind, a point he wanted to make. The truck had long since departed. Finally, one of the men moved over slightly, but enough for the officer to notice. Those nearest him noticed, too. The officer walked up to the man, drew his revolver, and at point blank range blew the man's brains right out of his head. Then he turned smiling to the rest of the shocked prisoners and said, "You see, that is what happens when you disobey an order here. Welcome to Babi Yar. We affectionately call this the Syretsky Camp, after your lovely suburb of Kiev, the Syrets District. This camp is in Babi Yar, and any infraction will buy you a spot in the ravine. Now, continue to stand at attention until our camp commander comes."

No one moved. Time dragged. Ivan's muscles began to ache. He feared he might faint, so he carefully wiggled his toes, flexed and relaxed his muscles. At least now the officer was talking to one of the guards, not looking for the slightest movement among the prisoners. Still, no one dared move.

At last a staff car drove up and stopped directly in front of the line of agonized men. Ivan dared not move his head but could see out the corner of his eye that the officer was driving the vehicle himself. On the front seat next to him sat a huge dog, a dark gray Alsatian. In the back seat sat a junior officer who—by all protocol, Ivan thought—should have been the driver.

The senior officer jumped from the driver's seat, not waiting for anyone to open his door. The Alsatian heeled without command at his side. The man looked to be about fifty years of age. His head was completely bald, lengthening his already long, thin face. He wore glasses through which he squinted. His uniform fit smartly, tailored to disguise his less-than-perfect body. The holster he wore, prominently displayed, was as polished as his gleaming boots. His voice was gruff, angry in tone. He spoke only German. The junior officer from the back seat walked with him, the dog between them. He repeated everything in Ukrainian that the officer said in German.

"Well, what have we here," he said, grinning down at the dead body. "Looks like you had to do some disciplining. I hope the rest of them learned a lesson from it." Then he walked down the line of men, counting until he got to the seventh— the man next to Ivan. He drew his own pistol and, without a word or flinch, shot that man in the head. "Now that is the second lesson for you to learn today. Your lives mean nothing to me. I would as soon shoot you all. One wrong move out of anyone and all your pleading will do no good. Also, if one of you does wrong, I might have your entire barracks eliminated. We can easily replace one or all of you, so it is up to you to keep each other in line." He paused for emphasis, then continued. "I am Strumbahnfuhrer Paul von Radomsky. I am the camp commander. Also, I want you to know Rex, here." He pointed to the animal at his side. "Rex, as you can tell, is a very well-trained dog. He is especially trained to rip the flesh off of a man at my command—especially the genitals. So make sure you do nothing to provoke me." With that, he turned and strode to the car. The dog jumped into its place, the interpreter into the back, and they drove off.

The first officer now took over again. "All right, find yourselves places in that building over there." He pointed to a row of huts similar to those the partisans had built in the family camp. Ivan hurried to the dugout hut as quickly as he could, realizing that the bunk space would be first-come. As he entered, all similarity between this and the family camp ended. Here, the stench was unbelievable. It went right to his stomach, and he thought he would be sick, but he couldn't turn around. He had to find himself a bunk, and he took one as close to the entry as he could. That was the only source of fresh air in the entire dugout.

The horrible dwelling was illuminated by a solitary kerosene lamp that hung from the ceiling near the rear. It took Ivan a few moments to get accustomed to the semi-darkness. The hut was only about two meters from dirt floor to sod ceiling. but in that shallow area the Germans had arranged to get in three levels of bunks. The bunks were shelves on which straw had been thrown. There was a ragged blanket for each space. The odor in the stuffy room was a combination of mildew, vomit, urine, shit and sweat. When Ivan chose his bunk, he lay down on it in hopes of getting a moment's relief from his fatigue. He lay there in misery, trying to figure out how a day so beautiful could end so tragically, when suddenly he came up off the putrid straw.

"Damn it to hell! This place is full of lice!" The straw, the blankets, the entire hut was infested.

"Everybody outside," came a command in perfect Ukrainian. Ivan was only too happy to get outside again. Everything about the hut repelled him. They all fell into formation outside the dugout. It was turning dusk. Ivan realized that he had not eaten since he shared breakfast with Sosha. Oh God, he prayed, please see over my dear Sosha.

"My name is Timtov. I am responsible for you. If you cause trouble, I might suffer for it, so it is up to me to see to it that you do no wrong." He brandished a whip with leather tails, each strand tipped with metal. "Disobey, and I will be the first one you will have to deal with. If it goes no further than that, you will consider yourselves lucky. Now you may sit here on the ground until the remainder of your dugout residents return from today's work detail. Then you will line up with them for the roll call before you are locked into your hut. Tomorrow at 3 a.m. your day will start with roll call and breakfast. At roll call, you will bring out your dead—those who have died during the night—and lay them in front of your ranks. Everyone must be accounted for or the entire group goes to the ravine. I don't care how many of you die during the night, and some of you will try to kill yourselves. That is your business. But in the morning, everyone—dead or alive—must be accounted for."

Everything seemed clear.

71

A week had gone by, and the partisans at the family camp had found out about Ivan and Sosha's arrest. They had no idea of their fate, but Ivan had been seen and recognized on the open back truck that was headed for Babi Yar. The partisans knew of the concentration camp at Babi Yar, but no one knew what the layout of the facility was. There had been much discussion of making a raid on the camp and freeing the inmates. It would be a very risky mission, and there was no guarantee that either Ivan or Sosha was still alive. Besides, the men's and women's concentration camps were separate, and it was doubtful that both could be liberated.

"I feel we have to try," Solomon argued. "Even if they are not there, we would still be freeing many other prisoners."

"Solomon, you are overly involved because they saved your life. Maybe you are right, but we cannot let our decision be an emotional one," Yorgi warned.

"Might I suggest that we discuss the idea with Diadia's group," Father Peter offered. "They carried out a raid on a small concentration camp once. They can speak from experience. And besides, such an endeavor would probably require a joint effort."

"A good suggestion," Yorgi agreed. "I appoint you and Solomon to go to their camp and make inquiries."

An hour later, Father Peter and Solomon were heading out through the forest toward Diadia's camp. Solomon was quiet and thoughtful. Traveling through the forest now, he was reminded of his own escape from Babi Yar . . . that flight through the woods for his life. How very long ago. He remembered few of the details but could still feel the terror as he ran blindly through those woods. Now he wanted to return to that ravine to save his friends and to avenge his people. He wanted to strike a blow at the one place that was to him a symbol of all that the Nazis stood for. Father Peter was sensitive to Solomon's torment.

"I suppose that next to Rachel, Ivan and Sosha were the most important people in the world to you," Father Peter said. As soon as he spoke, he was sorry that he had used the past tense.

Solomon thought a moment. "I guess they became my second family when Ivan pulled me out of that ditch and took me home to his storage cellar. It's kind of ironic, too, when you think about it."

"Ironic? How?"

"In a lot of ways. I don't know if you can understand them all, not being Jewish."

They came to some rough, thickly overgrown terrain that required considerable effort to traverse, so neither of them spoke. When they finally got through, they had to sit down and rest.

"Tell me what you are talking about," said Father Peter. "The ironies, I mean."

"Well, it's just that being in a camp of predominantly Jewish partisans, I am so close to three of the few gentiles among them. You must realize as a Jew I have always been leery of gentiles. Now my greatest concern is to get them out of the very place I would have perished in. If anyone would have told me, as a boy, that someday I would be traveling through the forest with a priest to save the lives of two gentiles . . . well, that would have been inconceivable."

"I guess we Christians have never done much to endear ourselves to the Jews."

"Father Peter, until Ivan and Sosha took me in, my idea was that a Christian was someone to be avoided. I think most Jews feel about Christians the way cats feel about dogs."

They got up and started to walk again. Solomon checked a captured German pocket compass. Without trails to follow, direction was all they had to lead them along to the camp of Diadia Misha.

"Did you really think all Christians were anti-Semitic?"

"Aren't they?"

Father Peter looked at Solomon in surprise. "What do you mean, 'Aren't they?' You still feel that way?"

"It's a matter of degree, but anti-Semitism has been drilled into the Christians from infancy. I think that if sufficiently provoked, ninety-nine percent would fall back on their anti-Semitic indoctrination."

"I can't believe you feel that way! Do you feel that way about Ivan, Sosha, or me?"

"Ivan and Sosha told me long ago that they didn't consider themselves Christians. He considered the Church a hypocrisy from the time he witnessed a pogrom that the local churchmen didn't condemn. I really think he and Sosha were not anti-Semitic. But I do not think that a person can embrace Christianity without embracing some degree of anti-Semitism."

"Then you must think me one," the priest said, obviously hurt.

"Father Peter, I think the world of you, and I honestly could feel toward you as a brother. If you were captured, I would want to do all I could to help you, and I know that you would do the same for me. I know what a risk you took when you helped save Jews who sought you out. I appreciate the enormous sacrifice you made when you left your parish. But in a way, you are the most dangerous type of anti-Semite—one who doesn't realize he is one, and certainly doesn't try or want to be."

"Solomon, you hurt me deeply. Please tell me you are making a joke—an ugly joke."

"Well, maybe the word anti-Semite is a bad one to use, but I use it for lack of another. Let me put it differently. The difference between you and Ivan and Sosha is that they were not practicing Christians. You are, and my grandfather—

blessed be his memory—told me from the time I was a child that every practicing Christian is to some degree anti-Semitic. In my lifetime I have not seen proof otherwise."

"Solomon, how am I anti-Semitic?"

"Don't you believe that for salvation, to be accepted in the eyes of God, to keep from spending eternity in Hell, to not be damned for all time, a person has to accept your Christ?"

"Well, it is basic . . ."

"And didn't you teach that to your parishioners?" Solomon interrupted. "In fact, do not all priests teach that to all Christians, from infancy on?"

"Yes, but . . ."

Again Solomon interrupted. "And how else do you think anti-Semitism is handed down from generation to generation, from century to century? What does the Christian think of the Jew who does not accept your doctrine? In the eyes of the practicing Christian, the Jew is an evil-doer, the nonbeliever, the damned, condemned to burn in Hell. Your faith propagates hatred of the Jews. If at any point in history society has needed a scapegoat, Christianity has helped provide it, and the priests have paved the way."

Father Peter was speechless. They walked on. Solomon began to realize that he had been a little over-zealous. He had gotten carried away with himself and hurt his friend.

"Father Peter, I'm sorry. I shouldn't have said all of that. God knows you have done much for us. It is just that we Jews have been made to live in mortal fear of Christianity. As children we felt daily taunts and beatings from Christian children, and as adults we feel the oppression of the Christian community. It's not only passed from fathers to sons, but from the Church to parishioners. I know there are others who deserve the blame far more than you, but, nonetheless, you must realize that most Jews are going to be forever mistrustful of all Christians, and the one in a hundred like you will have to bear some of the blame, rightfully or not."

They continued on a little farther in silence. Then Father Peter quietly said, "I'm truly sorry."

72

The news of Ivan's and Sosha's arrests reached Diadia's camp. What had happened and what could be done about it provoked long and serious discussions. In the end, Diadia summarized his position.

"Father Peter, Solomon, I hope you will understand the only position I can take in this matter. I hope that you and your group will not think we do not want to help or that we wouldn't help if there was any chance for success. But under the circumstances, the risk would not be justified. To begin with, your comrades were arrested in what has all the appearances of a retaliation roundup. That being the case, they were probably executed the same day. Now even if by some miracle one or both of them was spared, it has already been over a week since they've been interned in a concentration camp. That is longer than the average human being can survive in such a place. If we were successful in raiding the camp at Babi Yar, chances are we would not find them alive. Maybe we could save some others. To my knowledge, that camp holds a maximum of three hundred prisoners. If we were lucky, we might be able to break out ten percent—maybe thirty. That is the most we could hope for. To assault such an installation, almost in the middle of Kiev and the German army, especially since we know nothing of its layout and defenses, we would have to expect to lose almost twice as many of our people as we could contemplate saving."

Diadia paused to give the matter a last thought. He didn't like having to turn his friends down. "No, there is no way I can see to justify such a mission. It would be suicide. Only my emotions tell me to do it, and they are clearly wrong this time."

Solomon and Father Peter knew he was right, and they did not argue.

It was late. They would spend the night in Diadia's camp and start back in the morning.

It was actually mid-morning before Solomon and Father Peter started back to their own encampment. The day was warm, but the forest shade kept them comfortable. They had forced themselves to make the best possible time the day before as they were going to Diadia's camp. Now that they had resigned themselves to the fact that there was nothing they could do for Ivan and Sosha, they were making their way back home at an almost leisurely pace. The forest quiet was disturbed only by the chatter of squirrels, the incessant chirping of the birds, and the sound of their own footsteps on the leafy floor.

They were still a long way from their camp, perhaps four hours at this pace through the difficult terrain, an estimated eight kilometers yet to walk. They sat down by a small spring to rest, refresh, and take even more pleasure from the forest and its sounds as well as its intermittent silence.

"I feel bad about yesterday, Father Peter. I hope it won't destroy our friendship."

"Nonsense! Your point was well taken. I had never really understood before. It was something that needed saying— especially between friends."

"But I feel I let out a lot of pent-up anger on the wrong Christian. Actually . . ."

"Shh!" Father Peter interrupted. "Did you hear that?" He had his ear cocked to the wind.

"What? I don't hear a thing."

"Listen! It's that same horrible sound that haunted me in Kiev. I haven't heard it in all these months, that terrible sound of gunfire from Babi Yar. The wind must be carrying it all this distance."

"Yes, I do hear it. But that wind is in the wrong direction. Babi Yar is southeast of us. That wind is from due south." They both listened carefully. There was no question: the wind carried the sound of gunfire. "That is not only gunfire, there are explosions—grenades or mortars. It sounds like a battle."

Suddenly they both came to the same realization, but it was Solomon who voiced it.

"Dear God, that's the direction of the family camp!"

Both men jumped to their feet and started running and stumbling through the thick underbrush.

They ran for several minutes, the trees and scrub tearing at their clothes, scratching their skin. They tripped, fell, got up and ran some more in the direction of their camp. Finally, they were stopped by a small cliff they would have to climb, and their exhaustion caught up with them . Their breathing was labored, and they could hear nothing over the pulsing of their blood. Both slipped silently to the ground as they tried to get their breath back.

"This is insane," Father Peter finally found the strength to say. "We will never get back this way. We must use our heads. We are wasting too much energy. We must go by deliberate forced march. We must pull ourselves together."

"I don't hear the sound any longer. Do you think we just imagined it?"

"Not unless we are sharing the same nightmare. Perhaps when we get to the top of this ridge. It protects us from the wind. It might carry the sound over our heads, too."

They climbed the steep but short incline and at the top carefully listened. Silence.

"All right, Solomon, with a steady and forced pace we ought to make it back in about two hours. Running through this terrain will only slow us down, and we risk injury. Let's be rational. And when we get near the camp, let's use caution. If there is trouble back there, we will be unable to help anyone if we just stumble into the same situation."

73

It took them only one hour and forty minutes to get back to the family camp. When they reached familiar territory, they slowed their pace and used extreme caution.

At half a kilometer from the camp, they stopped. They remained hidden from anyone who might happen by and listened. Silence. The wind, though mild—more of a light breeze—still came from the direction of the camp.

"We should be able to hear some sound from the camp at this distance," Solomon whispered.

"I agree. I smell smoke on the breeze, and gunpowder."

"I'm afraid to think about it. God, I wish we could hear something!"

"We should hear something," Father Peter said, "either our people or the enemy. Do you suppose they have all been captured and taken off?"

"Let's go in and see."

"Careful, they may have posted guards or snipers."

"Let's separate, just in case. No point in both of us getting caught."

"You're right, Solomon. You go to the left; I'll go around to the right."

As Solomon crouched and crawled the last half kilometer toward the camp, he listened for any sound that would betray some form of life in the area. Even the forest animals were still. He constantly looked about and up into the trees, wary of ambush. When he had worked his way into about thirty meters from where the first dugouts of the family camp were, he stopped and raised his head above the low shrubs.

"Oh dear God, no!" He stood up, grief expelling caution. Where he had expected to see the first of the dugout huts, he saw it collapsed into a crater, smoke rising from its smoldering timbers. Now, standing, he had a better view of the encampment. Not a single hut was left standing. Smoke filtered up through the trees, carried on the mild breeze in the direction from which they'd come. Then he saw someone walking toward him through the smoke. He was about to drop back into his cover of shrubs when he recognized Father Peter.

"Come on in, Solomon," he called. "Come in, there is no one here."

Solomon went to Father Peter's side. There was not a building standing, not a body in sight, not a single person to be seen. Small trees were uprooted or broken off at their trunks by what must have been explosions. The larger trees were badly scarred by shrapnel and bullets.

"Whatever happened here was devastating. But there are no dead. Not ours, not the enemy's. Solomon, what do you make of it?"

"Only one thing: they found the camp. They must have surrounded the area and surprised us before we could make a move. They must have rounded everyone up and taken them prisoners, then just destroyed the camp so it could never be used again."

"That makes sense. But we must stop them somehow! If they get them out of the forest, they will just execute them all, either at Babi Yar or, more likely at a public execution in Kiev. What can we do?"

"I don't know. We have to think." The problem was overwhelming.

Solomon continued, "While we think, let's have a good look around. Maybe someone had a chance to hide or escape."

Together they started to walk through the entire area kicking over large planks and rubble that might be hiding a partisan—or a body. When they reached the spot where the radio shack had been, both came to a sudden stop.

"Oh, Solomon, tell me I don't see it."

Solomon was silent. He couldn't move. His heart beat furiously in his chest. His throat went dry and his mouth opened as if to cry out, but no sound came forth. He put his hand over his eyes.

"Solomon, we have to check. We have to take a look." And then Father Peter too was overcome. "Oh dear God in Heaven, don't let it be . . ."

Gathering their courage, the two walked to a large area of freshly turned soil. It looked to be ten meters by about fifteen meters. There was fresh dirt scattered all around its edges, and the black earth mounded gently toward the center.

"How could they have dug such a large pit?" Father Peter asked. "They couldn't have had much time."

"They had our people dig it themselves. It can't be very deep."

"Solomon, we have to be sure. You know what we have to do. Solomon, we have to check."

"I know. Oh please, Rachel, don't be there."

Slowly and filled with dread, they approached the turned earth. At its edge they dropped to their knees and with their bare hands began to dig in the cool, loose dirt. They had not dug more than a few inches when Solomon felt a hand. Withdrawing his own, he beat at his chest and cried out, "They're all in there, God, aren't they? All but me! Why? Why me? Why not me?"

74

The disaster was too huge to fathom. There was nothing to do but return to the camp of Diadia Misha. As they made their stunned way back through the forest, Solomon's pain was almost more than he could bear.

By the time they arrived at the camp, the partisans already knew of the disaster. The Germans wasted no time in broadcasting their triumph over the radio. They described the action in full detail and boasted that every man, woman and child at the partisan camp had been captured and killed. The only fact that was omitted from the broadcast was that the majority of the partisans were Jewish.

Solomon kept his grief to himself. Outwardly, he displayed hate and confusion. He insisted on going out on almost every mission. His new comrades could not decide whether he was determined to kill every German in the Ukraine or was seeking death for himself. In any case, he became a fighter with an insatiable fury. No action was too dangerous. The greater the odds, the more eager he was to go on the mission. Any Nazi, or anyone collaborating with the Nazis, was marked for death in Solomon's mind. Some of Solomon's fellows hesitated to volunteer for missions with him, feeling his eagerness for revenge might jeopardize the safety of others on the mission. But Solomon always returned. He never as much as received an injury. In time, the others realized that he had no intention of throwing his own or anyone else's life away. In conversation one evening, he replied to a comment with, "I cannot kill the enemy if I am dead. I have every intention of going on living until there are no more of those bastards left to kill."

By the end of the summer, it became quite clear that the days of the German occupation of the Ukraine were numbered. The partisans started to make plans of how best to reach the advancing Russians and join forces with them against the Germans on the front lines.

75

Ivan learned quickly. He became an expert in survival. Anyone less than an expert was dead in a week. Two things were necessary to cheat death at Babi Yar: expertise and luck.

On the average, twenty percent of the prisoners at the Babi Yar camp died daily. Some died from exhaustion or from being shot for minor infractions; others were just murdered at the whim of Von Radomsky or other camp personnel. Even the Kapos, prisoners used by the Germans to keep order in the camp, held the power of life and death over their fellow inmates. In fact, many of the Kapos were more brutal than some of the German guards. They were certainly hated by the other prisoners more than most of the German guards were.

Camp commander Von Radomsky had a favorite game which contributed significantly to the mortality of the prisoners. He would walk among the inmates after the daily evening roll call, up and down the rows. He had his daily luck number, as he liked to call it. Some days the number was chosen at random; other days it was determined by how crowded conditions in the camp became. If the attrition rate of the inmates did not keep up with the number of prisoners coming into the camp, the lucky number would be a low figure; if the total number of prisoners in the camp was less than the work force that was needed, the lucky number was high. After each day's roll call, in the late afternoon, Von Radomsky would drive up in his car, his interpreter in the back and his trusted dog in front, and would get the evening count from the officer in charge of that lineup. He would make a quick mental calculation, then announce for all to hear, "Today's lucky number is eight!" Then he would casually get out of his car, dog and interpreter following, and walk up to the first row of prisoners at a random spot. Unholstering his gun, he would start down the line of men counting, "One, two, three, four, five, six, seven—" and the next man would be shot. Without even breaking stride he would continue up and down the rows, counting and killing. He used two pistols for this game, and when one was empty, he would hand it back to the interpreter who would reload as they walked. This went on until he became bored. Then, so as not to stop anticlimactically, the last unfortunate winner of the lucky number was told, "Run or be shot." Not all ran, but most did. With an inaudible command, the Alsatian would pursue the terrified victim and bring him down, clamping his genitals between his powerful jaws. The downed runner would scream horribly, producing cheers and laughter from most of the camp personnel. It was the highlight of their day. If the dog did not finish the victim off, which was rare, he would usually be taken to the ravine and left there to die. Fortunately, death was far more merciful than the Germans and usually came quickly.

But even with all the daytime help death had from the Germans, most inmates died during the night. They fell exhausted and weak, sick and starving onto their straw at night and were found there dead in the morning. For morning roll call, the dead were taken out by those who had shared the huts with them and laid on the ground, in the ranks, to be counted with the others before being hauled to the ravine.

Each morning after roll call, the daily meal was given. It consisted of weak, muddy brown liquid cynically called coffee and dry bread made of potato peels and sawdust. A few days of this diet followed by sixteen hours of hard labor led to death for most of those not skilled in the art of survival.

Ivan made a point of associating himself with those who had lived the longest in the camp. There were some who had actually survived for months. It was from these, Ivan reasoned, he would learn what he'd need to know. The morning after he arrived at Babi Yar, after the first meal, Ivan had asked a man who looked better nourished than the others, "How have you kept from starving? No one can stay alive on this. You've been here weeks, and you look as well fed as anyone here."

"Are you willing to eat rats, cats, mice and other vermin?"

"If that's what it takes. But how do you get them?"

"Stay with me. It is the only way I know to get enough food to keep going."

After the brief feeding period, and before the work of the day was begun, the inmates were made to police the grounds.

"Stay near me, Ivan. We'll police the area nearest the fence. Remember that there are 22,000 volts in this fence. Don't touch it, but collect all the rats, mice, weasels, rabbits and other animals that have. In twenty-four hours, a lot of creatures meet death on those wires. Carry a stick to pull them off the fence and put the animals in your clothes.

Ivan was surprised to see how many of the survivors were doing the same. Mostly, the fence held dead rats, mice, and occasional squirrels. The prized larger animals were rare.

"Keep what you can scavenge until lockup tonight. It is up to you how you prepare it for eating. They can be cooked on the wood stove in the huts. If you are at a job where there is a fire, you might even be able to eat them during the day, but that is risky. Some of the Germans might consider that an infraction and shoot you on the spot."

76

Ivan was assigned to a variety of jobs. Almost every day he would be sent out on a different work crew. There seemed no pattern or logic to the way jobs were assigned. Some prisoners were sent to the same work every day, while others never did the same job two days in a row.

On his first day, Ivan was taken on a work detail dismantling some old Russian barracks. Each board was salvaged, each nail withdrawn, straightened, and placed in containers according to size. On the second day, he was placed on a work detail assigned to cut down trees and dig out their roots. Any tree in the vicinity of the camp that offered cover to a potential enemy or escapee was removed. For this they had to go outside the barbed wire fences, and they went under heavy guard. They were told that any escape attempt, even by one individual, would get everybody in the party shot on the spot. On the third day, he went back to dismantling barracks, and on the fourth he was put to work as a beast of burden. He and several others were harnessed to a heavy wagon, and all day they pulled that wagon around the camp while other prisoners loaded it with trash, sewage, garbage, and other refuse.

There were other jobs, but Ivan was never assigned to those. There were jobs from which prisoners never returned. Those who were taken to work on a secret project at one end of Babi Yar never returned. Once there, they would know too much of what was going on. They were kept at the project until their usefulness was exhausted, then they were shot, only to be replaced by others who knew they would never return. Even with this security, information had a way of filtering back, and before long everyone in camp knew that the project was construction of a factory—a factory that would make industrial soap out of human corpses.

For Ivan and ninety-nine other prisoners, all this ended on August 14, 1943. This group was selected for the most inhuman job any person could possibly devise—and the Germans devised it.

"What have we been selected for?" Ivan asked the man standing next to him in the line.

"I don't know. No one seems to know. It must be very secret."

"That is what worries me," Ivan replied.

"What do you mean?"

People never come back from secret assignments."

Just then, von Radomsky drove up with his two constant companions, the dog and the interpreter.

"Good morning. You are surely wondering why you have been picked out of all our guests here? Well, you are a very special group," he explained sarcastically. "You are the strongest and hardest workers, and for this you are to be rewarded." At that he started to laugh hysterically. The interpreter stood with a stupid smirk on his face, not knowing whether he should laugh too. After von Radomsky regained control of himself, he went on with his little speech. "I want to remind you that any infraction or escape attempt will end in the usual manner. Any hesitation to do your assigned work will be punished with a very special and painful death."

"It is obviously our end," the man next to Ivan whispered through his teeth.

"I think you are right. I just wonder what he has planned for us between now and that end."

A moment later Ivan found himself marching with the others to the gate of the concentration camp. Timtov, the leader of Ivan's dugout hut, was in charge of the group, along with seven other Kapos.

"Two Kapos for every twenty-five of us," Ivan noted. We've never had such supervision on a work detail before. What can they have in mind for us?"

"I don't know," came the whispered answer. "But I don't like it."

They were marched out through the double gates and up the road by which they had been trucked into the camp. When they reached the fork in the road, they turned into the ravine.

"Oh shit," Ivan heard the man in front of him say.

For the prisoners of Babi Yar, this had always been a oneway road.

"Today I join my Sosha," Ivan heard himself say.

It was a long hike into the ravine. The men walked in silence, each with his own thoughts—thoughts that he surely considered his last.

Strange, Ivan thought, how often during one's life one wonders what the end will be like. Now it is here. God, I don't even know the date. I hope they make it quick. Why aren't I upset? Damn these Germans. Why did they have to come into our lives? So this is really the end. How many have gone ahead of me here? I'm sure Sosha did that first day we were arrested. I hope she didn't suffer. I hope she was brave. I hope she felt at ease about it as I do now. I can't understand why I'm so calm. I guess they've worn me down. I guess I just don't give a damn anymore.

"Halt," Timtov ordered, and the procession halted.

They had marched to a far end of the ravine. The ground was sandy, mixed with clay. Looking around, Ivan noted shovels being counted out by German soldiers at the back of a truck some thirty meters away. Dirty bastards are going to make us dig our own graves, he thought.

"All right men," Timtov started, "we have a big job to do. Each of you will be given a shovel. You will dig in groups of ten or fifteen. You will unearth bodies that have been buried here. The Germans have decided that all who have been buried in Babi Yar must be unearthed and burned."

No one could believe his ears. It was absolute madness. Surely this was some insane joke, a ruse to get them to dig their own graves without suspecting. Everyone knew that there must be more than a hundred thousand dead in the ravine. Everyday they could hear the gunfire from dawn to dark. They heard it everyday at the concentration camp. It never stopped while the day lasted.

They had heard it every day in Kiev since the end of September 1941, when they had rounded up all of the Jews. How many days had there been since September of 1941? This was August 1943. How many days, how many thousands of bodies? Now these madmen expected them to be dug up and burned?

From another part of the ravine the sound of gunfire could be heard. They were still killing.

"Now get started. Everyone take a shovel and start to dig."

It was no joke. It was no ruse. It soon became evident that the Germans were expecting them to dig up bodies. All day they dug. First in one place, and then in another. By noon they had dug up enough ground to make mass graves for themselves several times over. The Germans were really looking for the dead. And the humor of it was, if one could call it humor, that in this ravine of death they could find no bodies. Was it possible that they could have started their digging in one of the few undefiled places? After twelve back-breaking hours, the only dead they had were those of their own that had died that day of exhaustion. At dusk seventy-three men, those who had not died, put down their shovels for the night. An extra ration of food was given them. Real bread and a bowl of soup that had potato and a bit of meat in it. It was real potato, not just the peels, and real meat—horse meat, to be sure, but real meat. That night they slept where they had been digging, in the ravine. They were exhausted, but for once with something in their stomachs. They slept like the dead they were searching for.

They were awakened at the first light of dawn. Again they got bread, real bread, and coffee that resembled the real thing.

By the time they were ready to start digging again, a truck had come with replacements for those who had died the day before. Again they dug all day, this time for sixteen hours, and again they had only their own dead to show for it at day's end. Thirty-nine died that second day.

On the third day, replacements came again. By noon they still had not uncovered any dead. At about 1 p.m. a staff car drove up, two officers in the back seat. One was a member of the present staff at Babi Yar; the other had been at Babi Yar in the beginning, when the Jews were slaughtered there. It was a quirk of the systematic German mind that made them insist on digging up the dead in the same order that they had put them into the earth. They were determined to dig up the first Jews they had slaughtered. But they could not find them.

"You damn fools!" the visiting officer called out. No one knew for sure whether he was addressing the diggers or their supervisors, but no one really cared. "You are digging in the wrong place! This is where we made them undress." Then he added, pointing to an adjacent area, "This is the place." He got out of the car, walked about sixty meters, and with his heel made a mark on the ground. "Dig here." The prisoners were brought over, and the next few shovels full of earth revealed the remains.

77

There was little dirt over the dead, and the pit gave them up by the thousands. The first bodies were in such an advanced state of decay that they came away in parts. The prisoners were sick from the sight and smell. They vomited. The Kapos vomited. When even some of the German guards began to vomit, they started guarding the diggers from a greater distance.

Ten meter-square areas were marked off on the ground. The bodies and parts were laid out in the area. On each layer of the dead was placed a layer of wood, and on that, another layer of the dead. Those diggers who died that day and who had died the previous days were also placed on the pyre. Thus they were placed until the pyre was about two meters high. Then petrol was poured over the entire pile and ignited. Flames licked at the sky beneath a thick black cloud of smoke. A new and horrible smell was added to the already existing stench. But after a short time, the flames died. The petrol and top two or three layers had burned off, but the mass below was packed too tight; there was insufficient draft to let the piles burn.

By dusk that night, there were six partially burned, smoldering pyres. When the food came, no one could force himself to eat. They escaped the horror in sleep.

Again, German ingenuity came to the rescue. The next day the replacements were accompanied by two hundred additional prisoners. The newcomers' shock was evident on their faces. While two hundred prisoners dug and carried the dead out of the pit, the remaining hundred were put on trucks. Ivan was among that one hundred.

It was still early in the morning, and already the sun was hot. The prisoner next to Ivan said, "The heat will take its toll. Many of us will die today."

"It makes little difference which day we die," Ivan replied. "Do you have any guess at where they are taking us?"

"None."

They drove only a few minutes when the truck stopped just outside of the old Jewish cemetery at the entrance to the ravine.

"Good Lord, you don't suppose they want us to dig up these dead, too?" the man asked, half joking.

"Well at least we'll know where to dig, if so," another answered.

"Get out! Hurry! Everyone out and into the cemetery," Timtov commanded.

"I can't believe it," Ivan said. "I think they really are going to have us exhume these corpses."

Once inside the graveyard, Timtov gave them their instructions. "At once, start taking down the grave markers. Take down each headstone and carry them over to the main gate where I want them neatly stacked. Now, you four," he said, pointing to the largest and strongest men he could see, "you will take them from that pile and stack them on the trucks. Two carry to the truck, and two of you work on the truck stacking. Four more of you are to take down the iron fence that is on top of the brick wall. Four volunteers, quickly!"

Ivan and three others stepped forward. Ivan wanted no part of desecrating these graves. He thought it strange after all that he had been through the previous day, but the thought of taking down headstones left him with an uncomfortable feeling.

The work was hard, but a pleasure compared with the work in the pits the day before. By noon the sun burned down without mercy. The temperature was well over a hundred, and there was no refuge from it. Even the Germans realized that to get the work done they would have to give the prisoners water, and in an unprecedented act of kindness they brought in a water truck.

As the men took their unusual break, they noticed a strange, muffled explosion. And a few minutes later another, then another. As the temperature rose, the explosions became more frequent.

"What in the hell is that?" Ivan asked the man he was working with, not really expecting him to know the answer.

"I've never heard anything like it. It's too muffled to be a very big explosion. I can't imagine what it could be. But with the Germans, there are a lot of things I can't imagine."

"I can't imagine what they want these headstones and iron fences for," Ivan added.

All day they worked. Truck after truck was filled with the materials which were driven back into the ravine. By dusk, the cemetery had been denuded. It looked eerie, a field of unmarked graves, unkempt and overgrown with weeds. The truck returned once more to take the prisoners back to their temporary living area in the ravine. As the sun set and the air cooled, the muffled explosions ceased.

When they arrived back at their area, they saw what their labor had been for. Makeshift furnaces were being built of the headstones, and the iron fence was being used for grates, which let the pyres draw air from underneath.

The pyres from the day before were restacked on the grates. They were packed more loosely, and three were ready for ignition. One of the Kapos was given a torch which he put to the stack of dead bodies, and it went up in a roaring flame. The same horrible stench filled the air. The other two pyres were lit.

Humans can get used to anything. That night when the food came, almost everyone ate. Ivan was sitting near one of the men who had remained behind on the pit detail.

"What was that noise we heard all day? Sounded like muffled explosions, all coming from inside the ravine. Do you have any idea?" Ivan asked.

"They were just that, explosions. We could see them. Never saw such a thing, and I hope never to again. We were working in the terrible heat, when suddenly we started hearing those sounds. They came more frequently, and we could see puffs of dust rise from the ground with each explosion. They were over there by that cliff."

"Well, what was it?" Ivan asked impatiently.

The man shrugged. "It appears the Germans used that area for their slaughter last week. The earth over the dead is very shallow. The sun reflecting off the cliff raised the temperature over there even higher than it was here and the heat beating down on the dead caused the gasses that form in the corpses to burst. Those bodies were actually exploding under the ground. Each time one exploded, it made a muffled poof and threw up a little dust."

The thought of it ended Ivan's meal. He gave his bowl to the man who had related the story and who was glad to take what was left of Ivan's food. Ivan rolled over on his side right where he had been sitting and went to sleep.

78

The bringing up and burning of bodies took almost six weeks—seven days a week, sixteen or more hours a day. To get the job done, the number of workers was increased to five hundred. And all the time that Ivan and the other prisoners were made to dig up and burn old corpses, new corpses were being added by the Nazis. Each and every day the shooting continued as the Germans brought in new victims. Each pyre had a hundred bodies in each layer, and there were sometimes twenty layers to a stack. The Germans decided two thousand bodies made the most efficient blaze. It took about two nights and a day to burn out one pyre completely. The prisoners worked all day to stack as many pyres as possible and that night would ignite them. The next day, while they still burned, new pyres would be stacked for burning that evening. On the second burning, when the ashes heaped under the grates, a crew of prisoners would sift through them for any gold or precious stones that might have escaped detection at the time of execution. What bones were found were brittle, and another group of prisoners was put to work crushing them. Then the bone and ash was bagged to be used as fertilizer.

Ivan estimated that each day they burned about ten thousand corpses. There were usually five pyres stacked each day. This pace continued for forty-one days—from August 19, when the efficient burning plan was accomplished, to September 28, when the digging was finally completed.

The nights were getting cooler in September, and after the first week of that month the Germans started taking the workers back to the dugout huts in the concentration camp for the nights.

As they rode back to the camp one evening toward the end of September, a relative newcomer to the work crew said to Ivan, "Do you know what I just calculated?"

"How many days to Christmas?"

"No! But do you know how many bodies have been raised and burned since you started this work?"

"No, I guess I never carried it that far. I just know we have done about ten thousand corpses a day."

"Yes, and that figures to about four hundred thousand bodies to date. There can't be too many left in the ground now."

Ivan wondered whether Sosha's body . . .

"How could they have murdered so many?" the young man asked.

"How? For them it was easy. They just sat day in and day out and pulled the triggers and released the gas in their vans. In the first week of their slaughter they murdered almost a hundred thousand Jews."

"Are you serious? In the first week?"

"The estimate I heard was ninety thousand and I believe it. The first pit we emptied was filled with their remains. When we had taken them all out, the bare pit was twenty meters deep, twenty meters wide, and over eighty meters long. The weight of the corpses on the top had so compressed the ones on the bottom that we had to hack them apart with shovels and axes to get them out. In a few cases the Germans went down and set small charges of dynamite to blow the bodies apart."

"Oh God!"

"Oh God, hell! Better ask, 'Where was God then?' After that first week, they imported more Jews; then Gypsies and Russian prisoners; then Communists and partisans; then just innocent men, women and children who happened to be on the wrong street at the wrong time." He paused, reminded of his own arrest with Sosha. "Anyway, by now they have killed over one hundred fifty thousand Jews and two hundred fifty thousand non-Jews in this hell hole, and it hasn't stopped yet. The last pyre will be ours, because we are witness to it all and we can't be left behind to give testimony to this . . . this . . ."

"How much longer do you think it will last?"

"Not long. When the wind blows from the East, it carries the sound of battle. The Russians are advancing. But rest assured, the Germans will get rid of us before the front passes back through Kiev."

79

It was a coincidence that the last of the bodies were exhumed on September 28, 1943, exactly two years to the day since the first Jewish roundup in Kiev. And as the last pyre was ignited, Ivan and the other survivors of the forty-one day ordeal knew that tomorrow would most likely be their execution date. That knowledge encouraged the only known mass escape attempt at Babi Yar.

There was nothing to lose. They would try an escape during the night. It would have to be spontaneous. It was too late to make definite plans. When they were locked in for the night, the men in Ivan's dugout considered their best course. Like prisoners everywhere, the men had over a period of time collected things that might come in handy. This night each brought out his secret treasures. There were some pliers stolen by the men who had been assigned to pull teeth from the dead. One had found a small hammer that some poor soul had taken to his grave with him in the ravine. There were pieces of wire, nails, needles, bits of string, a broken knife blade—but no weapons, and little that would be of much help in an escape.

"Give me that piece of heavy wire," one of the men said. "Maybe I can work the lock with it."

He went to the single door in the dugout and pulled the lock, which was outside the wire mesh door, to where he could manipulate it. To everyone's surprise but his own, the lock snapped open with ease. "Don't tell anyone what you just saw!

They might get the wrong idea of my past life," he said with a grin. To everyone's further surprise, he snapped the lock shut again.

"What the hell did you do that for?" someone asked.

"I just wanted to see if I still had the touch. It's too early yet. We must go after midnight when they least expect it. If the guard comes around and sees the lock off before then, we'll all be shot right in our bunks."

The next four hours were the longest Ivan could ever recall.

While they waited, a fog set in. It lay heavily on the ground to a depth of about a meter. The man who picked the lock volunteered to crawl in the fog to the other dugouts and unlock their doors. "I've done riskier things in my life," he said. "I think I can do it. Just give me five minutes after I leave the hut."

"And once we're out of our hut, what do we do?" someone asked. It was a reasonable question.

"All I can think to do," Ivan volunteered, "is to surprise the Germans. Overpower them and hope we can bluff our way out."

"That's crazy," a voice came from out of the darkness.

"Does anyone have a better idea?"

Silence.

"Okay. We outnumber the Germans ten to one at least. If we can eliminate a few before they give the alarm and get their weapons, we may be able to shoot our way out. If we can get lucky and get a few grenades, we might even be able to blow an escape route through the fences." Ivan paused. He knew it had little chance. "Besides, it beats just waiting to be shot tomorrow."

Maybe they won't shoot us tomorrow."

"Then it will be the next day. Only the agony of waiting will be prolonged."

The camp had been quiet for more than an hour. The guards were at a minimum.

"Now's the time!" the lock expert announced. He slipped from his bunk and had the lock off in a few seconds. "Five minutes. You have to give me five minutes." He was gone, somewhere in the deepening fog.

It was hard for the men to contain themselves. Five minutes are difficult to estimate, especially when every nerve and muscle wants to go. It may have been five minutes; it was probably less. Suddenly prisoners were running crazily in every direction. The alarm was sounded. A few Germans were downed by blows, but in the panic no one got any weapons. The Germans in the gun towers were, at first, helpless to fire. In the fog, they couldn't see who were their own men and who were the prisoners. The dogs were set loose and barked from under the fog. They tore into Germans and prisoners alike. The other dugouts had been opened, and three hundred and thirty prisoners ran crazily among a dozen equally confused German guards. Finally the guns in the towers started to fire—first at specific targets, then they just raked the area blindly. Screams, shouts, swearing, and gunfire mingled with the yelping of dogs and sirens.

The Germans made only one mistake in their surprise and confusion. They opened the gates to let in reinforcements, a truck and several motorcycles. The cyclists could barely see over the fog. In the few moments that those two gates were open, fifteen prisoners escaped by running against the traffic. They were out before the Germans knew what they had done.

Out of the three hundred and thirty prisoners in the camp on the morning of September 29, 1943, fifteen got out. For Ivan the waiting was over. He had been killed by the first blast of machine gun fire from one of the guard towers.

80

By the first week of October 1943, Russian guns could be heard almost daily in the Kiev area. Constant radio transmissions from Russian broadcasters encouraged all partisan groups to step up their activities against the Germans. They invited guerrilla groups to try to break through and join Russian forces where they could. In isolated areas, partisans actually took over small towns and villages, running out the Nazis and setting up their own governments. This created little islands of freedom inside the occupied territories.

Diadia Misha and his partisans remained in the forests, but they started to move eastward in hopes of joining the Russians. There was special motive on their part. Not only would this give the fighters a chance to join the Russian troops, but it would offer sanctuary to the non-combatants among them. The elderly, children, and non-fighting women would for the first time since the occupation be able to leave the forest and live among other people.

Cautiously, the group migrated through the forests north of Kiev. Then they turned in the direction of the nearest gunfire, and in the third week of October they passed out of occupied Ukraine into regained Russian territory.

Two hundred and eighteen Jews and seventy-seven gentiles walked into the Russian encampment. As soon as the Russians realized what and who they were, the partisans were received with enthusiasm. But, strangely, those who had just regained their futures, who had just walked out of the threat of eventual annihilation by the Germans, those who had just become survivors, showed little joy. That evening Solomon wrote in his diary:

"Today I walked out of the terror of German occupation. I'd thought—on those few occasions when I allowed myself to think I might survive the occupation—that this day would be a day of celebration. It was not. Physically I am alive, but I fear that I am dead inside. I think that part of me which feels died with all those others who were torn from life.

"I have nothing to celebrate. Today I came to the realization that I am alone in this world. I felt it almost the instant we walked into safety. I think we all felt it. Almost all of us have lost those most dear to us. Of the two hundred ninety-five of us, there were only three families partly intact. Diadia Misha and his son, Simcha, a father and two daughters, and a husband and wife with one of their three children still alive. Those people cried. They showed emotion. They still had something of their past; they have a future. For the rest of us the past has been slaughtered and we are alone with unknown futures. Our gentile comrades are a little more elated over their liberation. They may still have family to go back to after the Germans are pushed out completely. They will probably have homes to return to. They worry about their families who are still under occupation, but at least they still have hope of finding loved ones. They are victims of oppression and political tyranny, but only we Jews are victims of genocide. We have no loved ones to return to; we have no homes. We are adrift. I feel more uncertain today than I did yesterday. Yesterday I knew what I had; today, I have no idea what tomorrow offers me. Yesterday I knew I had to fight against the German oppressor. Now what do I do?

"Suddenly I realize today we were liberated by the people from whom we thought the Germans were liberating us two years ago. I am back among the same anti-Semites who for centuries have slaughtered my people with their pogroms. Will they now be different? Has their inbred hatred changed? What will it take to reawaken it? How soon?

"Already our fighters are planning to turn back to the west and chase the Nazis out of our lands with the Russians. Somehow I no longer feel it my homeland, but I will join them. I may not have a country, but I still have my hate. And vengeance still tastes sweet."

PART V
THE AFTERMATH

81

Solomon sat in dusty confinement behind barbed wire. His thin face showed abysmal depression. Incarcerated with him were thousands of other Jews who shared his feelings, or had been by circumstances pushed beyond them to indifference: those were the suicides. Then there were those who didn't take their own lives but died from sheer lack of will.

Solomon just sat there. No reason to move. Staring at the barbed wire and the armed guard on the other side, he recalled the utter helplessness that he had not felt since the night of September 29, 1941, when he and his family were being held under armed guard in Babi Yar. They were among those who didn't make it to the pit the first day of the massacre but knew what was in store. There was no way out that night either.

Just a few weeks earlier, he'd thought he would have a new life. But now—hell, what was the use? At the moment Solomon was sure of only one thing: *There is no place for Jews in this Christian world except under their thumbs, behind barbed wire, or in the ground.*

A group of seven children walked by, supervised by a girl in her early teens. Solomon guessed the younger ones at four or five years old. It was hard to be sure; malnutrition left most of these little ones small for their age. They should be in kindergarten. Not behind barbed wire. Barbed wire was invented for animals, not human beings . . . certainly not children. What kind of a world uses barbed wire for children?

He watched them walk around the corner of a row of tents under the watchful eye of their guardian. Orphans, all of them. None had ever known the joys of childhood, only survival and fear. They had succeeded where their families had failed. Now Solomon was a fellow inmate with them and thousands of other Jews. Why? Why was it that the world could not leave the Jews in peace?

A few weeks ago, Solomon had part of the answer to "Why me?" At least he thought he understood, "Why not me?" It was his job, he was convinced, his obligation to all those who died to make sure the world knew. But now he wondered who in the world would be willing to listen.

Jews were coming together in this camp from all the other death camps of Europe and the occupied territories. Atrocities were coming to light. Babi Yar, in relation to some of the others, was a minor offense. The figures were in: eight million gentiles, six million Jews. Out of every ten Jews in the world, the Nazis murdered four. Of the eight million gentiles slaughtered, some were political enemies of the Third Reich, some were outright partisans and saboteurs; some refused the immoral, unprincipled occupation governments, or spontaneously acted on conscience. Only the Jews and the Gypsies were slaughtered because of their birth.

And there was that inevitable question, "Why did God do it?" And there was an answer, "God didn't do it; man did it." And that left Solomon asking, "God, why did you let man do it? Why six million Jews?"

Nothing would ever placate Solomon's bitterness toward the Nazis or toward the German people who let the Nazi ideology take root. He was bitter toward all the anti-Semites of the world. And he was bitter toward the rest of the world, the "good Christian world," because after all the crimes against the Jews, the "free world" apparently didn't give a damn. How could a world that gave a damn about what happened to the Jews under Hitler allow this further incarceration of Jewish survivors, these children who still had never experienced freedom? How could a world that cared keep people who had suffered so much behind barbed wire? Hadn't the world learned anything? Solomon wanted to scream the question at the British soldier on the other side of the barbed wire. While the rest of the world was free, including most of the Nazis, the Jews were still behind barbed wire, this time as prisoners of the allies. How could the British hold them here on the island of Cyprus?

Three years had passed since Solomon walked out of the German occupied territory to fight alongside the Russians; there was still no place for the Jews. Of course, it really is different, he thought. There are no gas chambers or crematoriums, and now the guards are supposedly our friends.

Solomon reflected on the years since he and the partisans walked out of the Ukrainian forests in October 1943.

They'd fought their way back to Kiev and liberated the district from the Germans on November 5, 1943. He and Father Peter went together through the city and its surroundings. The priest found many of his old parishioners and acquaintances who greeted him with open arms. Solomon found no one. The city had no Jews left; there was no one nor anything to attest that a hundred thousand had ever existed. Their property had been confiscated by either the Nazis or the Ukrainians. A few gentiles from the Podol area where Solomon and his family had lived remembered him. One or two talked to him, but most preferred not to linger in conversation.

"Tell me, Father Peter, is it my imagination or do they really try to avoid me?"

"I have to admit, you cause them obvious discomfort."

"What is it that bothers them?"

"I think their conscience. After all, they probably think you blame them."

"I think I do."

"I guess I can understand that, too. But they also probably fear you a little. After all, we have come back with the liberating forces, armed to the teeth. They have known nothing but oppression from all of their previous liberators. Who knows what they expect you to do? After all, you carry a machine gun slung over your shoulder. Maybe they think you plan to loot their homes."

"As they looted the homes of Jews."

"I'm sure they did some of that, and that would only add to their fears."

Father Peter's parish had no priest. At the request of his congregants, he unofficially took over the leadership of his flock. He wrote to his superiors, but could not get an answer. Each noncommittal reply suggested that his letter would be forwarded to someone in a position to take the matter under advisement. It made him bitter. The Church would not back him when the Nazis were occupying the district and now would not commit itself. It occurred to him that the Church didn't really care what was right. Perhaps it wanted not to declare its stand until it was certain which turn the war would really take.

After a few depressing days in Kiev, finding no one or anything from his past, Solomon decided to move on with the Russian forces. He would stay with them until they pushed the Germans beyond the Ukrainian borders. His decision was made when he went to the old Jewish cemetery and could not even find his grandmother's grave. The headstone had been taken. He could not bring himself to go into the ravine to the last place where he saw his family. Kiev held nothing for him anymore.

82

Major Hans Oberman left Kiev along with the rest of the staff officers just a day before Solomon, Father Peter, and the Russian troops broke through the faltering German defenses. To the other officers, it seemed a strategic retreat; to Oberman, it was the beginning of the end for the Third Reich. Oberman was no fool; he was wise enough to keep his opinions to himself. No German could be trusted. The only intelligent thing to do was to keep his eyes and ears open for opportunities that would save him in the future—the not too distant future.

Good fortune was not alien to Oberman, a man who knew how to make the best of his opportunities. He had built a reputation for his superior, the Colonel, as a master at destroying resistance movements. It was quite natural that the Colonel should be transferred to an area where there was a hotbed of resistance activity. It was also natural that the Colonel would request that his chief aide, Oberman, be transferred with him. And it pleased the Colonel that Oberman was perfectly willing to let him take full credit. Oberman, of course, reaped other benefits more important than fame. Oberman's philosophy was that if anyone screwed up, the man with the reputation would hang first.

The hotbed of resistance where the team was transferred proved to be Holland. Major Hans Oberman was delighted. He looked forward to getting out of the Ukraine. Let the Bolsheviks have it back. Uncultured slobs, these people. How I long to get back to real people. Europeans.

Oberman was thinking of other things besides good company. He was contemplating how to insure his future. He knew that no matter what the future held, wealth was going to help. His family's wealth was considerable but not easily moveable. If he could liquidate his property, turn it into cash, in Holland he could turn his cash into diamonds. Easily transported, they were an international currency with a much surer future than the German Reich's mark. Besides, these Ukrainians had nothing of any real value. Perhaps in Holland he could increase his wealth. Extortion was a game he was in a good position to play. In Holland, the stakes made it more worthwhile.

Amsterdam was the city to which the Colonel and Oberman were assigned. "God, it's a whole different world," Oberman said to his Colonel. "I had forgotten what civilization was like."

The Colonel sat with a rather blank expression on his face, looking out of the window of the staff car as it drove past the Dutch city's many canals. Oberman doubted his superior even noticed the difference. The old fool is little better than the Ukrainians, Oberman thought. Oh well, that too is part of my advantage.

Oberman found himself a comfortable, spacious apartment with an abundance of old-world class. He furnished it with his favorite things, then set about selling everything he didn't need. When he could, he traded for diamonds and other precious gems. When he was forced to trade for money, he quickly converted his cash into the little stones elsewhere. When he had sufficient smaller stones, he traded up for larger, more precious gems. It would be easier to carry the larger stones than a large number of little ones. He kept a number of smaller ones to bargain with, but his real fortune was in the rare large stones, prized by buyers of quality anywhere in the world. By mid-summer of 1944, Oberman had turned almost his entire fortune into easily transportable and negotiable jewels.

He had also been doing well at his job: ferreting out

resistance groups. But now he was turning his back on as many as he was arresting. Where he could, he took extortion in exchange for opportunities to escape. The resistance movement in Holland was altogether different from that in the Ukraine. Here in Holland, it was almost universal. In the Ukraine, the Germans looked down on the people; here, the Dutch looked down on the Germans. These people had courage. They were not anti-Semitic. They didn't give up their Jews to the Germans if it could be in any way avoided. They suffered, but with pride. Even the Church resisted in Holland, despite the stand of the Vatican.

As time passed, Oberman was more certain that Germany's chances of winning the war were approaching zero. To express such feelings was considered by many as treason, so he kept his thoughts to himself. But he started seriously thinking about how to get out of Europe. He didn't know what repercussions there might be after the war, but he would take no chances. He was quite certain that any Germans taken by the Russians would pay dearly for their part in the war. He figured the Americans, English, and other powers would be a little more forgiving, but he thought it would be wiser to observe this from outside of Europe. He would always have the option of coming back if there was to be no retribution. If he stayed, he might not have any options. His problem now was to make the proper arrangements so that when the time came he would be ready.

83

Oberman did not speak out; he listened. By the beginning of 1945, the Germans were withdrawing on all fronts. Oberman was returned to Germany. Now there was considerable talk of German defeat. Everywhere officers talked of ways to escape the advancing enemies. Oberman kept his mouth shut. He listened and gathered information. His fortune was a small pouch hidden where he could get it quickly. The more he heard, the more he realized that for him and other Nazis, salvation would come from the Church.

There was little question in Germany where Vatican sentiments lay. The Vatican had remained silent through the years. Never did the Holy See cry out against the policies of the Third Reich. Atrocities were never criticized. The Nazis were allowed to do their work without any show of indignation. But though the Vatican didn't speak for or against Hitler's policies, it showed support in other ways.

Oberman heard that when Germany occupied Rome on September 10, 1943, the Nazis ordered the roundup of all Jews trapped in the city. The world waited for the Vatican to protest the arrest of these eight thousand Italian citizens. There was a resounding silence. In spite of Vatican indifference, many of Rome's clergy gave refuge to the condemned Jews, hiding as many as they could. The less fortunate were sent to Auschwitz or shot right there in Rome. Because of the outrage around the world at the Pope's silence, the Vatican later issued a statement that three thousand Jews were hidden from the Germans in the Vatican itself. This was a lie. Of the eight thousand Jews threatened by the Nazis, some two dozen did find refuge in Vatican City.

Though the Vatican made no official statement, Archbishop Constantini voiced Vatican sentiments in 1943 when he said, "We wish with all our hearts that the Germans will bring final victory and the fall of Bolshevism." He hailed the brave soldiers who were fighting "Satan's deputies in Russia." Oberman kept in mind this statement by a leading churchman, a confidant of the Pope.

Christian support for the Nazi policies was further demonstrated by what Oberman recognized as previews of how the Church would help in the future. After the Americans and British landed forces in Europe, many German soldiers and officers were helped back to their own lines or hidden by priests; many were smuggled back to their troops disguised as Jesuits and Monks. Oberman was quite sure the Church was not displeased with the job the Nazis had done to combat communism and destroy Judaism in Europe. He was quite sure that the Church would show its gratitude by helping Nazis escape persecution after the war. He set about to avail himself of its services.

84

In the first week of April 1945, about a month before VE Day, Major Hans Oberman took off his uniform for the last time. Dressing as a middle-class German citizen, false papers in his pocket and the pouch of diamonds under his clothes, he left his apartment to go to confession. He closed the door and didn't bother locking it.

There was no staff car awaiting him at the front door this time. Casually, he walked the three kilometers to a small church in the outskirts of bomb-shattered Berlin. Upon entering, he strode straight to the confessional. After a short wait a priest appeared.

"You wish to confess?" the voice of the elderly priest trembled through the screen.

"I seek the salvation only this sanctuary can give to the misjudged servants of God," Oberman said, speaking each word deliberately.

The old priest immediately recognized the phrase.

Two days later, Oberman was hidden away in a monk's cell at a monastery in the Austrian Alps. He remained at that monastery for eight weeks, spending his time reading and relaxing. He found it boring after a few days, but there was no alternative. He showed no surprise at the announcement of Germany's surrender during his third week at the monastery. Each day at the cloister more and more German officers came to be hidden by the monks. They were kept separate; no one was told the identities of the others. Since most of the Nazis passing through the monastery now were very high-ranking officers, they were passed through quickly. It meant that Oberman was kept at the first refuge for weeks longer than most. It couldn't be helped. Those of high rank, wanted for war crimes, had to be moved out first. Never was Oberman asked to make payment for the services he was receiving from the Church. It was, after all, Christian charity.

The war in Europe had been over for about four weeks when one morning a knock came earlier than usual at Oberman's cell door.

"Please come in. I am awake."

The door opened and a monk, robed in brown, entered the humble quarters. "Today is your day," the monk announced. He placed a garment similar to his own on the table next to Oberman's bed. "Please dress in these today. Later you will get a new identity and proper papers."

"Where will I be going?"

"You will be told what you need to know when you get there. It would not do for you to know the next point on the escape route in case you are picked up."

At mid-morning Oberman set out with seven other refugee Nazis along a country road in the direction of Innsbruck. A group of monks sworn to silence accompanied them. The walk would take three days at an easy pace. The nights would be spent in safe houses established along the way.

They had no difficulties on the road to Innsbruck, and once there they were met by a mountain guide. For another week they were hidden in a third-rate boarding house. At the end of the week, they walked to a small village near the border. There the guide had provisioned the party for the most difficult portion of their "pilgrimage" to Rome. For the next few days they would be crossing the rugged Brenner Pass to an inn on the Italian side of the border. There they would rest from the ordeal.

Two days later, they were all safely hidden in a convent in

Northern Italy. From there the Nazis were taken out, one or two at a time. They received new identities and were driven to Rome. Again Oberman was the least important, so he was not taken to Rome for almost three weeks. Christian charity again took care of all expenses.

In Rome he was passed on to Collegio Croatto, a seminary operated by a group of Yugoslav priests. From there, contact was made with the Titular Bishop of Aela, a close friend and confidant of Pope Pius XII. That Bishop was a last contact before the infamous Bishop Alois Hudal, who operated the Vatican rescue mission. In the years to follow, Bishop Alois Hudal would make possible the escape of more than fifty thousand wanted Nazis, among them Martin Bormann, right-hand man to Adolph Hitler. Bishop Hudal moved the fleeing Oberman along with the other Nazis into Teutonicum monastery, within the walls of the Vatican. There Oberman received yet another identity and a matching International Red Cross refugee passport.

In two more days, Oberman found himself on an Argentine ship. While on board, he was given a choice of South America or Syria. Oberman chose Syria. He wanted to stay nearer Germany and the continent he knew. The thought of going to South America distressed him. He imagined it a primitive land of natives and jungles. He further suspected that in a few years all would be forgotten, and he would be able to return to his homeland. Besides, he wasn't even sure yet that he would be among those wanted for prosecution. He figured that he could make some investments in the Middle East and parlay his fortune while in exile.

He disembarked the Argentine ship in Barcelona, Spain. When he got off, he had yet another identity and a new passport, this one the most valued and versatile in the world—a Vatican refugee passport. He was put aboard a ship for Lebanon and the Mediterranean Sea. In Lebanon, he was met by a priest of a church in the Christian sector. That priest was assigned to transport fugitive Nazis across his country into Syria. He also offered those Nazis positions as consultants to the

Syrian army. Oberman accepted an advisory position in guerrilla warfare and terrorism.

85

Immediately after Solomon decided to leave Kiev, he rejoined the Russian forces chasing the Germans out of the Ukraine. Many of the partisans actually enlisted in the Russian army. Diadia Misha joined, went to Officer's Training School, and received a commission of captain. Many of the Jews preferred not actually to sign up. Before World War II, Jews were made to suffer terribly in the Russian Army; the reputation of their mistreatment lived on. Jews had been conscripted for periods as long as twenty-five years, and most never lived to see discharge. So Solomon and several of his Jewish comrades were satisfied to fight along with the Russians as civilians, able to walk away as soon as the war was over.

Originally, Solomon intended to fight only until the Germans were out of the Ukraine, but he fought through the winter of 1943 and into the summer of 1944. Then he felt compelled to return once more to Kiev. He really didn't understand why. Perhaps it was homesickness, though no one was left who meant anything to him except Father Peter. He recalled the emptiness he'd felt when he had returned there in November, and he asked himself, why should it be different now? He had no answer, but he had to return—perhaps just to be absolutely sure. In November the city had been freshly liberated; maybe now things would be more normal. Though almost everyone he cared about was dead, their memories lingered in the Kiev district.

He reached the city in the last week of June 1944. Hardship and poverty were evident everywhere. A few Jews were now returning, coming out of the forests, out of hiding, out of concentration camps which the Russians had liberated. Two or three thousand out of a pre-occupation population of nearly a hundred thousand had come home to salvage what they could of their lives.

"Look how many have returned" could be heard in street conversations everywhere.

"How come so many survived? I suppose they want to move back into their homes now."

"I thought they killed them all."

"They're lucky to be alive. Why do they come back here now?"

There were certainly those who felt compassion for the survivors and wished them no further harm or hardship, but they were a silent minority.

"It is not up to us to give them back their property," the majority complained. "The Germans ran them out. To the victors go the spoils, and we are the victors." Anti-Semitism was growing, flourishing. "Damn Jews. Want to take over everything."

Of the few Jews who returned to the city, Solomon knew none from before. He went to the only friend he knew, Father Peter. As he approached the little parish church, he wondered whether his friend still held the pulpit there.

"Solomon! Welcome home, Solomon! Dear Solomon," he heard as he turned into the walk. Father Peter was coming around the side of the building.

"Father Peter! It is good to see a familiar face again. Thank God you're still here."

"I was tending my garden. I saw you walking up the road but couldn't believe it was really you. When did you return to Kiev?"

"Three days ago. But I couldn't stand it any longer. The city's terrible! I had to get away."

"Why didn't you come sooner? You are always welcome

here, you know. Don't you, Solomon?"

"I was sure you would welcome me, but I wasn't sure you would still be here. I'm so glad you are." The two men embraced.

"Solomon, come in. Let me make some tea and lunch. You must be hungry. We have much to talk about."

Solomon had forgotten what welcome was like. Not since leaving the forests had he felt it.

Father Peter filled a chinik with water and put it to boil.

"Well, what have you heard from the Church? Will they let you keep your parish?"

Father Peter answered as he went to a shelf to take down two glasses, "I've heard nothing. I'm doing my work here. My parishioners need me, but I don't know if I'm working officially. I don't know if the Church wants or needs me."

"They're noncommittal?"

Father Peter measured some tea into a perforated container, "Not even noncommittal. They are silent."

"What will you do?"

The priest sat down to wait for the water to boil, "I don't know. I can't go on like this much longer, though. Soon I will have to make a decision. But enough about me. What are your plans?"

Solomon sat silently for a moment. He sipped the tea Father Peter had just poured. "I'm not sure either. I felt I had to come back here once more before I could decide anything, but now I know: Kiev is as dead as my past. Still, where will I find it better? We Jews have had no real home since the year 70, when the Romans ran us out of Palestine."

"I remember you talked of going to Palestine when you were in the forest. What happened to that idea?"

"Things were different then," Solomon replied, choking up a little. He still had to fight back tears when he thought of Rachel. "Things were different."

"Give yourself time. When the war is over, then it will be different. The world will surely learn its lesson!" Father Peter did not speak with full conviction.

"What I have seen and heard in the city these last few days

. . . well, I'm just not sure."

"I have heard it, too, but things are difficult now. When things improve, the atmosphere will be better."

"But we Jews can't go through life waiting for good times! We can't live in constant fear. And there aren't enough of us left to withstand another pogrom."

"Pogrom? You can't believe that will ever happen again?"

"Pogroms are our destiny."

"If so, then all our struggles have been in vain."

Solomon answered dejectedly. "What is, was; what was, will be. It is our destiny."

86

Solomon stayed at the church with Father Peter. Most Jews who returned to Kiev found corners of destroyed buildings to dwell in. They lived in rubble while trying to reclaim, trying to start anew. As more and more Jews returned to the city, the anti-Semitism became organized. Through some of the congregants of Father Peter's parish, Solomon heard that a pogrom was actually being planned by a radical group of organized Jew-haters.

"They intend to finish what Hitler started," Solomon told Father Peter.

"But they are a minority! The rest will not let it happen."

"Like they stopped the slaughter in Babi Yar?" Solomon snapped back. Father Peter was stymied. Solomon continued. "A small minority is all it takes. Then the masses come out to see what is happening, and the next thing you know there's a mob. The mob will kill. Once a pogrom starts, they don't care who they kill. The smell of blood makes them wild."

"I will go to the commander of the city," the priest said. "I know him. Perhaps he can help."

"I doubt it. He is a Russian."

"What else can I do?"

To Solomon's surprise, the commandant was an understanding man. Furthermore, he was aware of the problem, had already taken steps to break up the threat. The pogrom did not materialize, but there were numerous incidents of confrontation and many fights, all spontaneous between individuals.

In September 1944, Father Peter received a letter from a priest he had gone to school with. About the time Father Peter returned from his schooling to start his work, his friend took over a small parish in a Polish Kielce. They had corresponded infrequently through the years. This was the second letter since the two cities' liberation. He let Solomon read the letter in his rectory. From the letter, Father Peter and Solomon discovered the relative good fortune of the Jews of Kiev. In 1939, before the German occupation of Kielce, twenty-five thousand Jews lived in that city. Like Kiev, Kielce was devoid of Jews at the time of its liberation. As in Kiev, a few Jews drifted back to the city that had been their home: only two hundred from the death camps, the forest, and the interior of Russia. But even two hundred were too many for the Polish anti-Semites. When the Jews tried to reorganize their community, the anti-Semites also organized. Their efforts culminated in a full-blown pogrom. Jews who'd survived the Nazi occupation died at the hands of Poles who also thought the Germans were inhuman animals.

"You see?" Solomon asked. "Nothing has changed. It's not only here in Kiev or in the Ukraine; it's everywhere in Europe and Russia! We'll never be free as long as we have no country of our own."

"Solomon, I fear you are right," Father Peter admitted.

Over the next few months into 1945, conditions grew worse for the Jews in Poland, the Ukraine, and in the liberated areas of Europe. There were few left after the Holocaust, but their minority position only encouraged harassment. Father Peter's disillusionment with the Church was deepening. He could get no response from anyone.

"They'll make no commitment until the war is completely over," Solomon kept saying. "Though I can't believe they could still hope for a Nazi counteroffensive."

"I just don't understand it," Father Peter said. "But I know I can't continue like this. Even if I get Church support, I no longer respect the hierarchy. Such hypocrisy! Too much has happened. Too much has changed."

"What else can you do?"

"I can teach. I could teach history. I would like teaching. But that has its problems, too."

"Which are?"

"I certainly could not teach in a communist state. I am still Catholic. I can't give that up! I could compromise my principles with the Church." Father Peter shook his head and laughed bitterly. "I can't tolerate either one and for the same reason. The Church and communism—they both make the same intolerable demands!"

"What if you were to move to a non-Communist country?"

"I have considered it. A big step. There are language problems, and I would have to leave everyone I know."

"Father Peter, have you ever thought of going to Palestine?"

"You mean on a pilgrimage? Of course."

"No. I mean to stay!"

"To stay? Of course not!"

"Well, think about it now. After all, your faith began there! Surely there must be ample opportunities for . . . a man like you: to teach, to write, do research. I think it might be your answer!"

87

By the time the war ended in mid-1945, the idea of leaving had totally absorbed Father Peter. He had talked it over with his friends, and several reluctantly agreed he should make the move. Father Peter would accompany Solomon to Palestine.

The first problem that faced them was getting out of the Ukraine. Exit visas were not easily come by. Even applying for an exit visa was risky, because it alerted the authorities and put one on a list of possible enemies of the state. Finally, Father Peter and Solomon agreed to slip out of the country secretly. One advantage they had was that much of the country was in transit: soldiers and refugees were returning, displaced persons were trying to find places to settle. The Jew and gentile joined the flow of transients toward the border towns of the Ukraine.

They made for the mountain town of Glybokaya in the south. From there they crossed the border at night to the Romanian mountain town of Putna. Father Peter had several priest acquaintances in Romania who willingly helped them to cross that country. Security in Romania was not strict, and they had no problems getting into Hungary. As they traveled west, the number of people in transit increased and security was more lax. The two men traveled now as priests; as members of the clergy they escaped scrutiny by security people. They left Hungary and crossed into Austria under the protection of the forests. Once in Austria, they considered their problems behind them.

The first thing they did was present themselves at the headquarters of the U.S. and British occupation forces. They had no difficulty proving their identities from papers they had brought with them out of the Ukraine. They were given asylum when they announced that they were defecting. They received new papers allowing them to stay in the west, work permits, and a list of all available aid societies that had been set up for refugees and displaced persons. They were sent to a special office for those who wanted to resettle in other countries of the non-Communist world. Austria was a major staging area for resettlement.

"Your papers, please," the official requested. "You wish to go to Palestine? You wish to live in the Holy Land, Father?"

"Yes. We seek a new life in the place of our beginnings," Father Peter replied as he handed the official his own and Solomon's papers.

"Let's see. You are from the Ukraine—the Kiev district. That should be no problem. We have few requests from Ukrainians to enter Palestine; the quota should be far from filled." He searched a looseleaf book before him containing columns of countries and figures. "Ah, here it is. Oh my, they have never filled their quotas. Since the war, not even two percent of it. You will have no problem at all." He took some papers from a drawer in his desk and handed them to Father Peter. He said, "Each of you fill out one of these forms completely and accurately, then bring them back here. We'll process you together so you won't be separated."

"Thank you, sir," the priest replied. "You are a great help."

The form asked a number of questions: place of birth, date of birth, family name, given name, middle name, date of application, citizenship, race, religion, education, profession, skills, political convictions, criminal history. There was a section on health history, family history, personal history, and a section for the whys of wanting to resettle. When both he and Solomon had finished the chore, Father Peter gathered up all the papers and returned to the room where "their" official worked. He had just finished with a family group, so he turned his attention immediately to Father Peter and Solomon.

"Ah, you are finished. Let me see your forms. This is only the first in a tedious series of steps, but it is the most important of all; and if it is not properly done, you'll have difficulties later."

He scrutinized each form point by point and gave an affirmative nod. He mumbled "fine," and "very good," and "seems in order," and initialed each page in its proper place—until he came to Solomon's. His face grew stern.

"Oh my!" he shook his head, reopening his book of countries and figures. "Oh dear me!" He turned a few more pages and checked in another place. "This presents a problem. Mr. Shalensky, Solomon Shalensky—being with the priest, I assumed . . . well, I assumed you were with him."

"I am," Solomon said.

"Well, yes, of course. But I mean to say, of his religion . . . aaaah . . . his religious conviction."

"What are you getting at?" Father Peter demanded.

"Well, Father Rochovit, Mr. Shalensky comes under another quota list. It is the way the British have set up the quota. Jews are under a different listing."

"What are you saying? We are Ukrainian! We are both from Kiev!" Father Peter was almost shouting. "You yourself said the Ukrainian quota was far from filled."

"For Ukrainians, yes. But not for Jews. I am truly sorry, but I have no control over the matter. Jews are under a separate quota system. The British will not let you in, Mr. Shalensky. The Jewish quota is filled—and the list is very long."

"You can't be serious," Solomon said. "You distinguish between Ukrainians and Ukrainian Jews?"

"I don't, but the system does. Your friend can be on his way within the week; but you, as a Jew—well that will take a long time, I'm afraid."

"How long?" Solomon demanded.

"They take a few thousand a year," the man shrugged. "And the waiting list seems endless."

"My God! What madness is this?" Solomon raged. "It's the Jews who need the refuge of Palestine! There is no place for us in Europe or Russia—and now the British tell us we can't enter

Palestine? What would you have us do?"

The official's face colored. "There are the displaced persons' camps where you will be taken care of until something can be worked out."

"Displaced persons' camps? Something worked out!"

"Please, I understand that you are upset, but these are the rules."

"You understand?" Solomon retorted. "You don't understand shit!" He leaned across the official's desk and looked him in the eyes. "How long will it take the non-Jewish world to learn? It's quite obvious why we no longer want to stay in Germany, Austria, Poland, or the Soviet Union. How can anyone ask us to stay where our families were butchered, gassed and burned, turned into soap and fertilizer, their corpses raped of gold teeth and hair to further the economy of what you called civilized nations? Oh, you are shocked and outraged that the Nazis could have done such things, but at the same time you're sorry the job wasn't finished!"

"You can go, but not to Palestine."

"All right, where can I go?"

The official's face grew even more florid. He picked up his book and leafed through it as if looking for an answer. "Well," he stated finally, "except for returning to the Ukraine, where they have to accept you back, there is no place that will take you right away. However, there are a number of countries which have much shorter waiting lists. You could get into Holland, Denmark, or Sweden in a shorter time. Maybe even America."

"But what about this week? Or next?"

"No place."

"And if I were to go to one of those countries, could I then go from there to Palestine?"

"Not as a Jew."

There was nothing left to be said. Solomon turned and walked away from the desk, bitter and frustrated. Father Peter picked up all of the forms and followed Solomon out of the building.

"I can't blame you for the way you feel," the priest said. "It would be easy for me to say I know how you feel, but the more I see of how the world treats you and your people, I begin to realize that no gentile will ever know just how it feels to be Jewish."

"You want to know something funny, Father Peter? All my life I have wondered about something, and the answer has always eluded me. I remember my grandfather saying that the most precious thing we had was our birthright. Well, I understood that we were Jews by birth, but he spoke of 'birth right'—'birthright,' implying it to be a privilege. As a child growing up, I wondered what privilege he saw in it. Was it a wonderful privilege to be everyone's scapegoat? To be spat on and beat up by the goyim? Was it a privilege to have to live in ghettos and worry about every drunken group of goyim starting a pogrom, or just having fun breaking our windows and looting our stores, raping our sisters and mothers? Well, now it all comes clear to me. Finally, when my birthright allows me to spend my days in a displaced persons' camp, I realize what my grandfather understood so long ago. My birthright allows me to live with a clear conscience! As a Jew, I don't have to carry with me the gentile's guilt. I haven't the shame of contributing to the bigotry, bloodshed, and hate that has contaminated this planet for the last twenty centuries. It is my birthright to be oppressed throughout history, but I think that is easier to live with than the guilt of being the oppressor."

88

That evening, tempers cooled and perspective regained, Solomon persuaded Father Peter that the only thing to do was for the priest to go ahead to Palestine.

"It would be pointless for you to stay here. Go ahead! Get settled in the new homeland! Write to me of it. At least I can know from you what it is really like. And when I do get there, I'll have settled friends to help me out."

There really was no alternative. By the end of the week, Father Peter headed toward Palestine and left Solomon considering life in a displaced persons' camp.

It was not easy for a Ukrainian Jew to find a place and a way of making a living in postwar Austria. At least in the displaced persons camp he would be among his own people; he would have shelter, food, and medical aid should he need it; and unlike the concentration camps, he could always leave if it didn't work out.

The displaced persons' camps really were far different from concentration camps, but for those who had survived concentration camps—especially the children—they kept the nightmares alive. Any form of confinement and regimentation, however lax, was a reminder. But for the displaced Jews, the DP camps were the best alternative.

The DP camps came under the auspices of the United Nations Relief and Rehabilitations Administration. At war's end, only 50,000 Jews came out of the death factories alive. At first, they joined the streams of refugees returning to their places of origin, but before long they found that, unlike the non-Jewish refugees, they had no place to return to. In addition, there were those who had survived the war in hiding, in partisan groups, and a few who had succeeded in posing as "Aryans." The DP camps brought all of these Jews together. Since Jewish communities were prevented or discouraged from re-forming in postwar Europe and Russia, they began to form in the DP camps. There the universal problem was recognized, and out of that universal problem grew universal Jewish purpose: to open the doors of Palestine and re-establish it as their rightful homeland—the Jewish State, Israel.

President Truman, on June 22, 1945, appointed Earl G. Harrison to report on the conditions and needs of the displaced persons in Germany—particularly the Jews. On August 1, 1945, Truman received the report. It described the harsh and crowded conditions. "The first and plainest need of these people," the report read, "is a recognition of their status as Jews. Refusal to recognize the Jews as such has the effect of closing one's eyes to their former persecution.

"For reasons that are obvious, most Jews want to leave Germany and Austria. The life which they have been forced to lead has made them impatient of delay. They wish to evacuate to Palestine now. I come to but one conclusion: the only real solution of the problem lies in the evacuation of all non-repatriable Jews in the DP camps, who wish it, to Palestine."

President Truman transmitted the report to General Eisenhower, Supreme Commander of the U.S. Forces in Europe, to be acted upon. Conditions in the camps were immediately improved. UNRRA appointed Jewish refugees to posts in the administration of the camps. Most importantly, President Truman recommended to the British Government that one hundred thousand immigration certificates be issued, allowing Jews in the DP camps into Palestine.

The British refused.

89

By the time Solomon made his way to a DP camp—it was on the German side of the Germany-Austria border—the improved conditions were already being enforced. He found a highly organized society within the camp. A kindergarten was being operated for those too young for regular school. School-aged children were being taught in Hebrew and Yiddish as well as in the language of their origin. For most, it was the first formal schooling they'd ever had. There were also ORT vocational schools for adults, teaching skills needed in Palestine. Agricultural schools were also established. Everyone who didn't know the languages tried to learn conversational Hebrew and Yiddish, which would be their native tongues. Newspapers were published by the DPs themselves, and the Zionist Organization actually set up an office in the camp to help the Jews prepare for their future. In an extensive survey carried out by UNRRA, it was found that 96.8 percent of the Jews desired and intended to go to Palestine. There was only one problem: the British refused to let them in.

On December 5, 1945, the British closed the doors of their European occupation zones to refugees. The ban was for all refugees; almost all other DPs had found a place to settle and start anew. Only the Jews had no place to alight. Of course, this placed an added burden on the DP camps of the American zone. Also, more and more Jews were coming out of the Polish and Russian zones because of renewed anti-Semitism in those countries. In the first few months of 1946, one hundred forty thousand Jews fled Poland alone; after the bloody pogrom in Kielce, on July 4th of that year, ninety thousand more Jews abandoned their homes in terror. The pogrom in Kielce had murdered nearly one out of every four Jews resettled in the city, and most of the others had been severely injured.

International opinion and pressure did not impress the British. They had barred the door to Palestine, and that was all there was to it.

Solomon had been attending one of the ORT trade schools in the DP camp. He was learning auto and tractor mechanics. He thought that when he got to Palestine, it would be a valuable skill on a Kibbutz. The work had its challenge; it not only enabled him to make a contribution, but it gave him time to himself when he could think.

One morning in the spring of 1946, a young man approached Solomon's work bench. "You are Solomon Shalensky?"

"Yes. What can I do for you?"

The man was about Solomon's age, twenty-two or twenty-three years old. He spoke Yiddish, the language understood by most of the DPs.

"I am with the Jewish Committee. We are making inquiries into the conditions in the various camps. Could we talk someplace privately?"

"What can I tell you?"

"I have been lent an office upstairs. Do you mind if we go there to speak?"

"Not at all," Solomon replied, wiping the grease off of his hands and putting his tools away. There was something about this young man that did not quite ring true. He wore a short-sleeved shirt without a tie or coat. He was neat, but certainly not dressed in the business-like manner of most officials. The young man seemed to have something on his mind, but somehow Solomon did not believe it to be camp conditions. There was no conversation on the way to the office. When they got there, the young man ushered Solomon in. It was more a storage room than an office. The man closed the door behind him. The room contained a table and two chairs—nothing else.

"What do you want of me?" Solomon asked. "I feel it is something other than camp conditions."

The stranger smiled. "Of course I'm not interested in camp conditions. I am interested in emptying the camps. Let me introduce myself. I am Eliazer ben Drobkin. The Jewish Agency provides us with a front, an excuse to enter these camps, but I am really with the Haganah."

"Haganah? The Jewish army of Palestine? You are really with Haganah?"

"Yes, with a special section assigned to bringing 'illegals' into Palestine."

"Illegals?"

"Yes, illegals. It is the British name for those who enter Palestine without papers—or at least without *legal* papers."

"You are making an overture? Recruiting me to enter Palestine illegally?"

"You do come to the point quickly, don't you?" Eliazer grinned.

"Why wouldn't I go? What fool would turn down such an opportunity?"

"It is not without risk, Solomon. Many get caught. If that happens, you will most likely be interned in a British prison camp on Cyprus. Believe me, the conditions here are much nicer than on Cyprus. Also, you will be taken off the quota lists. It may end your chances for ever getting into Palestine legally. It is something to think about."

"I have just given it all the thought I intend to. I want to go. What must I do?"

"You just did it."

Solomon laughed. "I did?"

"You will be contacted," Eliazer told him. "Now go back to your work and say nothing of this to anyone."

"May I ask why you came to me for this privilege?"

"There will be time for that later. Just return to your work and say nothing. If anyone asks you, you just told us of the general conditions here and how much you love it."

90

Nothing happened. Nothing more was said. Several weeks passed, and Solomon began to think he had imagined the whole thing, except that there were several other DPs he knew of who had also been interviewed about "camp conditions." But none spoke to each other about the incidents. They all did as they were told and said nothing. Solomon knew of at least seven who had been interviewed, but he had no idea how many others might have been picked. He was dying to talk to someone about the matter, but too much was at stake. He was not about to do anything that might spoil his or the others' chances. At long last, another stranger came to his bench one morning and said, "Solomon Shalensky?"

"Yes."

"We finally have the results of the survey on camp conditions you took part in. You remember the survey, don't you?"

"Of course. What came of it?"

"That is why I am here. All those who are interested can hear the results. I assume you are still interested?"

"Absolutely."

"Good. Tomorrow morning, leave the camp as if you were just going to town. Take only what you consider essential. No luggage—only the clothes you wear. Come to this address before seven in the evening, but not before noon." he handed Solomon a folded piece of paper. "And again, say nothing to anyone."

Solomon arrived at the address in the early afternoon. It was a bookstore. Eliazer ben Drobkin was there, greeting each DP as he entered the store. They came throughout the afternoon, and as quickly as they arrived they were taken away by another Haganah member. The DPs came from several camps, so that not any one camp would turn up with a large number missing in any one day; a few absentees per day was considered normal attrition in most camps. From the store, Solomon and two others were taken to a farm just on the other side of the Austrian border. It was a safe house run by the Haganah. The tight security was not so much for fear of the local authorities, for the DPs had every right to move about the country. Security was kept strict so that the British would not be on the lookout for a large group of "illegals" getting ready to run past their patrols off the Palestine coast.

Solomon and the growing group stayed three more days at the farm. When the last of their number arrived, they totaled thirty-nine. Just enough to fill a bus which the Haganah simply chartered to take the DPs to the Italian port city of La Spezia. Numerous other groups of DPs were waiting there, and others were yet to come. The Jews were hidden in several nearby farms.

On the evening of the third day after Solomon's group arrived at La Spezia, a dilapidated Greek freighter steamed into port. It loaded its cargo and moved to another pier to await its turn for a drydock overhaul. Its crew was given a two-day shore leave, and the captain and skeleton crew of hand-picked men remained aboard. A messenger was sent to a member of the Haganah with the code phrase, "Awaiting new manifest."

That night, seven hundred sixty-seven Jews of all ages and nationalities were loaded on to the waiting ship. They were stuffed into cargo holds, crew quarters, officers' cabins, any place where people could be put below decks. At a quarter past midnight, the skeleton crew fired up the boiler and the engines began to crank. As soon as the ship had cleared the harbor, the Jews were allowed on deck. A message to the port authorities had said the ship had been given clearance to another dry dock which could save several days and that the captain had found a cargo at that other port. By dawn the ship was well out into the Mediterranean Sea on its illegal voyage.

The ship did not head directly for Palestine but churned toward Lebanon. Vessels headed in the direction of Palestine were watched by British patrols from the air. Once sighted, the ship's progress was charted daily. The crew and passengers watched for aircraft, but fortunately none was sighted. As they approached the waters off Palestine, the Captain started to run an erratic course which slowed their progress but would confuse any British patrols that did happen upon them. Slowly he worked his vessel into position to run the British blockade that night. At dusk he dropped anchor and waited. They were still out of sight of land. The next two hours seemed an eternity.

"I don't like it. It's been too easy," the Captain said to his crew chief. "I've done this several times now, but I feel very uneasy tonight."

"Perhaps we should not try tonight," the second officer replied.

"No. The longer we are in these waters, the greater the risk. We go in thirty minutes. But I still feel uneasy."

Thirty minutes later, the anchor was hoisted and the ship's crew began their struggle against the current. The Jews were headed home.

In another hour, a light flashed from shore at a prearranged interval and the captain set his bow in its direction. Thirty minutes later, the light flashed its code again, and the captain knew he was still on course.

They were within minutes of their destination when a crew member on watch yelled out, "Patrol boat closing in from starboard!"

No sooner had he called out than the approaching vessel turned on its powerful searchlights. Pandemonium broke loose on deck.

"I'm going to make a run for it!" the Captain shouted. "Full ahead!"

"We can't outrun her!" the bewildered second officer

exclaimed.

"No, but I can damn well ground her. These are shallow waters with a sandy bottom. As soon as we hit, lower every lifeboat loaded to the top. A few of these tormented souls may get ashore. The rest are headed for Cyprus anyway. What the hell do we have to lose?"

As soon as the ship grounded on the sand, six lifeboats were let down. The patrol boat started after them but only caught up with one before the others were in water too shallow for it to follow. The five successful, overloaded boats landed nearly a hundred lucky Jews on the sands near the ancient town of Caesarea. The other Jews picked them up and whisked them off under cover of night.

A few Jews who'd been captured jumped off the grounded British ship and swam for shore. No one ever knew just how many tried that or what their fates were. The Greek Captain and his crew were incarcerated in Palestine at the old prison of Acre. The remaining DPs were taken to the interment camps on the island of Cyprus—Solomon among them.

91

Solomon's eyes lifted briefly to the barbed wire. His gaze fell back to the ground. His thin face was worn.

Barbed wire confined him. A British soldier guarded him and fifty thousand other Jews.

How quickly they've forgotten.

These are the liberators? They liberated us from the Nazis. They imprison us here on Cyprus. God, why can't we just be allowed to live our lives in freedom? There are Jews in this camp who have faced death at the hands of the Nazis every day for the past decade. Now they are thrown into this hell hole by our allies. There are children who have not known a day free of fear in their lives.

The sun burned down on the island. There was not even a breeze. The interment camp was a tent city quickly thrown up to hold the displaced Jews. Palestine was their only hope. But Palestine was in the hands of the British, and the British had closed the doors to the only country that would take the Jews of Europe. Now Cyprus was their concentration camp. For many who finally gave up hope, Cyprus became their death camp. Attempted and successful suicides were commonplace. Some of the elderly who had survived Hitler could no longer struggle against this last disappointment. Without hope, the soul died, and shortly after, the body.

"They have already forgotten."